Buckling Down
By Moira Keith

When two hearts are on the line, it's double or nothing.

Levi McKenna heads to Las Vegas with one simple goal: win the rodeo and cement his place in rodeo history. Then Lady Luck throws a wild card into the deck—Sydney Hart. Time and distance haven't dulled the sharp edge of their attraction, but thanks to a long-ago promise, she will always be forbidden fruit dangling just out of reach.

Sydney wants to believe in fairy tales and happily ever after, but her past relationships leave her doubting such things exist. She's ready to give up on love...until Levi walks into her bar. The man who's always held the missing piece of her heart. Love may not be in the cards, but that doesn't mean a girl can't flirt.

Neither expected passion this hot, this fast. Yet once the cards are dealt, the only thing left to do is play them out—and see if they have a winning hand.

Warning: this book contains a sassy heroine, a scrumptious hero, blood, sweat, tears, not to mention...sex laced with Vegas heat.

Strong, Silent Type
By Lorelei James

Tough. Taciturn. And a fool for letting her go...

Wyoming rancher Quinn McKay thought he'd only have to bide time until his levelheaded wife came to her senses and called a halt to this "trial separation". He never believed the marital rough patch would drag on for a coon's age.

Libby McKay knew when she married the gruff, laid-back cowboy that he wasn't prone to blathering about his feelings. But three months have passed and her stubborn-as-a-mule husband is still living by himself in the horse trailer. It seems he'd rather hold onto his pride than hold onto her.

Quinn realizes Libby is determined to move on if he doesn't loosen his tongue and he'll lose the only woman he's ever loved. In a last-ditch effort to keep her in his life, he offers her one weekend of uninterrupted sexual decadence.

Reigniting the passion is easy. The hard part comes after the sheets have cooled and they find out if what remains is strong enough to survive past mistakes.

Warning: Old-fashioned groveling leads to smokin' hot sexual encounters—steamin' up the truck windows, rockin' the horse trailer—proving even an old married dog can learn naughty new tricks.

The Real Deal
By Niki Green

He held the reins to her heart once—and this time he won't let go.

Willa Tate left Millbrook, Texas, years ago—along with her future, her fiancé and her heart. Now, as one of the headlining acts at a hot burlesque club, she looks into the crowd, sees a familiar face staring up at her—and her past comes crashing back.

Chase Kiel has some hard questions for the former love of his life. He spent forever looking for her, and now he wants answers—even if he has to throw her over his shoulder and drag her back to Millbrook to get them.

He'd find it a hell of a lot easier if the chemistry weren't still there. If they didn't still fit together like keg of dynamite and fuse. If he didn't want not only his answers...but her heart.

Chase is still certain he and Willa belong together—and convincing Willa of it will be his pleasure.

Warning: This title contains explicit, powder-keg-hot sex, language that ain't fit for your mama's ears, and a hot cowboy with a Texas-sized heart.

Wild Ride

A Samhain Publishing, Ltd. publication.

Samhain Publishing, Ltd.
577 Mulberry Street, Suite 1520
Macon, GA 31201
www.samhainpublishing.com

Wild Ride
Print ISBN: 978-1-60504-566-5
Buckling Down Copyright © 2010 by Moira Keith
Strong, Silent Type Copyright © 2010 by Lorelei James
The Real Deal Copyright © 2010 by Niki Green

Editing by Heidi Moore
Cover by Scott Carpenter

Buckling Down, ISBN 978-1-60504-519-1
First Samhain Publishing, Ltd. electronic publication: May 2009
Strong, Silent Type, ISBN 978-1-60504-521-4
First Samhain Publishing, Ltd. electronic publication: May 2009
The Real Deal, ISBN 978-1-60504-522-1
First Samhain Publishing, Ltd. electronic publication: May 2009
First Samhain Publishing, Ltd. print publication: March 2010

Contents

Buckling Down

Moira Keith

Dedication

In loving memory of my grandmother, whose love for life and literature continues to inspire me.

To my family for always believing me capable of far more than I ever dreamed possible, for their support and patience while I spent countless hours in front of the computer. Lastly, to my sisters Sara and Riss, thank you for coming along for the ride from word one.

Chapter One

Levi turned on the TV in the bedroom of the hotel suite and flipped to the local news. He was thankful to be out of the noise that engulfed Las Vegas's many casinos. It gave him a chance to steal some time to unpack and settle in before the rodeo got under way. Glancing at the TV, he caught an interview with one of the many young rodeo hopefuls he'd seen at registration. The new guys made him feel old at twenty-seven. But running around as though they were the latest rock band to hit the scene wouldn't win them titles—he should know.

Experience had made him somewhat of an expert on the subject. Still, everyone had to learn in his or her own time. A fast rise to fame had caused him to lose sight of why he'd started this journey. Finding himself near the bottom of the standings had knocked him straight. This would be his turnaround year, the year he regained control of his life from his overbearing personal assistant. The year he finally claimed the Nationals title. Levi clawed his way back into contention, worked hard to qualify for Nationals and had made it by the skin of his teeth.

After he placed the last shirt in the drawer and the empty suitcase in the closet, he sank down onto the bed and closed his eyes. Listening to the reporter drone on almost lulled him to sleep, until he heard his name.

"In local news, rodeo and film heartthrob Levi McKenna arrived for the NFR this afternoon. He politely shunned reporters' questions regarding his latest breakup, but his assistant confirmed it. Levi McKenna is back on the market. The rodeo runs through..."

Levi shut off the TV. *Damn that woman and her big mouth.*

Women and tabloids were just another form of publicity in Lisa's eyes, and until recently he'd never given it a second thought. However, "eye on the prize" was his new motto. A woman on his arm would only serve to distract him from the big payoff. Irritated, he threw the remote across the room. Every time he made some progress, his assistant would have some new commercial or movie deal for him to look at and he'd let the dollar signs sway him. Lord knows the woman knew her work, but Levi had one rule when he started out—the love life remained off-limits and was not fodder for the gossip hounds. He'd let it slip. Not anymore. The assistant would be gone at the end of Nationals. If he still needed one after the rodeo, he'd have to re-establish the ground rules. *Damn news.*

"Hey Levi, open up!" a husky shout carried through the door, followed by a heavy-handed knock. Levi considered ignoring the man, but thought better of it. He opened the door. Justin Trent stood in the hallway, towering over Levi's five-eight frame.

Justin peered over Levi's shoulder to the interior of the room. "Must be nice living the high life, huh?"

"You could have booked a suite if you wanted. It's all about choices. What's up?"

"Some of the guys and I are going to check out this new bar in town. It's supposed to be a pretty hot joint for the local country set. Plus, they're sponsoring the bull riding competition. Thought we should show a little support. After the news report, we figured you might want to join us."

"Great. Bad news travels fast." Levi raked his fingers through his hair and thought about sitting in his room stewing. Dealing with Lisa while he was angry was never a good idea. He needed to cool off before he faced her. A few beers with the guys before the hectic rodeo schedule began might be just what the doctor ordered. "Where is this bar?"

"Just off strip, some joint called *Cowboy Up*. The band's singer is supposed to be pretty hot." Justin waggled his eyebrows in an awful Groucho Marx impersonation.

"Tempting." Levi groaned. "When y'all leaving?"

"In thirty. Do what you need to do and meet us down in the lobby." Justin walked away and called back over his shoulder, "Of course, the guys may leave without you. They figure without you there they stand a better chance with the ladies."

"Right, so why invite me?" Levi mumbled, closing the door. A bar named *Cowboy Up*? Probably run by some yahoo who'd never been to Texas. What would Sin City think of next? He headed for the shower. No doubt it would be a long night.

✳

Thirty minutes later, he sat in a limo with guys he had run the circuit with for years. The talk ran from girls to sports, wives and kids. Levi, not in a talkative mood, opted to sit back and listen as a few of the older guys entertained them with stories of their home lives. A handful of them were married or in serious relationships, something which seemed to elude Levi. As of the last breakup it could stay that way.

"You've got to be kidding me," Levi muttered to himself. The limo pulled up to the bar, where a sign advertised *Cowboy Up* in typical gaudy Vegas fashion.

"Don't be such an ass, Levi. Try to enjoy yourself, or pretend to. Remember all it would take is a call to Lisa, and your location would be dropped on the news." Justin slapped him on the back.

"I'd prefer you didn't." Levi slid out of the limo, turned his attention to the driver, and slipped him a fifty. "Thanks, we'll catch a cab back."

"Sir, my instructions from the hotel are that I wait."

"Suit yourself." Levi shrugged and headed into the bar. Glancing around, a guy couldn't help but notice the eye candy in tight jeans. He silently recited his new motto, "Eye on the prize". Peanut shells crunched under his feet as he moved through the bar.

"Over here, buddy." Justin waved him over to a corner booth large enough for the group to sit comfortably. Pulling an authentic cowhide-upholstered chair from a nearby table, Levi placed it at the end of the booth and settled in.

Justin dug his hand into the bucket of peanuts on the table as he yelled, "You get first round, hotshot."

The waitress stopped at the table, popped her gum and winked at Levi. "What's your poison?"

With a round of beers ordered, the waitress, who seemed better suited for a fifties diner than a country bar, disappeared into the crowd. Ten minutes later, the guys all had beers in hand. Usually the slow service would have been something to complain about, but the joint was packed.

Levi raised his beer to each guy around the table. "May the bulls be kind this week."

Justin shook his head. "The bulls are going to give you a run for your money, hotshot, but I'll toast to that. There's nothing like a little friendly competition to keep things interesting. Maybe you should practice on the mechanical bull over there."

Bottles clinked together and Levi took a pull of his beer. Following Justin's gaze, Levi looked at the piece of machinery—the bull appeared as if it hadn't been broken in yet. "Yeah, looks like it's getting a lot of use."

The waitress made her way up to the stage where band members were settling in. Justin smirked. "Hope she's not the singer."

Levi agreed as the waitress began to speak into the microphone. "All right y'all, you know what to do." The customers began to clap to the rhythm of Kellie Pickler's *One of the Guys*. A sweet southern voice laced with Texas twang came through the speakers.

"Watch out, Levi's a real sucker for a true southern girl," Justin said. A few of the guys at the table whistled and Levi followed their stares over his shoulder towards the bar. He could not believe his eyes. The singer stood on the corner of the bar in a black tank top and low hip-hugging jeans that revealed a glimpse of her stomach. Long legs were accentuated by the fit of her jeans and red cowboy boots. Levi stared at her like a deer caught in headlights. She hopped off the bar and worked the crowd better than any entertainer he had ever seen.

"Sydney," he whispered when those familiar light gray eyes locked on him. A smile crossed her face. The auburn haired beauty from his childhood made her way through the tables towards him. "Eye on the prize," he reminded himself.

Damn if she wasn't getting a reaction out of him. Desperately, he tried to remember the pact he'd made ages ago. Sydney sat on his lap, plucked the cowboy hat from his head, placed it on her own and wrapped an arm around his neck as she sang. Her body pressed against his. Focusing on anything other than the feel of her ass against his lap, the curve of her breast pressing into his chest and the sweet magnolia scent wafting off her skin was an impossibility. After the longest minute of his life had passed, she winked, slowly slid off of his lap and headed towards the stage. Wolf whistles filled the air as she finished the song.

"Well, that's definitely the best entertainment we've seen all evening. Seeing a woman have that kind of effect on Levi is worth a round of beers. I'm buying. Earth to Levi..." Justin nudged him. "Might want to wipe the drool from your chin and put your eyes back in your head."

"I don't believe it," Levi murmured, staring after her.

"Believe what?" Justin asked, looking puzzled. "Game face on, Levi. Fans approaching."

A few bar patrons asked for autographs. Levi never turned away fans, though he hoped to finish before Sydney disappeared from view. The band began to play again, but a male voice came through the speakers. Levi flicked his gaze up to the stage, located his hat and watched as it moved towards the bar.

"Excuse me guys, time to go fetch my Stetson." Levi rose from the chair but lost sight of his hat as he made his way through the crowd. As he leaned against the bar, he spotted Dusty Hart, another face from his childhood, at the opposite end.

"Syd, get your ass back here already. Did you fail to notice the people three deep around the bar?" Dusty yelled out.

"Jesus, Dusty, no need to go birthin' any cows." A familiar, feminine voice answered back. Levi chuckled. She was still full of piss and vinegar. Glancing down the length of the bar, he caught a glimpse of Sydney's long legs as she swung them over the bar, before dropping down into the trenches. Captivated by her movements, he watched as she took drink orders, tossed empty bottles over her shoulder to the trash, and made her way down the antiqued pinewood separating them. After all these years, it was harder to deny the attraction he had for her. Sydney continued towards him, exchanging drinks and money faster than he had ever seen.

"Hey angel, can I have my hat back?"

Those beautiful eyes met his and a sultry smile that promised nothing but trouble crossed her lips. "Are you kidding? I've got Levi McKenna's hat. You know I could make a pretty obscene profit off this hat."

"But you won't," he said, turning on the smile his assistant referred to as a real lady killer.

"That smile might work on them Hollywood girls you've been hanging out with, but I am immune to your charms, Mr. McKenna."

A voice called out, "Hey Sydney, how about a kiss?" Though the tone in the man's voice was playful, Levi's jaw tightened. A slow intake of air eased his tension.

"You're in the wrong place, mister. A few clubs downtown might be able to give you the action you're looking for." Sydney looked at Levi and rolled her eyes. "Some people. So, back to the hat, what makes you think I won't sell it?"

Trying to hide her discomfort, Sydney pushed past the remark but not before Levi saw it. "Call it a hunch."

"I guess we'll just have to see about that, cowboy." She handed a few beers across to a waitress, then turned and blew him a kiss. "I might just hang on to it as a memento."

"Fine by me," Levi thought, looking around. Dusty was no longer in sight. "So where'd the big man run off to?"

She jerked her head towards the opposite end of the bar. "Busy, but I'll get him. Dusty, you got a guy down here wants to talk to the owner."

"So deal with him," Dusty yelled back.

"He doesn't want to talk to me." She winked at Levi.

Dusty's voice grew louder, laced with irritation. "Well, why the hell not? You're nicer than I am and much better to look at. Just take care of it, Syd."

Levi watched the ease with which Sydney switched discussing fashion or sports, depending on who she served. The woman's love and ability to talk about both made for a combination Levi found intoxicating and damn sexy. Of course, he had always found her an enticing little package. Nothing compared to southern charm in his book, and she had it in spades. Even the curses dripped with it as they fell from her tongue.

"Dusty, get your ass down here already!"

"God damn Sydney, you're an owner. Tell the guy to get over it or take his macho bullshit out of here."

Levi could hear the frustration in his friend's voice, but

knew he wouldn't leave Sydney to deal on her own. An exasperated sigh escaped her and Levi had to forcibly bite his tongue. Dusty slowly moved in their direction, stopping occasionally to refill drinks.

"So what's the deal, guy? Too macho to deal with Sydney..." Dusty's voice trailed off as recognition slid across his face and his good-humored personality took over. He chuckled, "When the hell did you get to town?"

Levi studied his watch. "About four hours ago."

"Here for the rodeo or slumming?"

"Rodeo. A few of the guys are at the corner table." Levi looked towards the stage when the band began to play again.

"So, I need a rodeo in town before I can get your ass out here for a visit?"

"Hardly. Just been busy."

"So I gathered. I follow the news. Movies, women and bulls leave little time for much else."

"Can't believe everything you hear or read, man. You know that."

"True," Dusty looked past him with a hunger in his eyes. Only one thing in the world, so far as Levi knew, elicited such a reaction from his friend. Dusty's wife, Becca, stepped up next to him with a tray full of empty glasses. She still looked at Dusty as though he were the only man in the room. When she leaned over the bar to give Dusty a kiss, a pang of longing for what his friends shared crept up before Levi could stop it. "Becca, you're as beautiful as ever. When you planning on leaving this lug and running away with me?"

"Why? You plan on growing up and settling down in the near future?" she asked, hugging him. "It's good to see you, Levi. Where is she, Dusty?"

"Follow the trail of drooling men." His tone held irritation, but Levi didn't blame the guy. His sister had always been eye catching. Dusty turned back to him. "We make more money the nights she hops behind the bar. Damn guys ogle her like she's serving them naked, though. It's disgusting and yet, it's hardly the worst part."

Before Levi could ask what could be worse, Justin strolled up and slapped him on the back.

"Hey, Levi."

"Justin, this is Dusty Hart, the owner of the bar."

Justin shook Dusty's hand. "Hey man, the singer is hot. I bet she makes you a lot of money in this joint." Ignorant to the expression on Dusty's face, he turned back to Levi. "We're thinking about checking out some of the casinos, you game?"

"Nah, I think I'll hang here and catch up with y'all later."

"Mind if we take the limo?"

"Go ahead. I can catch a ride or call a cab."

Justin's exaggerated wink before he left could only mean one thing—he suspected Levi's reason for staying. Levi shook his head as Justin walked away. "Sorry, Justin's mouth rarely checks with his brain first."

Dusty shrugged. "No problem. So you're gonna hang around?"

"Until you get sick of me or kick me out." He settled onto the nearest cowhide barstool. "So what's worse?"

A female voice came over the microphone and Dusty looked to the stage where Becca now stood.

"You'll see."

"She sings too?" The look Dusty shot him quickly shut him up. Becca began to sing. A few bars later, Sydney joined her sister-in-law on stage and their two voices melded together in perfect harmony in a heart-wrenching song Levi'd heard only a few times since it had been written. It was Syd's mom's song. One Charlene Hart had written about a love gone bad only a few short weeks before her new husband had ended her life. Trying not to stare at Sydney, he pulled his gaze away and peered around the bar. Considering the way the other men were gawking at both women, he could understand Dusty's feelings. "Yeah, I can see why this is worse."

"Would you enjoy watching your wife and baby sister being stared at by a bunch of men? Drooled over like they were a couple of perfectly cooked cuts of prime beef?" Dusty sighed. "Becca likes when Sydney sings with her band though, and I'm not such an asshole I'd stop it."

"Could be worse. They could be dancing in a club downtown."

"Don't even go there." Dusty's glare could have frozen him to the barstool and he quickly threw his hands up in submission. The girls left the stage, smiling as they headed to the bar.

Levi took a sip of his beer. "So this is why you haven't returned my calls?"

"Figured I babbled about it long enough. It was time to shit or get off the pot." Dusty chuckled. "If it's any consolation, it was on my to-dos, just never quite finished the damn list."

"How's Syd been? She seems happy. Ever walk down the aisle?"

"Nope. She has poor taste in men and is still a regular asshole magnet, with her last one turning out to be the worst yet."

"What was so wrong with him?"

"Controlling and manipulative with a jealous streak that would put my stepfather to shame about sums it up. She has that same scary wild streak our mom had." Dusty's voice softened as Sydney approached. His friend's eyes held a protectiveness Levi was all too familiar with.

Sydney stopped close enough for him to touch. Sitting on his hands to avoid trouble suddenly seemed like a good idea. She elbowed his side.

"Ouch! What was that for?"

"Staying away so long." Resting her arms on the bar, she looked to her brother. "I need a round for the guys up front." She turned her attention back to him. "I watched you last year. You did pretty well, until Devil bucked you after two seconds and Justin walked away the winner."

Hearing she closely followed the rodeo circuit shocked him. "Devil's the worst bull to ride, and Justin got lucky last year."

"Please, Justin Trent is going to give you a run for your money. He holds more titles than you and doesn't have your distractions."

"What distractions are you referring to?" Turning to face her more fully, the sight of her casually moistening her lips sent a wave of desire burning through him.

She didn't seem to notice. "Take your pick, but I was referring to the buckle bunnies and media. No one seems to be interested in much else when your name comes up anymore."

Levi tried not to let the comment bother him. "Last year— was it the brunette or blonde?"

"The blonde. She miraculously appeared on your arm whenever a camera was near. Think she had a bit part in your

last movie." Sydney scoffed. "Meant a lot to ya, huh?"

"You don't hold anything back do you, angel?"

"No point. Life's too short and you aren't around that much."

Dusty's laughter interrupted them as he set the last shot on the tray. "Here, Syd."

Levi watched her disappear into the crowd with the drink order and turned back to find Dusty shaking his head. "She's got your number."

"Unfortunately."

"Catch up at closing?"

"Yep." He took another drink from his beer and thought about what Sydney had said, while Dusty went back to tending the crowd. Damn if she hadn't been right, a fact that bothered him more than he wanted to admit. Just another affirmation of what he needed to do.

✳

Three hours and a barely touched beer later, the bar had closed. Tossing his towel to the last bartender, Dusty walked away from his post. "Come on, let's grab a table."

Levi followed Dusty to a booth in the corner. The bar, now practically vacant, seemed like a ghost town. Becca and Sydney worked diligently to move the tables, revealing the dance floor he hadn't known was there. "You really seem to be doing well for yourself."

A smile crossed Dusty's face. "I'm no Levi McKenna, but I do all right."

The grass always seemed greener. Levi shrugged. "I'd trade places with you any day of the week."

"I'm not offering up my life for trade. It took a lot of hard work to get all of this. Life is good."

"I'd call you a damn fool if you said otherwise." Levi glanced towards the bar where Sydney had disappeared. Yep, given half the chance he would trade it all.

Chapter Two

Absent-mindedly wiping down the bar, Sydney watched as Levi talked with her brother. They fell into the old groove so easily after years of little more than a few phone calls. Becca came over with the last round of empties from the tables and tossed them in the trash. The weight of her sister-in-law's gaze made her squirm. "Why are you staring?"

"I could ask you the same thing. He's nice eye candy." Becca nudged her. "You don't plan on being a miserable old spinster surrounded by a bunch of cats do you?"

"Oh, come on." A very unladylike snort escaped her. "Need I remind you of my last adventure in romance? Tyler didn't exactly turn out to be Rhett Butler."

"True." With a dreamy-eyed look, she stared out at Dusty. "But you can't judge all guys by Tyler."

"Okay, what about the one before him, the devil in blue jeans? Oh and we can't forget the CEO, the snowboarder, the banker, the musician or the poker player." Sydney sighed. "I'm just like my mamma after all I guess."

"Don't say that! Your mother was a lost soul who made one wrong choice that ended her life. And I doubt the Charlene Hart I knew would want you subjecting yourself to a life without love."

The truth in Becca's words stung. The woman knew her too well. "I'm hardly lining up at the door to the nearest convent, Becca." She took in a slow breath. "Just saying I might need to change my strategy a bit."

"Sweetheart, strategy's hardly your problem. It's your taste in men." Becca winked at her. "Maybe, the one you're searching for is right in front of you."

"Right, my brother has one rule—no dating his friends. Last I checked Levi's still on the friends list. Dusty would have a complete conniption."

"True, but how do you know Levi's not the man to ride you off into the sunset? You might never know if you don't test the waters." After a long appraising look, Becca sighed. "You're hopeless. I'm taking this to the office."

Register drawers in hand, Becca turned towards the office. Opportunity to punish the meddling reared its ugly head and she took the towel and whipped Becca with it.

The loud crack of the towel against blue jeans caused her sister-in-law to jump and nearly drop everything. "Damn it, Sydney!"

"Serves you right." She went back to cleaning up, ignoring the evil stare cast in her direction. Date Levi McKenna, what a laugh. Obviously marrying her brother had taken Becca's I.Q. down a notch or two. Jerry, the last of the bar staff to hang around, brought up the stock she'd asked for and they set about preparing the bar for the following evening. When they finished, she headed back to the office.

Becca had the radio on, money spread all over the desk, appearing as frazzled as Sydney'd ever seen her. The laugh threatening to escape her was quickly stifled. Her sister-in-law exceeded at everything except the books, proving the woman wasn't as perfect as she believed her to be.

"So how bad did you screw it up?" Taking Levi's hat off, she set it on the corner of the desk.

"Damn it, why can't I figure this out? I graduated top of my class, married one of the few decent men in Vegas and help run a successful business. Yet, I can't get the damn books to balance." Becca's pencil sailed across the room.

Sydney moved around the desk, bringing the extra chair with her, and studied the receipt tape. They had been busy. With the rodeo in town, it would continue. "Good thing we had extra help tonight."

"You wouldn't have known it. Dusty still acted like we were short handed." Becca laughed. "I'm amazed he's actually planning on leaving the bar in Jerry's hands for a few nights."

"Me too, but I've learned to never look a gift horse in the mouth." Staring over Becca's shoulder at the computer screen, she looked at the numbers before studying the receipt tape again. "Where in the hell did you get this number from? Move over will ya?"

When Becca had done as she'd asked and moved her chair out of the way, she moved up to the computer and began keying in the figures.

"You know, Levi's single again."

The statement caught her off-guard and she cursed as she keyed in the wrong numbers—distraction at its finest. Her mind reeled at the thought of Levi and the muscles that had felt so good when she'd leaned into him earlier. No doubt about it, she was in trouble. "Stop bringing him up, he's off limits."

"You've considered him." Her sister-in-law giggled like a school girl who'd just heard the latest gossip and Sydney shook her head in denial.

"You're not pulling the wool over my eyes. I saw the way you drooled over him tonight."

"I'm not blind, especially where he's concerned, but it changes nothing." Trying to move on from the conversation, she keyed in a few more figures and hit total. Comparing it with the register balance, she turned to show Becca.

"Wow, is that right?"

"Yep, proving yet again people love two things." She smiled at Becca's quizzical look. "Cowboys and beer. The only thing to top it off would be if we added some real Texas barbeque, but this is Vegas, not the Lone Star state."

"You still miss Texas?" It was a question she'd heard many times over in recent months. A southern girl at heart, she longed to go back, but she couldn't bring herself to leave.

"Yeah, I still miss it."

"You plan on going back?"

"Depends. Are you trying to get rid of me?" Her brother's constant worry for her had to wear on their marriage. She had difficulty dealing with it herself at times.

"Hardly. You've just never been a Sin City kind of girl." Becca got up and walked to the couch at the back wall of the office. After finishing up the deposit and entering the totals in the ledger, Sydney grabbed Levi's hat off the desk and joined Becca, loving the feel of the leather couch as she sank into it.

"You can take the girl out of Texas, but you can't take Texas out of the girl."

"Huh?" The expression on Becca's face didn't surprise her.

"Nothing, just something my mamma used to say. Truth is, I'd go back in a heartbeat, but what would I be going back to? My family's here." She ran her hands over the felt of Levi's hat.

"You thinking about your mom?" Becca rested her head on her shoulder.

Afraid words would fail her, she simply nodded. The two of them had become close, even before Dusty had popped the question and she'd come to treasure the friendship more with her mother gone. Girls back home had been far more interested in playing the part of the southern debutante and had had no interest in getting dirty on the ranch, where she'd lived and breathed the ranch life.

"So what's so great about the rodeo?" Becca said, obviously changing the subject.

"It's probably easier to list what's not great about it. I can't believe you've lived here for fifteen years and have never been to the rodeo."

"What can I say? I've lived a very sheltered life."

"Well, you can't stay married to a Texas man and not go to the rodeo. Didn't you read the manual he came with?"

"There's a manual?" The mock surprise in her sister-in-law's voice made her smile.

"In fact, it should be a rite of passage for all women. Bulls, horses and cowboys' asses in tight jeans are hardly things a girl should go a lifetime without." Reclining deeper into the leather sofa, she let out a sigh. She knew she couldn't pass up the opportunity to see real cowboys again.

In her twenty-four years of life, she'd seen many, but five years away from Texas had left her suffering some serious withdrawals. Three years ago Dusty had bought rodeo tickets as a last minute surprise, which had left them sitting in nosebleed central. This year it would be Gold Buckle seats, thanks in part to the bar's generous sponsorship. Best seats in the house. Close enough to see the blood, sweat and tears. "Becca, we'll be close enough to pinch their butts if we want to."

They both fell into a fit of laughter that was interrupted when Dusty poked his head through the door. "You girls have a little more beer than you should have?"

"Nope," they both said in unison, trying to reign in their laughter. Dusty shook his head in disbelief. Sydney tried to answer him with a straight face. "We're just talking about butts."

"God help me, I don't know if I have the strength to survive another rodeo season." Dusty leaned against the door. "Syd, you did mom's song justice tonight, she would have been proud."

"Thanks. I just wish she was here to see me sing it."

"Me too," His voice went a little soft and he cleared his throat before continuing. "Do you mind driving Levi back to the hotel?"

"Not at all," she blurted out a little too eagerly, earning a look of warning from him. "What?"

"Just drive him to the hotel and go home."

Standing up, she put Levi's hat on her head, saluted her brother, followed it with a clipped, "Yes, sir," and went in search of her passenger.

$$*$$

Leaning against the bar, Levi looked at ease as he talked with Jerry. His jeans were tight enough to look good, without ruining the illusion of what might lie underneath them, though sitting on his lap had given her a pretty good indication. Paired with the black T-shirt that seemed to cling to the upper part of his chest and the sandy blonde head of loose curls, it was a damn shame he was off limits. Well, she had to give Becca credit. Her taste in men remained intact.

Levi peered at her with those baby blues and winked. "Come to return my hat I see."

"Nope, came to take you back to whatever fancy ass hotel you're staying in, Mr. Rodeo Heartthrob."

"I'm staying at the Mirage, which was hardly my first option, angel." Straightening up, he shook the bartender's hand. "Thanks for keeping me company, Jerry."

Yep, Texas knew how to make 'em and they just didn't make men the same anywhere else, she thought as she slid into her jacket. Levi stepped up behind her and rested his hand against the small of her back. "After you."

As they walked, the sensation of warmth spreading through her elicited thoughts of what could be. She shook them off knowing they would lead to nothing but trouble and heartache. When they stepped outside, Levi began to chuckle.

"What's so funny?"

"I'm going to take a wild guess here at which car is yours." He confidently strolled towards Becca's convertible Mustang. She smiled and shook her head. Cocking his head slightly his eyes widened in surprise. "No?"

"Guess again, hotshot." Walking past him, she headed towards the forest-green super duty pickup. A white folded piece of paper on the windshield stopped her. She ripped the paper out from under the wiper, opened it, then tossed it towards the trash and missed. Cursing under her breath, she picked it up and threw it in the bin before heading back to the truck.

Levi looked at her. "Problem?"

"Just an asshole who doesn't know when to quit." Unlocking the truck, she climbed in and settled into the leather seats. Satisfaction—the kind that came from something hard won—washed over her. This truck had been the first thing she'd bought and paid for with her own money.

"Seem to remember you having a thing for assholes." He climbed in next to her.

She stuck the key in the ignition and pulled out of the parking lot. The gaze from her passenger weighed down on her, but she refused to look at him and hoped he would get the message.

"Okay, not something you care to discuss. So what have you been doing with yourself?"

Realizing how childish she was acting, she conceded. Outside of her family, the only other person in the world who knew much about her life now sat beside her. "I've been having a thing for assholes."

"No Mr. Right yet?"

"Nope, not with the men I pick. How about you? No new flavor of the week?"

"To my assistant's dismay." Levi shifted in the seat. "No, there's no new flavor of the week. Didn't really want the flavors being offered to begin with."

"So what do you want?"

The long look he gave made her squirm. Finally, he

answered. "Something out of my reach."

"Probably not dating the right women." Having seen the many women he had been paired with over the last few years, along with the fact she'd practically grown up with the man, she felt it was a fair statement. Her thoughts drifted to her last failed romance with the ex who wouldn't leave her alone. She'd been blind not to see their relationship for what it was—a reenactment of her mother's and stepfather's. Unlike her mother though, she'd gotten out before it was too late. "Of course, I'm a fine one to give advice considering my track record. I must be cursed," she mumbled.

"Somehow I doubt that. You just have to stop being—how did Dusty put it? An asshole magnet."

She sighed. Only Dusty could put it so eloquently. Her brother had a point. If there was an asshole in the room, she seemed to hone in and take him home. The city passed them by as she drove, and she found it soothing to be sitting next to Levi. She pulled the truck onto the strip and headed towards the hotel.

"Are you taking a trip down memory lane?" Levi asked, jarring her out of her moment of self-pity.

"Not much for conversation, am I?"

"We obviously aren't talking about the right subject. Let's see—does prom ring any bells for you?" His smile was infectious.

"Yeah, actually, it does. Some cowboy came in and saved me from a night of embarrassment. If I recall, that was a pretty fun night." Sydney glanced over, watching the neon lights of the strip play across his face. God, he was handsome. Just a little eye candy to soothe the soul, she'd always thought so.

"Yes, it was. I don't think I laughed or had as much fun at my own prom."

"Somehow, I doubt doing a favor for your best friend and coming to his little sister's rescue was entertaining for you." The look she sent dared him to lie.

"Well, let me see if I can recall the events for you, angel. I think we were late to the prom because I had to scrounge a suit together at the last minute. I showed up without flowers or a corsage. You walked out in a very sexy strapless gown, and I tripped over my own two feet..."

"You did look ridiculous in your uncle's baby blue suit.

Where a southern gentleman ever bought a suit like that is beyond me."

They both laughed.

"I couldn't tell you, angel. He left me that damn suit in his will. Needless to say, the night continues to hold the record for most fun I've had on a date, by far. They've all been downhill since then."

Reflecting on that night and their obvious misfortunes in dating since then laid the groundwork for a bet. "I'll try to stop dating assholes if you stay away from the blonde bimbos." She pulled the truck into valet parking at the Mirage and stopped. She spit in her hand and held it out to him. "Deal?"

"Gross and completely unladylike, Sydney." He chuckled, spit in his hand and shook hers. "It's a deal, angel. Thanks for the lift."

"You're welcome. Thanks for the enjoyable trip down memory lane."

"Welcome," he said as he leaned towards her and kissed her cheek, grabbing his hat from her head. "I told you I'd get my hat back."

He started to open the door to the truck, but hesitated. "Syd, are you and Dusty going to the sponsors' cocktail party tomorrow night?"

She shrugged. "I thought about it, but I didn't want to go alone and Dusty and Becca are working the bar."

The devilish smile she'd seen so often growing up slid across his face. "Feel like keeping me out of trouble?'

"Depends. How fancy is it?"

"Requires tickets to get in, not open to the general public kind of fancy."

"I'm not wearing the strapless."

"I'm not wearing the baby blue suit, so I think we're good. Meet me here at five-thirty then?" Another quick peck on the cheek and he climbed out of the truck. "Thanks, angel."

She felt her cheeks flush as she watched him disappear into the hotel. Not for the first time, she wondered what things would have been like if he and Dusty hadn't been friends. Would Levi's name be another on the list of heartbreaks she'd suffered, or was Becca right? Had her Mr. Right been under her nose all along?

A relationship with him would come with its own set of problems. She couldn't be sure if the playboy image was real or fabricated. In her opinion, relationships didn't belong in the spotlight and she wouldn't be just another notch on his belt. Then there was her overprotective brother, who seemed quite partial to having her wind up the spinster with cats if it meant keeping her from guys like Tyler.

*

The whole way home, she dwelled on the mistakes she'd made in her life. Becca was right. Her mother wouldn't have wanted her to give up on love. After Tyler, the option held some appeal, but she was a dreamer like her mom and as such, not quite ready to give up on finding her own happily ever after. When she pulled into her street and saw the unwanted car in her driveway, she wished the drive had lasted longer.

The never-ending debate began, get out of the car and face the ex or go to Dusty's. If she got out of the car, she would never get off the merry-go-round she was on. Nope, she'd walked away once and still bore the scars of a battered heart, but she wasn't stupid. She turned down a side street to avoid the house. Why couldn't people accept when things were over? From inside her purse, the phone began to chirp a familiar ring. She dug around for it, opening it as she pulled it from her purse. "What, Dusty?"

"You should have been home already."

Classic overprotective Dusty, she thought. It didn't surprise her anymore. "No shit, I'm on my way to your house. There's an unwanted visitor at mine."

As he hung up, she could hear his swearing. She tossed the phone up on the dashboard. If she couldn't get rid of the Mr. Wrongs in her life, how in the world would she ever find Mr. Right? And what the hell good did a restraining order do when people refused to obey it?

Fifteen minutes had passed by the time she pulled her truck into her brother's driveway. Becca, appearing a little worse for wear, waited for her on the porch swing. She felt bad because her brother had obviously gotten Becca all worked up.

As Syd climbed out of the truck, her sister-in-law stood and shook her head.

"Guess maybe you should have stayed with the cowboy in the hotel."

"Only you, Becca."

Becca walked over, slipped her arm around her waist as they walked into the house. A raised voice came from the kitchen, where Dusty was on the phone. Relief slid into his eyes when he saw her.

"Dusty, calm down."

"Yeah, thanks officer." He slammed the phone down. "Don't tell me to calm down, Syd. There's no damn way I'm going to sit here while some asshole camps in front of your house. He shouldn't even be there. What in the hell's he doing there, anyway?"

"Jesus, you act like I invited him. If I wanted the man there I surely wouldn't be standing here now, would I?" She loved her brother and understood his concern and desire to keep her safe. She was even thankful for it, but it was a little trying at times when he took his frustrations out on her.

As the family mediator, Becca took her cue. "Dusty, why don't you go grab us all a beer."

Soon they were all seated around the table. Silence hung heavy in the room until her brother finally broke it. "It was good to see Levi again. I mean other than during our family tragedies or in the newspapers and television."

Good seeing Levi was an understatement in her opinion. She was really looking forward to going out with him. A fun night with a guy hadn't been on her agenda in a long time and she would take her fun where she could get it, even with someone who was off-limits. *Shit.* Glancing at her brother, she quickly decided on the best course of action. "By the way, Dusty, I won't be stopping by the bar tomorrow night. I'm going to go to the sponsor thing after all."

His eyes fixed on hers, accusation in them. "With Levi?"

"Call it a repayment for a last minute prom night date."

Chapter Three

Levi sat on the bed, his back propped against the headboard, hat in his hands. The scent of magnolias clung to the felt as a reminder of Sydney. If she'd been any other girl he would have flirted, sent a sexy smile her way, probably even managed to steal more than a kiss on the cheek by the end of the night. Lord knows it was tempting. She embodied his idea of the perfect girl. He reached over and set the phone for no calls, sank further down into the bed and rested the hat over his face. For the first time in a long time, he was looking forward to a cocktail party.

∗

Pounding and hysterical calls from a woman on the other side of the door woke him up the next morning.

"Jesus, Lisa, give me a second," he yelled, pulling on jeans and a T-shirt.

Levi opened the door to his red-faced assistant, who pushed her way past him with the cell phone pressed to her ear. Damn thing was like another appendage. He didn't think she went anywhere without it, including the bathroom.

"Yeah, it's sitting in my briefcase—I'll run it by him." She hit a key on the phone and tossed it, along with her purse, on the coffee table, making herself at home as she sank into the couch. "So, who's the girl?"

"What the hell are you babbling about, woman? It's early. I would like a shower and a meal before attending the media circus you have me participating in." Levi pushed his hand through his hair in exasperation. The woman infuriated him.

"The girl, the truck, valet—any of this ringing a bell?" Lisa tapped her finger on the back of the couch to signal her impatience. "My phone has been ringing non-stop with papers wanting to get the scoop."

"Yeah, it rings a bell and the girl is none of your business."

"Hello? Remember me? I'm your assistant. You hired me to deal with this crap so therefore, anything concerning you is my business. If it can be captured on film, written about in a paper or reported on the news, I think it qualifies as my business. And you two were captured on film a few times." She snatched the phone up, opened an email and shoved it at him. Levi hesitated before taking the phone. The tiny display held a picture of him kissing Sydney's cheek. Damn it.

"Where did those come from?"

"Thought you'd be more interested in where they are going." Lisa tossed the phone back on the table, waiting for a response. Levi glared at her. "They're going to be in the local paper, television and no doubt the national news will pick them up shortly thereafter."

"God damn it, Lisa! You will call them all back and tell them to pull the story. They will not put this girl's picture all over the news."

"I didn't know you would be so upset about it. It's great. 'Rodeo and film heartthrob steals heart of unknown local girl'. You know how the press loves that crap."

In his whole life, he had never wanted to wring someone's neck so badly. "She is not unknown to me, damn it. We're not talking about one of the girls you set me up with. You will call and pull her picture, or I will not do the publicity events today and you will be left standing there like an ass."

He hadn't been so blunt with her before, but Sydney hardly deserved to be thrown under the bus by money-grubbing photographers, or an assistant who thought all publicity was good for his image. Publicity was not all he cared about and it had taken him a little too long to realize it. When Lisa didn't move, Levi grabbed her cell phone and shoved it at her. "I'll go a step further. If those pictures appear *anywhere* you're out of a job."

Lisa hesitated, then took the phone and hit speed dial. "Pull the story." She hung up and let out a huge sigh. "There, are you happy? I don't understand what the big deal is. She's just another girl that will do wonders for your image, just like all the others."

"That statement is exactly why it's a big deal."

"I don't agree with this." The frustration on her face was evident. Lisa didn't like being told what to do. Knowing her as he did, there was no doubt it would be handled, regardless of whether she agreed or not. She could be conniving when it suited his career, but she was also loyal and worked hard for him. "There's a new movie deal on the table."

"Not interested. We've discussed this."

"Just hoping you might change your mind. You should have options waiting for you if you decide to hang up your chaps." She picked her purse up. "I have a date lined up for you tonight. You need to be ready by five-thirty. Why are you shaking your head?"

"I can get my own dates, so please stop trying to hook me up with every floozy you find."

The Irish blood in the woman normally had her spoiling for a good argument, but when she refrained, he knew something was off with her. Upon closer inspection, he noticed the bloodshot eyes, the messy hair and sweats.

"Something's going on with you. What is it?"

"Just stuff back home. It's fine, really." She calmly stood and headed for the door, but turned back towards him. "I'll have room service send up your usual breakfast. Get your shower. We're running a little behind schedule. I need you at the events pavilion by eleven."

Without waiting for an answer, Lisa walked out the door. When she was gone, he headed for the shower and ran things over in his mind. Relying on her to handle everything had become second nature and it worked out well for both of them in the beginning. With her ambition and take-no-prisoners attitude, she dealt with everything he despised, like agents and the media. But his career goals no longer extended beyond the rodeo arena. Life was all about the road to the title from here on out.

Levi stepped from the shower. Focus, that's what he needed. He had allowed it to slip away from him, but it wouldn't happen again. This was going to be his do-or-die year. If he finished the Nationals without the title, it would be fate's way of telling him it was time to move on.

✳

Thirty minutes later he was dressed, in the car and on his way to the events center. God, he hated these media events. Other guys got to discuss their careers, while Levi got to talk about whatever had recently hit the papers regarding his love life and any recent movies he'd been in. He needed to play this right if he was going to keep focus where he wanted it.

The driver stopped in front of the media and fans awaiting his arrival. Time to put on the old game face, he thought as he stepped from the car.

Lisa got things started as Levi took his seat at the table, staring out at the throngs of fans and reporters. Media was something he could do without. They didn't have anything to do with what happened in the ring between him and the bull. A little fact he had to occasionally remind himself of. The first round of questions began as flashes went off and fans stood on the sidelines in wait.

"Levi, what happened to the last girlfriend?" A young, female reporter asked when Lisa pointed. This game he'd become quite adept at playing, despite his discomfort.

"It ended, the way many relationships do."

"What about the girl you were with last night?" another reporter chimed in. "She going to be the next on the long list of girls you have been with?"

When Lisa started to speak, he stopped her and took a deep breath. This was his show. "She's a childhood friend and I ask that you respect that. Now, if this is the direction the line of questioning is going to take, then there's no point in continuing."

"What are your plans while you are in town?"

Levi smirked. "Did y'all forget Nationals are going on? I plan on winning myself a title."

Laughter erupted from the sea of reporters. Another spoke up. "Your luck hasn't been very good since you won your first big title. How do you plan on stealing the title from Justin Trent?"

"Stealing? You can't steal a title. The only way to win in this game is by being better than the others you are up against. I am."

A familiar TV reporter raised her hand. "Justin Trent has been on his game all year. How can you say you are better?"

"Darlin', obviously I managed to qualify. Besides, I have confidence in myself. Your head has to be in the arena, if it's not then you go down. We're not out there riding Shetland ponies. These are creatures that could crush your bones if you aren't careful. You can't approach them like you're taking them for a ride through the countryside. If your heart and head are not in what you're doing, you can't win. I plan on winning. Thanks for coming out." Levi stood, signaling there would be no more questions. Stepping away from the table, he caught sight of Lisa in a heated discussion with a reporter. Considering the reporter couldn't seem to get a word in edgewise, Levi figured he'd done something to earn the tongue lashing she was giving him.

Fans stood patiently behind the barricades, waiting for his autograph and he indulged them, only walking away when he'd finished. Sydney stood to the side, waiting. She smiled and he headed towards her.

"I think you handled the circus very well, Mr. McKenna."

"Watch out, angel. These vultures will swoop in, snap pictures, and before you can say boo—you'll be branded as just another one of my bimbos." He winked at her.

"It would be a change from the blondes and wouldn't Dusty just love that. Local bar hussy hooks up with rodeo heartthrob." She grinned. "Just here dropping off some logos."

"You're really going to sponsor the bull riding competition?" Levi failed at keeping the surprise from his voice.

"Obviously you don't pay much attention to the sponsors, so I won't take offense. Yeah, we had planned on it when we opened the bar." Slipping an arm through his, she walked with him towards the events center. "Why do you seem so shocked?"

"Just think it's a lot of money to throw away."

"You call it throwing it away. We call it a good investment in advertising." She reached for the door, and he brushed her hand away.

"Angel, didn't Dusty teach you anything? A southern girl never opens the door for herself when a gentleman is present to do it for her."

"Gentlemen are few and far between in this hellhole."

Sydney smiled and it made him feel capable of dealing with anything. Amazing the effect some things had on people, he thought as they walked through the center. This felt almost too comfortable. Levi saw Justin Trent headed their way.

"Hey Levi, I thought you handled yourself real well out there. But I am hardly going to hand the title over to you." Justin stopped, looking Sydney over slowly from head to toe. Sydney, apparently not bothered by the once-over, looked back at him.

"Well, if it's not the reigning champ himself, Justin Trent," she said in that damn southern drawl, her eyes twinkling as she gazed at Justin. He had half a mind to shake some sense into her. If it were any other girl, he wouldn't have been bothered.

"Hi there, you're from the bar last night, right?" Justin smiled when she nodded. "You have a great voice."

"Aw, how sweet of you to say."

Levi grabbed hold of Sydney's arm. "Well, I think we need to be moving along."

"It was nice to meet you, Justin. I hope I get the chance to see you again while you're here."

Looking past her to Justin, he shook his head.

Justin laughed. "I'm sure you will."

With every intention of putting as much distance between them and Justin as possible, he set a quick pace as they walked away. The expression on her face showed displeasure at being dragged away. Half-expecting a tongue lashing, he braced himself, but all Sydney did was gently pull her arm from his grasp. "It's bad enough I have to deal with Dusty's over protectiveness. I hardly need it from you."

"Sorry," was all he could manage to say. Admittedly, he was a little taken aback by his behavior.

Truth sucked. Sometimes it bit him in the ass. Other times it eluded him. He knew why he'd hauled her off like a barbaric caveman staking his claim, but he wouldn't say it. To speak the words out loud would be a confirmation he could not afford.

Biting her bottom lip and studying him with a scrutinizing gaze, she was apparently considering the depth of his sincerity. "Well, you've apologized, so I guess you deserve a chance at redemption."

Looping her arm through his again, she led him along the

corridors without any further comment. Calm washed over him while they walked. The leisurely pace, as though they had all the time in the world, gave him a sense of normalcy he found comforting.

"So where are you headed?"

Sydney shook her head. "Not telling. It would ruin the surprise."

He looked at her and she smiled. Warmth spread through him, and he wanted to wrap his arms tightly around her. God, where had his restraint gone? Sydney, his best friend's little sister, was and always had been off-limits. Her voice pulled him from his thoughts.

"I think you need to be reminded of why you started this journey."

"Really?" he asked as they walked through the back doors of the event center where her truck sat. His phone rang but when he went to answer it, Sydney grabbed it from him and hit the power button before sliding the phone into her back pocket. "What are you doing?'

"Saving you from yourself," she said, handing him a piece of paper and then climbing into the truck. "Meet me there in two hours." Before he could ask any more questions, she pulled away.

Chapter Four

Sydney's life had been built around guarding her heart. Risk and chance—two words with the potential to tear down her carefully constructed wall. Becca made it sound so easy. She sighed. The ghosts of failed relationships still haunted her. If she didn't take this chance, as Becca had suggested, would she regret it? Worst case scenario—her heart would get broken. Sydney Hart would be just another name on the long list of girls who'd gambled on love with Levi McKenna and lost. Deep down, she knew she'd overcome the heartache. Each time it had become a little easier. Still, she wasn't sure if she should take the chance. Working on Becca's father's small ranch usually helped her sort through things, but waiting to see if Levi would show, her mind simply ran in circles. She dispelled the thoughts and moved to the back of the trailer to unload the hay bales.

"You know, I would've been here sooner, but I really try to avoid manual labor." Levi appeared on the opposite side of the trailer. "So you lured me here to do your chores?"

His teasing demeanor made it difficult to keep a straight face.

"I hardly need the help of a sissified country boy." Lacing her fingers through the wire, she hauled another bale off the trailer. His laughter followed her, and he climbed up on the trailer to help. Her gaze lingered over him, and when it met his she felt her skin flush with embarrassment. Quickly, she set her sights back on work. When they'd finished, Levi leaned against the trailer.

"I'm not complaining, but how was that supposed to help me remember why I chase rodeo titles?"

"Oh, this isn't why I invited you, but when you climbed up on the trailer I was hardly going to stop you. Besides, I needed the help." Handing him a bottle of water, she smiled and jerked her head towards the barn. "Come on."

The scent of hay, dust and horse manure always made her feel at home. Grabbing Levi's hand, she pulled him past the open barn doors and around to the corral. She opened the gate and stepped inside, approaching the horse, who nudged his nose against her in greeting.

"I know, boy," she said, running her hand over his muzzle. "I brought you a visitor."

"I don't believe it." Levi stepped past her, pride evident on his face.

"I thought your dad told you. He drove him out here last year. Said Dante had chosen me, and it wasn't right I left him behind."

"No, he told me he'd sold him." Levi ran his hands over Dante's coat as he examined the horse he'd helped her train. "How's she been treating you, Dante?"

In response, the horse nudged his head against Levi's arm. Dante loved a good run and they'd ridden him double before. Taking her time, she ran her hand over his back before saddling him. She slipped her foot into the stirrup, mounted in one lithe movement and looked down at Levi. "Ready?"

Levi mounted the horse behind her, slid up close and reached his arms around her to take the reins. The stallion began to dance beneath them, but Levi quickly took charge and Dante settled. Levi whispered against her ear, "You ready?"

She nodded, and he nudged Dante's sides slightly. The Appaloosa relished being out of the corral, and Sydney could feel him begin to loosen up underneath them. Dante was surefooted and sped across the rocky ground as they headed towards the canyons. They came to a small stream created by the recent snow that had dusted the higher elevations of the valley. Levi pulled back on the reins and halted Dante at the water's edge. They each dismounted, and Sydney led the horse to the water to let him drink.

"Well Dante, you give a great ride, just like I remember." Levi ran his hands over the horse's muzzle in appreciation and then ground tied him. Sydney sat on a rock and looked out at the beauty of the canyon.

"Do you mind?' Levi asked, straddling the rock as he settled in behind her. He rested his head on her shoulder. The scent of his masculine cologne enveloped her. God, he smelled wonderful.

Maintain control, she reminded herself.

Levi let out a slow breath and it tickled the side of her neck. "It's pretty here. I mean, I've seen pictures of the canyons, but they don't do it justice."

She tilted her head back to get a better view of him. Looking into his deep blue eyes, she knew drowning was a great possibility. He leaned towards her, stopping with his mouth hovering over hers. The thought of kissing him made her toes curl, but temptation and desire waged war with her more cautious side.

"Can I kiss you?" His warm breath teased her lips as he spoke, a seduction of her senses that clouded her mind and sped her pulse. Without waiting for her response, he closed the remaining distance between them and pressed his lips to hers. The kiss was gentle, his lips barely touching hers, yet it held a promise of passion and tenderness. He ran his tongue across her bottom lip, tasting, tempting, then he kissed her deeply. When she responded, Levi ran his hand up her arm to the back of her neck and held her to him. *More.* One mere touch of his lips to hers and her last thread of control threatened to unravel. The flame she had tried to douse flared through her, but she forced herself to exercise restraint. This road she could not take, no matter how right it felt. Once she did, there would be no bread crumbs to find her way back. She pulled away from him.

"Thank you," Levi said.

Panic and irrational thoughts crept up on her. Emotional distress could be dealt with later. Right now, she just had to make it through the rest of the day.

They arrived back at the ranch and settled the horse. The emotional battle within her raged on. She wanted to spend time with him, but prayed he'd have to leave and keep her from making a potential mistake. "So, what's the agenda?"

"For starters, I would like my phone back." He slipped his

hand into her back jean pocket and retrieved the phone, turned it on and walked out of earshot.

Allowing him the privacy he obviously wanted, she headed off towards her truck to wait for him. The smell of cornbread and chili drifted from the house, reminding her she hadn't eaten.

The passenger door opened and Levi hopped into the cab beside her. "Sorry to make you wait."

"No big deal. Am I dropping you at the hotel?"

When he nodded, she headed towards the strip. On the drive to the hotel, the silence between them was awkward and she considered calling off the evening. It probably would have been the safest option for both of them, but she knew she'd regret it if she backed out.

"What are you wearing tonight?" he asked, taking in her attire. "Can't have you showing up in those curve-hugging jeans and tank top. It wouldn't quite be fair to me. If I have to get gussied up, so do you."

"I've got something." The question broke the tension in the cab of the truck and she caught him studying her out of the corner of his eye, a smile on his face. "It's not the strapless, so don't get your hopes up."

"Oh, I anticipate every moment of the evening, especially your outfit."

"Great, nothing like adding high expectations to make a girl nervous." Easing the truck into the drop-off lane of the valet, she started fidgeting with her keys.

"I'll see you at five-thirty, but call me when you get home." He winked as he got out of the truck.

"What do you have up your sleeve, Levi McKenna?"

There was no answer. Instead, he grabbed his cell, closed the door and headed into the hotel, calling back over his shoulder, "Don't be late."

*

Fifteen minutes later, Sydney pulled into her driveway. A floral delivery truck sat parked at the curb, and the driver stood at her door. He turned to look at her as she climbed out of the truck and retrieved the dress and shoes from the passenger side. "Miss Sydney Hart?"

"Yes." She eyed the driver suspiciously. Floral deliveries had not ranked high her list of favorites thanks to the ex.

"Can you sign for these?" The driver shoved a clipboard at her and she scribbled her name down. He glanced at the clipboard then back at her. "It's quite a large arrangement."

"Okay, give me just a sec to set this stuff down." Sydney unlocked the door and walked in, leaving it open as she turned off the alarm. After laying the garment bag on the back of the couch, she returned to find the delivery guy standing in the doorway with an oversized arrangement of magnolias.

"Here you are, Miss."

"Thanks," she said, trying to balance the flowers as she closed the door. Sydney set them on the coffee table and her phone rang. She snatched it up. "Hello?"

"You didn't call."

She snatched the card from the flowers and sank into the couch when she heard Levi's voice.

"Sorry, I was a little busy wrestling with flowers." She smiled at the words on the card that simply read, "My angel."

Levi chuckled on the other end of the line. "I couldn't resist. See you at five-thirty. I'll meet you at the bar downstairs."

The line went dead and she sat staring at the flowers. He was unbelievable and full of surprises. Keeping this within the boundaries that would save them both from Dusty's wrath would be more difficult than she had originally thought. She glanced at the clock. Damn, where did the time go? "Time to get dolled up," she thought as she forced herself off the couch and down the hall.

$$*$$

Levi fidgeted as he finished dressing. God, he hated wearing suits. They felt so restrictive. Not like the everyday jeans and T-shirts he found comfort in. Feeling as though he were about to embark on a first date, he nervously glanced at the clock and ignored Lisa's barrage of phone calls. Foolish is what it was. He'd taken Sydney out before, even if it had been to help her out, and now she was returning the favor—coming to his rescue—though he'd be lying if he said he felt nothing for her. His cell phone rang and his nerves went into overdrive when he saw Sydney's number.

"I'm in the lobby and making my way towards the bar, cowboy." Her intoxicating voice came through the line before he had the chance to say hello and his gut clenched.

"You were supposed to call when you got close."

Picking up his wallet, the tickets and the key card, he pulled the door shut behind him and stepped into the waiting elevator.

"I am..." her voice was low and sultry, "...close to the bar. You never specified how close I had to be."

"Order a drink and charge it to my room. I'll be there shortly." He hung up the phone and stepped out of the elevator. Glancing around, he was thankful there were no reporters. They were probably camped out by the banquet hall, waiting for some good shots. Knowing Lisa, she probably had it orchestrated right down to which photos they would take and when. Funny how a quick rise to fame and fortune had made him easily dismiss the important things. Not too late for a change though.

✳

Levi entered the bar and sought out his date. He caught sight of Sydney sitting at the opposite end, talking with the bartender and watching the game on TV. She glanced up, smiled and gracefully slid off the barstool.

"Do you like it?" she asked nervously, as she smoothed her hand down to straighten the dress.

Like was hardly the answer. Levi smiled and indicated for her to turn around. He wanted to take in the full view of the dress. Sydney obliged. Eye catching hardly described the dress that revealed a tasteful amount of cleavage, hugged her at the waist and showed off enough leg to tempt him to ditch the cocktail party.

"This is just something you had hanging around?" He managed to sound somewhat composed and was thankful.

"Not exactly. You don't like it?" She sounded irritated.

"Angel, if I couldn't appreciate a dress like that, I don't think I could call myself a man." He smiled. "Shall we?"

Placing his hand against the small of her back, he led her

through the casino. Heads turned as they walked and for once, they didn't even seem to notice him.

✳

Levi had to concentrate on where he placed his hands. The hotel security kept the media under control, and he didn't hesitate as they walked past. Pictures were inevitable though.

The cocktail party ended up being the typical boring social event he had always hated. Thank God, Sydney had come with him. Occasionally, she would lean into him, remind him to smile, or make comments that left him biting his tongue in futile attempts to hold his laughter. Needing a break from the socializing, they headed to their table, where Justin sat with Lisa at his side. Levi held the chair out for Sydney and then took his seat beside her. He didn't bother to make introductions.

"What's your deal? Are you dating my assistant?" He asked Justin.

"Needed a date and Lisa said she would come." Justin leaned back in the chair, arm slung over the back of Lisa's and his eyes locked on Sydney like she was the ultimate prize. "What's your deal?"

Levi lifted the beer bottle to his mouth, trying to buy a bit of time, but Sydney jumped on the question.

"Levi's and mine?" A smile played across her lips. "I plan on getting him liquored up and using him for sex."

The nonchalant way the words came out of her mouth caused Levi to inhale his beer, but Justin's laughter and Lisa's bulging eyes made up for the discomfort. Levi leaned into Sydney, brushed her hair off of her shoulder and whispered, "Careful, angel, I might just hold you to that. This socializing crap is very boring."

"Pizza and movies?"

"You're on." He slid his chair back and held out a hand for her. A night with Sydney, doing something they'd often done when they were younger, seemed so normal and right up his alley. Lisa's phone rang and she held up a hand. He didn't want to wait, but stopped cold when he saw his assistant's face turn ashen and the phone slip from her hands. "Lisa?"

Moving to her side, he picked up the phone and closed it, but not before seeing the name on the caller I.D. She took the phone from him. "Just some news about my dad, but I'll be fine. You guys go enjoy your evening. I've got Justin for company."

Levi waited a moment, wanting to be sure she wasn't just being stubborn before he turned back to Sydney. "So pizza and movies it is. Shall we?"

∗

The hot pizza in his lap provided only minimal distraction from the woman seated next to him.

"What movie do you want to watch?" Movies had always been a topic of debate when they were younger, but they agreed on his favorites. When he gave no answer, she smiled. "You can't be serious. *Die Hard*? All of them?"

"You can't watch just one. It's against the rules."

"Man rules maybe."

Laughter came a lot easier the past few days thanks to Sydney and he realized how little of it he'd been doing lately. They drove up a street where every neighborhood entrance had a gate to keep people out and the houses behind them indicated money. He kept waiting for Sydney to pull up to one of the gates, and was surprised when she pulled into a neighborhood that looked inviting and modest. Levi knew Sydney could afford a more elaborate home, probably even one very similar to the gated homes they had passed.

It shouldn't have shocked him when she parked the truck in the driveway of a small single story with a modest front porch. Light yellow siding, white trim, shutters and a porch swing reminded him of home. A southern oasis in the middle of the desert. Sydney had managed to capture her southern roots, carve out her little piece of home, and it suited her. He made a mental note to spend some time with her in the swing while he was in town.

"This is your place?"

"Yep, why do you sound surprised?" Sydney opened the front door. "It's not much, but it's mine. Make yourself at home."

Setting the pizza on the small table in the dining room, he took the liberty of strolling through the living room. The walls were decorated with photos of her and her mother, Dusty and Becca's wedding and Dusty and Levi when they were younger. The denim-upholstered couch looked inviting and he imagined her cuddled up against him while they watched movies. He sat in the oversized chair, pulled his boots off and placed them by the door next to her discarded heels.

Absent from the home were expensive art pieces or electronics. He'd become accustomed to women who wanted more than they could afford. Everything always had to be bigger and better, nothing was ever enough. Now, he sat in the home of a woman he'd known most of his life, surprised by her comfort in the simple things. No, she didn't fit in the same category as the other women he knew. Then again, he'd always known that. The sound of keys hitting the counter echoed through the house and he followed the noise to the kitchen. She stood on tiptoes, retrieving plates from the cabinet, the mass of auburn curls released from the up-do now trailing down her back. Longing to run his hands through the silken strands, he needed a distraction and headed to the sink to wash up.

"Beer or sweet tea?"

"Truly a tough call—sweet tea made by a true southern woman or a beer. Seeing as we are having pizza, I think I have to go with a beer." He loosened his tie and unbuttoned the collar of his shirt.

"Man after my own heart, nothing beats pizza and beer." Pulling two bottles out of the fridge, she seemed to reconsider her statement. "Well almost nothing."

She hit the play button on the answering machine and turned to lean against the counter. The light in her eyes faded and tension crept into her when the messages began to play. Anger had seeped into her eyes along with a hint of fear.

"Sydney, where in the hell are you? You're not at the bar or at home, because I checked—" Sydney reached over and hit the delete button. The same voice came through on the next three messages and Levi watched as she erased each one.

"Is that the asshole?" Common sense told him it was, and he wasn't happy about it. The guy sounded a few cards short of a full deck and hardly someone he wanted calling Sydney. She nodded but wouldn't look at him, so he tipped her face up.

Staring into the depths of those haunted eyes, his career, the title, Dusty—it all meant nothing. All he wanted was to take away the fear and hurt he saw in her. "Sometimes taking back control means knowing when to take a different path," he thought to himself.

Her lips were slightly parted and her breathing became more rapid. He claimed her sweet mouth with his and took what he wanted from her. A slight moan escaped her as he slid his hands down around her waist. Leaning into her, he trapped her against the counter. With her body pressed against his, realization slapped him in the face. In all the years he'd known her, he'd never doubted his attraction to her, but he didn't truly know her. What was in her heart, or what kept her going day after day? But he wanted to know all of it, because it made Sydney who she was.

He cared about what happened to her and how things affected her. This woman did not compare to any of the others he had known in his lifetime. Deep down he had to acknowledge what he'd known since the night he took her to prom. Sydney Hart was "the one that got away" and he'd be a moron to let it happen again. Releasing her mouth, he looked down at her. "So...still thinking about assholes?"

With languid, sensuous eyes, she shook her head. "Nope."

"Good, then let's grab a slice and go watch a Bruce marathon."

Chapter Five

The intoxicating smell of magnolias surrounded him when he woke. They had fallen asleep somewhere around the middle of the first movie, or was it the second? With her body cradled against his on the small couch, it was difficult to think. He tried to move without waking her, but Sydney stretched lazily and opened sultry, smoky eyes to look at him. Waking with her in his arms was nice. "Good morning, angel."

"Good morning. Sorry, you're probably stiff. Not going to help much today at the rodeo." When she sat up, he quickly pulled her back against him and pressed his lips to hers.

"Thank you," Levi said, his arms locking around her, so he could enjoy the feel of her as much as possible.

"For what?" She still had that I'm-not-fully-awake-yet look about her and he found it endearing. Even more charming was the fact that she hadn't rushed to brush her hair, change clothes and make herself presentable the moment she woke.

"Yesterday, it was nice to just be myself. There aren't many people I can do that around. You did exactly what you said you were going to."

"Really?" Skepticism lined her voice. She crossed her arms on his chest and propped her chin on them. "I did?"

This was right. He knew it in his gut. The playboy image had always been just that—an image. Waking up with a woman, the intimacy of the little moments, those were things he didn't usually allow himself. Looking into those eyes, he was confident he'd found what had been missing in his life. She slid from the top of him and headed to the kitchen. After running his hands through his hair, he smoothed his wrinkled dress shirt and followed her to where she was busy putting the coffee on.

He watched her from the doorway. "You know why I started the title chase?"

"Do you want me to give you the reason you want people to believe, or the truth?" She pulled out ingredients from the fridge and got to work making breakfast. Taking a seat on one of the stools at the breakfast bar, he watched as she moved through the small kitchen.

"Tell me both and I'll let you know if your insight into Levi McKenna is right or wrong." It was childish, but he taunted her, daring her to take her best shot.

"Okay, if that's how you want to play it." Grabbing a whisk from the container near the stove, she started mixing up a batter. "From the beginning you've always said you do this to make your daddy proud. But I know Caleb McKenna, and this is not what he needs or wants from his son. The truth—deep down—is that you have something to prove to yourself."

He smirked, but it didn't dissuade her from continuing as she poured the batter into the muffin pan and started the gravy. "Laugh, but if you're going to go out there, the least you can do is be honest with why you're doing it. The only thing that keeps you from claiming the title is you."

"Angel, you are right on both counts. I tried to convince myself and everyone else that I did this for my dad, but it is something I have to do for myself. I need to know I can do it."

"Then do it." She checked the biscuits and threw a few eggs in a pan.

"You make it sound so easy. How many national titles do you hold there, little lady? Stashing buckles somewhere?"

"No, I gave them to my buckle bunnies. Look, you're making this harder than it has to be."

"You know, Syd, I've never given my buckles away. To me, that was like letting a girl wear your letterman's jacket in high school."

"Really?" The disbelief in her voice stung.

"Yeah, there's just something special about a girl wearing those things."

"Aw, I never knew you were so sentimental." She handed him a plate. The coffee pot beeped, so he got up and poured two cups as she put her plate together. Sliding onto the stool next to him, she looked at him, a crease in her brow. "Can I ask you to do something for me?'

"Sure." The quick answer elicited a giggle from her that went straight through him.

"No matter what happens, block out everything else, just have fun. Promise me that much. There's no point in doing it otherwise. At the end of the day if Devil bucks you, or Justin Trent walks away with the title—if you can look back and think 'damn that was fun' then it's all that matters."

"Syd, in all the years I've been doing this, you are the first person who has ever given me such good advice." He sopped up the last of the gravy from the plate. "And any woman who can make biscuits and gravy like that has got to be onto something."

∗

For thirty minutes, he'd flipped through channels like a madman, torture at its finest, as he'd tried to keep his mind off of her in the shower. To say he'd failed miserably would be an understatement. She walked into the room and Levi switched the TV off, his mouth gaping open. When a woman could render him speechless just by entering the room, wearing nothing special, he knew he was in trouble.

"Ready?"

Suddenly, formulating words proved a difficult task, so he sat there for a minute, and attempted to make his brain fire on all cylinders. "Hotel—cold shower," were the only words he could manage and he felt like a babbling idiot.

A deep blush rose on her cheeks, but the smile indicated her pleasure at his reaction to her. "I'll get you to the hotel for the cold shower, but maybe we'll have to work on that stuttering problem." She disappeared into the kitchen for her keys and purse. They walked out of the house and she pulled the door closed, locking it behind her.

"So our tickets are for all of next week, but I figure you can drop me at the bar and take my truck. Come by the bar later to pick me up and if you do well the beers on...." Her voice trailed off and he practically tripped over her when she stopped cold in front of him. "Son of a bitch!"

Sydney stared at the broken windows on her truck. What an asshole! Tyler knew how much she loved her truck. She moved closer to survey the damage. A folded up piece of paper on the front seat sat amongst the broken glass and she reached for it.

"Syd, you should probably just leave that and call the cops."

"Why? I know who did it." She picked up the paper by the corner and it fell open.

"Who's your new boyfriend, Syd?"

Levi peaked over her shoulder at the note. "How did he know you had anyone with you?"

"Tyler's made a sick hobby out of watching me." Flipping open the cell phone, she dialed the police.

"That is fucking creepy, Syd."

"Tell me about it." She waited for the dispatcher to come on the line. "I need to report vandalism."

After giving her address to the dispatcher, she and Levi sat on the porch to wait.

"Sorry about your truck."

"It's just a truck." Though she sounded calm when she spoke, she felt like she was on the verge of breaking. Her fury over her truck paled in comparison to the fear welling up inside her. Tyler had never damaged anything of hers before and this felt like a direct threat. Levi pulled her closer and she leaned her head against his shoulder, accepting the comfort he offered, but he couldn't sit with her all day "I'll call you a cab."

"You can't expect me to leave you sitting here by yourself." Protectiveness laced his voice and it soothed her fears a bit.

"Sitting here with me is hardly going to get you the title. Besides, I have to call Dusty. If he sees you here, the busted windows on my truck will be the least of my concerns." This was going to send her brother over the edge and she dreaded making the call, but did it anyway. Becca answered as the cop car pulled in front of the house. Giving her hand a squeeze, Levi headed out to meet them.

"Hey Syd, what's up?"

"Can you ask Dusty to stop by the house?"

"He's at the bar sorting out an issue with the morning delivery. Why? What's wrong?" There was a hint of panic in her sister-in-law's voice.

"Can you come by then? It would probably be better if you

were here anyway. You could help me handle my brother. Look, I have to go. I'll explain when you get here." She hung up the phone and stepped towards Levi. "Becca's on her way. With the cops here, I'm sure I'll be fine until she arrives. Will you come by the bar later?"

Levi pressed his lips to her forehead and caressed her arms. "Count on it. You aren't going to stay here tonight, are you?"

"No, I'm sure I'll stay at Dusty's." Gain her independence only to have it taken away again. Levi called for a car and then stood by her side while she gave her report to the police.

A car pulled up to the house and she assumed it was Levi's ride. After they had finished with the police and thanked them for their time, she walked him to the waiting car. Pulling her into his arms, he tried to reassure her. "Syd, nothing is going to happen to you. I promise."

"I know." Putting on a brave front was a lot harder when she wanted to fall apart. "It's just very intrusive and a bit unnerving."

Becca parked in the drive and stepped out.

"I'll see you later." He kissed her goodbye, and when he pulled back, her gaze met his baby blues and she smiled. Glancing past him, she saw Becca's eyes wide with shock. Devilish smile in place, he winked and disappeared into the car.

Becca walked over to her, watching as the car pulled away. "You want to tell me what the hell is going on? I pull up to find cops here, you sharing a kiss with the forbidden cowboy, and it's only nine in the morning."

"You failed to notice the broken windows on my truck." Slipping her arm through her sister-in-law's, she led her to the porch. They took a seat on the swing and Sydney tucked a leg underneath her as she settled at the opposite end.

"Jesus, Sydney, did he come here last night?" Her sister-in-law nervously ran her fingers over her car keys. There was little doubt as to who she meant.

"He left a few messages yesterday. This morning, we walked out to busted windows and a note in my truck. I never talked to him." If she didn't steady herself, it would be evident how scared she really was. "You want some tea?"

Becca nodded slowly and she stepped into the house, returning with the tea and a dust buster just as her sister-in-law snapped her cell phone shut. "Well, Dusty's on his way over. Spill the beans about Levi before he gets here."

"Come keep me company while I try to clean up some of this mess." She headed towards the truck and her sister-in-law followed. Using the little vacuum to suck the glass out of the truck seats, she struggled to avoid looking at Becca.

"So are you going to talk or am I going to have to tell Dusty I saw you together?" Becca's smile tempted Sydney to throw the vacuum at her.

"It's nothing. I took him riding yesterday. After that we went to the cocktail party and came here for pizza and movies." The attempts at keeping the girl talk about Levi limited were futile. There was no escaping this conversation.

"Dusty should be here any minute. I could always tell him you tripped and Levi caught you with his lips."

"If you do, I will be forced to tell him I followed the sisterly advice you so generously provided."

"Fine, keep the juicy details to yourself. Just tell me one thing—is he a good kisser?" A flush crept across Becca's face. "Just asking."

"Weak in the knees give you an idea?" Her sister-in-law's laughter eased her nerves slightly. They were just cleaning up the last of the glass when Dusty pulled up. He got out of the car and hurried over to her.

"Syd, are you okay? Why didn't you call me? Did you call the cops? If I see that asshole around I am going to kill him myself."

"Calm down. I called the cops, then your house. You weren't home but Becca came over. It's done. I'm fine."

"You're staying with us. I don't like the idea of you staying here by yourself. What if he decides to break in next?"

Typical of Dusty. He jumped right to a worst-case scenario. Of course, the thoughts were based in reality, but she'd tried to avoid thinking exactly what he was imagining. While Becca tried to calm him down, she went and locked up the house.

When she returned, he tossed her his car keys. "You take my truck. Becca will follow me to the dealer to drop yours off."

She considered arguing, but it would have been pointless, so she hopped into the driver's seat of the Ridgeline. Sitting in the sissified version of a truck felt awkward. How her brother had ever let Becca talk him into it escaped her. She started the truck and headed off towards the bar. No doubt it would be a long day.

*

The Friday crowd had already begun to make their appearance. Jerry looked up from behind the bar, a worried expression on his face. Great, sympathy was not what she wanted. Forcing a smile, she put on the perky routine. "Hey Jerry, I see the usual Friday riffraff is here."

"Yep, every last one of them, present and accounted for." Never one to pry, he wiped down the bar. "So what's on the playlist tonight?"

"That's Becca's department. I only sing if she wants me to. The rodeo will be on ESPN though." Sitting on a barstool, remote in hand, she surfed until she got to the channel.

"Why am I not surprised?" Jerry shook his head as he poured a few beers for the customers seated beside her. "That's what I get for working with Texas folk."

"Oh, you love working for us or you wouldn't be here." When Dusty and Becca came in, she slid off the stool.

Jerry winked at her. "Actually, I'm secretly in love with you."

"Um, you're cute and all, but you're old enough to be my dad."

"Syd, stop giving Jerry a hard time and come back to the office," Dusty said as they walked through the bar. Punching Jerry in the arm as she passed, she followed her brother, expecting a scolding or tirade.

Her brother closed the door behind them. Instead, he pulled her to him and hugged her tightly. Concern, she'd expected, but he seemed more emotional than she was used to.

"I'm glad you're okay."

"I'm fine, Dusty, really." She stepped out of the hug, but he held onto her hand, giving it a light squeeze and offering her a smile before he let go. Hesitating for a moment, he walked away from her and over to the desk where two wireless microphone headsets sat on its surface. A smile crossed his face. "I thought you girls would have some fun with these."

"I thought you hated when we sang," Her sister-in-law's

face lit.

"I don't hate when you sing. What I have a problem with is the men ogling you both. Actually, I quite enjoy listening to you sing."

Sydney watched Dusty walk over with the device in hand. He hit a few buttons, and tucked the wireless pack into her jeans pocket. "There you go. When you're ready, press this button and you are live. Jerry and I set everything up before Becca called. By the way, your truck won't be ready until tomorrow, so just hold on to my keys."

"Great, thanks."

Becca looked at her. "It's your call tonight, baby girl. Tell me what we're singing."

"I think I will be feeling a little Brooks and Dunn at some point tonight." The groan her sister-in-law let fly made her laugh. "Oh come on, it's for the rodeo boys. You know the bar will be packed with them tonight."

Chapter Six

The bulls were not playing nice. Of course, if they had been, the fun and excitement wouldn't be there. Levi had a good ride, made it the eight seconds and scored well. Justin managed to get bucked, but escaped the fury of the bull unscathed. The bullfighters had their work cut out for them tonight. He ambled over to where Justin stood leaning against the rails, watching the last rider of the evening.

Focused on the rider in the arena, Justin didn't look at him when he spoke. "Nice ride."

"I thought Spit Fire would buck me. I could have done better." His mind hadn't entirely been where it should've been.

Justin chuckled. "Are you ever happy? My ass ends up on the ground, you effectively put yourself in the lead and you're complaining?"

The last rider barely made it out of the chute before Devil bucked him. The bull, a notoriously difficult ride, had been his downfall last season. Cringing when they saw the rider's hand still wrapped in the bull rope, they both held their breath as the rider got loose and the bull charged after him.

With a slap on the back, Justin straightened and adjusted his hat. "Well partner, let's get this over with. I could use some beer and good music tonight."

As they walked through the arena, Levi absorbed the atmosphere. The smell of the animals, sweat, blood and adrenaline all still permeated the air while cowboys stood nursing their injuries. Just weren't real rodeos without those things present. Though he'd been pleased with his performance it was too early to guess the outcome. There was no room for cockiness or grandstanding and it would be hard to downplay once Lisa had him on display for the media.

"Looks like your fan club awaits." Justin indicated the media milling around the staging area. "Chin up. It's still early in the game, but if you keep it up, you just might beat me. Then there will be plenty to gloat about to the press."

"I plan on beating you, Justin. But gloating is not my style."

Limping a bit from his fall, Justin laughed. "Are you heading back to the bar tonight? The guys want to go back and catch Sydney singing again."

"Yeah, as soon as this circus leaves town." Oh, he would definitely be there, keeping a close eye on Sydney.

"The media used to be your friend. Change of heart?"

"It's a distraction. One among many."

"So duck out. I would. Never did like publicity crap anyways." Justin shrugged. "The guys have a car out back if you want."

"Sounds like a plan." He turned and walked out with Justin, with little else on his mind beyond getting to the bar as quickly as possible.

$$*$$

Several minutes later, they were at the bar. They walked in and Sydney spotted him and waved. Justin shot him a look.

"Don't say it."

The warning did nothing to derail Justin. "We'll be over here, Romeo, when you see fit to join us."

Heading towards the bar, he noticed Dusty walking down the back hall. Sydney hopped up on the bar, wrapped her hands in the front of his shirt, and pulled him close. When she pressed her soft lips against his, he practically moaned.

"Nice job tonight, cowboy," she said, taking his hat and dropping back to the floor as Justin walked up next to him.

"Well, if that's all it takes to get a kiss from this little lady, I might have to try harder."

"It takes more than a few belt buckles, Mr. Trent." She lined up beers and pushed them across the bar. "First round is on me. We got something special for y'all tonight."

Then she winked and headed towards Becca. Justin helped

him take the drinks back to the table and, as he slid into the booth, he looked towards Levi and shook his head.

"What?"

"You are so done for," Justin laughed.

"What are you talking about?" Not really wanting Justin to answer because he knew what he meant. Sydney always hit him where it mattered most, something he'd never wanted to admit.

Pulling a chair up to the same table they'd occupied before, he claimed the end of the booth as his own. Soon after, the band began to play. The guys around the table hollered and whistled as the girls began to sing the newly adopted theme song for the NFR, *Cowboy Town*. He searched for Sydney, and Justin smacked his head.

"Ouch!"

"Look at the bar, numb nuts." Justin pointed to where Becca stood on the bar. Still looking around for Sydney, he couldn't see her through the crowd. Becca caught his eyes and tossed her head towards the opposite end of the room. She sat on the mechanical bull, her body matching every slow movement as it rocked underneath her, a seductive feast for the eyes he could not look away from. The girls finished the song and hopped behind the bar. The crowd hollered for more.

Becca still had the mike on. "Y'all haven't had nearly enough to drink for us to sing another set. How about our rodeo boys in the corner, y'all ready for another set?"

The guys around him answered with a few yelps and Becca's laugh carried over the speakers. "All right Syd, should we give them more?"

"Are you kidding? They don't want to hear me."

"Who thinks Sydney should fly this one solo?"

"What did I do to deserve torture?" The bar filled with whistles, hoots and hollers. Looking out over the crowd, he truly enjoyed watching the people react to her. Justin was right. He was down for the count and enjoying every minute of it. He yelled out, "Lay one on us, Syd!"

Weaving her way through the room with a tray of beers, she stopped at their table, handed the beers out and the band began playing. Leaving the empty tray behind, she made her way through the bar as she sang, keeping the beat with her hand against her hip. He imagined all the possibilities as he watched her move to the music. When the song had finished, he loaded up the tray with the empties on the table and carried it to the bar. Dusty took the tray from him.

"Sorry about that." Dusty handed him a beer. "Hey, congratulations on today. Obviously you got your head back where it belongs. Whatever you're doing, keep it up."

He planned on it, but wouldn't be sharing the details with Dusty. The bar had begun to empty out and Levi kept the stool warm while he waited for closing time.

"Hey, cowboy." Sydney perched herself on the stool next to him. A loud clunk drew his gaze down to where her heels had hit the wood floor. Two perfectly manicured feet rested on the rung of the bar stool. He didn't have a foot fetish, but whenever she revealed any bit of skin, it sent his mind into overdrive. He wondered if his thoughts were visible on his face. The images were difficult to shove from his mind as her brother walked over, wiping down the bar as he did.

Sydney pointed to the TV, where on screen a reporter stood in front of the events center. "Dusty, turn it up."

"There's been a change of direction here at the T and M events pavilion, with Levi McKenna shocking rodeo fans by showing he can still be the man who burst onto the scene just five short years ago. Speculation says one of these two women is responsible."

Levi choked on his beer when the first picture came on the screen. It showed him standing with Lisa in the valet parking, his jacket draped around her as she stood leaning into him while they waited for a cab. The next was an image of Sydney and him exchanging a kiss that was more than friendly.

The reporter continued, "It would appear that Levi McKenna is doubling down in Vegas and the odds are in his favor. All the fans can do is hope that Lady Luck continues to smile on him."

Dusty turned off the TV and the look he sent in Levi's direction told him to expect trouble. "Sydney, go help Becca with the books."

"Dusty, there's no need to overreact." She unsuccessfully tried to diffuse the situation. "Don't be such an ass."

"Go to the back now!" Dusty barked at her and Levi watched as indecision played across her face. If his friend wanted to argue, she did not need to be present. Sliding off the stool, her hand rested on Levi's thigh as she slid into her shoes. Then she turned and headed down the hallway towards the office.

"Bar's closed folks, everyone out. You too, Jerry," Dusty ordered.

Levi stayed put, waiting for the unavoidable fight between him and his oldest friend. Things hadn't become too serious between him and Sydney, but he wanted more than friendship from her. So he would take whatever Dusty dealt him and try to get the man to understand his intentions. No matter what, giving up the one woman who made him feel the way she did would not be an option.

Once the last patron had left the bar, Dusty locked the door and spun around to face him. "You have your fucking nerve! Some friend you are. You breeze into town, take one look at Sydney, and forget the pact we made."

"We made a pact when we were kids and we aren't talking about your ten year old kid sister anymore. She is a consenting adult." Even knowing it would come down to this, he still respected his friend's determination to protect his sister. But he had no intention of backing down.

"You will leave her alone. If our friendship means anything to you, walk out that door and forget all about her." Dusty came towards him and he stood up. He continued through gritted teeth, "I want you to leave."

"Why don't you be honest about what's really bothering you. It's not that I broke the pact as much as it's what you think those pictures imply."

"If you think I'm going to let her be with a womanizer like you, just to end up another notch on your belt—"

Levi threw a right hook before Dusty had finished. He didn't want to fight with Dusty, but if it would enable him to be with Sydney free of guilt, so be it. Sometimes there were sacrifices worth making.

"You asked for that. I'm not seeing anyone besides her and I have no intentions of hurting her. As long as she's interested, I am not letting her go either." He headed for the door and hesitated. "You should know me well enough to determine fact from fiction. We've been friends a long time, and I've never regretted it. For years I've fought my feelings for Sydney because of our friendship. I'm not doing it anymore."

*

Sydney stood with her sister-in-law and watched Levi leave. Dusty rubbed his jaw and she couldn't help but smile.

"Son of a bitch," he muttered, as he leaned against the bar. "You can stop lurking, girls."

They both stepped into the bar. Becca's arms were crossed over her chest. She knew what it meant and never wanted to be on the receiving end of that anger.

"You are such an ass!" Becca blurted out.

"You don't understand." He walked behind the bar, grabbed some ice and held it against his jaw.

Becca took a deep breath. "Explain to me why this is a problem?"

"He's not right for her."

Grunting in frustration, Becca threw her hands up in the air. "Don't you think it's her choice to make? Ever since Tyler, you practically suffocate her with your protectiveness. You can't keep her from dating."

Recognizing the look on Becca's face, Sydney knew the time had come for her to defend herself. Lord knew her anger surpassed her sister-in-law's and her brother would not get off easy.

"I'm a grown woman. When are you going to stop babying me? I don't give a shit about rules or pacts that were made when we were kids. I'm fully capable of deciding who to date and handling my own mistakes."

"I know you are, but your taste in men is horrible. You know Levi's reputation. Hell, it hasn't changed much since high school and I can't stand idly by and watch you continue to do this to yourself."

"So you're saying Levi is the wrong choice for me?" She shook her head in frustration. "I love you, but you're an idiot."

"What do you want from me? I should stand on the sidelines while you ruin your life?"

"It's my life and I have to have believe there's a chance I can be as happy as I see you and Becca. Don't I deserve that?" She walked past him, but he caught her arm.

"Don't do this." His eyes pleaded with her, but she yanked

her arm from his grasp.

"You're my brother and Levi isn't some guy I met in a bar. He's your friend. A fact you should remember the next time you want to believe what you hear about him. The girl in the picture was his assistant who'd just gotten some bad news and outside of a few kisses and spending some time together, nothing has happened between Levi and me. Your stupid rule and my refusal to take a chance..." She sighed. "I'm tired. Each time it takes a little longer for me to drop that wall and let someone in. You know what my greatest fear is? One time, the wall won't come down."

Tears ran down her cheeks and she paused to take a slow, calming breath. "I'll drop your truck off in the morning."

$*$

He was in the parking lot, talking on his phone, kicking up gravel and leaving little clouds of dust in his wake when she walked out of the bar.

"Come on cowboy, let's go," she called to him.

He hung up the phone. "Dusty means well, Syd. Don't fight with him because of me."

"Fine. Stay in the parking lot all night." Hopping into the truck, she instantly regretted the tone she'd taken. He climbed in the passenger side and she started the engine, speeding out of the parking lot, fishtailing a bit as she turned onto the street. "Sorry, you didn't deserve that."

"No apology needed. Where are we headed?" He leaned his head back against the seat.

"Going to my house is probably not the best idea and we wouldn't be welcome at Dusty's. That leaves your hotel."

Levi raised his eyebrows and she laughed. "What did you expect me to say?"

"Not that."

"I didn't really expect you to hit my brother either, but hey," she said and winked. "By the way, you throw a nice right hook."

"I wish it felt as good as it looked. Are you hungry? We can stop and get something." His unease seemed to match her own.

"Not right now. If I get hungry though, I am sure the hotel has restaurants." If they didn't get to the hotel soon, she was afraid she'd lose her nerve. Memories of the kisses they had shared over the last two days had her licking her lips in anticipation.

The tension in the car could have been cut with a knife, and the weight of his gaze didn't make her nerves quiet any. She pulled into the hotel drive and spotted the news vans camped on the property.

"Keep going straight." He instructed. "Pull around to the back parking garage."

Parking the truck at the back of the hotel, it appeared they were in the clear. He got out and she took a deep steadying breath before following. She had never stood up to her brother or fought for what she wanted. It felt bittersweet. He took her hand as they walked towards the elevators.

"You okay?"

"Yeah," she replied as they stepped into the waiting elevator. When the doors slid shut, she gazed up into his eyes as he leaned in and kissed her. His body pressed against hers, pinning her against the wall of the elevator and her pulse began to race.

"You smell good," Levi whispered as he moved his lips along her neck. The elevator stopped and he stood next to her with a guilty expression on his face. Some of the people who entered the elevator recognized Levi and a few asked if she happened to be the girl mentioned on the news. When they reached the casino floor, Levi grabbed her hand and slid his hat forward on her head, leaving her line of sight obstructed. He led her quickly through the casino until a security guard stopped them.

"Mr. McKenna, the press has been camped by the main elevators all evening. We'll escort you through." The guard called on the radio and they were quickly flanked by security.

"Appreciate that." Levi pulled her in close to him as they walked along, pushing their way through the casino. They barely made it into the hotel elevator before the press swarmed in. The guards formed a protective barrier as they waited for the doors to open.

Once they were ensconced in the safety of the elevator, she let out a huge sigh. "Is it always like that?"

"Only when they think they can get something to help ratings or sales. Not having Lisa here to intervene explains their presence."

Tilting her head up, he forced her to look into his eyes and she forgot what they had been talking about.

Chapter Seven

Levi fished the key card out of his wallet. Damn, he could never get the thing to work on the first try. The little red lights finally changed to green and he opened the door. Sydney moved past him and ignored everything but the large picture window that overlooked the strip. Housekeeping left the shades open at his request and the sea of lights seemed to lure her over.

"Wow." Sydney stared out into the night as he stepped up behind her, moved her hair out of the way and resumed kissing along her neck. She moaned softly. "Well, this isn't bad either."

He slid her jacket from one shoulder and relished the feel of her silken skin beneath his fingertips.

"Better watch out, I may never leave," she practically purred as he moved over her skin. He pushed the jacket from the other shoulder and let it fall to the ground between them. Levi turned her around, pressed her up against the window, laced his fingers through hers and pinned her hands over her head.

"Promise?" he asked. Sydney's breath played over his lips and tempted him to take more.

"Uh-huh." She moaned.

He slipped his hands under the back of her tank top and slowly glided over her skin. Pressing his mouth to hers, he kissed her until his mind clouded over and she melted into him. In a swift movement, he lifted her off the floor and carried her back to the bedroom, tripping when he hit the edge of the bed. Laughter bubbled from her as she sailed through the air and onto the mattress, but his failed attempt at being suave left his ego a bit bruised. "Glad I could entertain you."

"Sorry." She crawled towards him and knelt on the bed.

"Condoms?"

Sticking his hand in the back pocket of his jeans he pulled two out and tossed them on the nightstand. Shooting a quick glance at the nightstand and then back to him, she asked, "Only two?"

"I wasn't sure I'd even have a use for one, but I was hopeful."

"Good thing." She reached up and slowly began to undo the buttons on her tank top. Unable to resist the temptation before him, he began to help her. His hand received a stinging slap along with a glare of warning. "Mr. McKenna, you do not need to have a hand in everything."

The slow pace was both achingly difficult to endure and a feast for the senses as she undid each button. With the tank top gaping open, revealing her smooth stomach, his eyes drifted up to discover the absence of a bra and he silently uttered thanks for having one less article of clothing to remove. The mere glimpse of her breast peeking out from behind the edge of the fabric tested his patience. He reached out, grabbed the waistband of her jeans and pulled her to him. "You can literally drive a man crazy teasing like that."

Her eyes glinted. "There are rewards for being patient."

"Yeah, and now I am collecting." He undid the button on her jeans while he kissed along her smooth shoulders. She gently nudged him back and stepped off the bed. His eyes devoured every movement as she slid her jeans down her long, lean legs. "You're beautiful."

He captured her mouth again as her fingers threaded through his hair. Sliding his hands along the curves of her waist, he didn't stop moving up until the tips of his fingers brushed along the outside of her breasts. With one hand, she reached down to his jeans, popped the button open, and began to ease them over his hips. A low growl escaped his mouth as her tongue danced sensually with his. God, he couldn't get enough of this woman. He removed his jeans, scooped her up and laid her gently on the bed.

Her heart raced beneath him. Having never noticed the flecks of violet present in her eyes, he now had one more thing to commit to memory. The desire to touch her had been unquenchable for so long. Now, every caress fueled rather than satiated. Like an addict who could never get his fill, he'd never wanted someone so badly. Moving his mouth over her body, he tenderly made his way to her breast. He flicked his tongue across her nipple, driving his need for more. As he ran his hand lightly over her skin and between her legs, her breathing became more rapid. When he slid his fingers inside, her back arched and he watched as pleasure shot through her body.

"Levi..."

"Should I stop?" he asked, making no attempt to slow the rhythmic torture he was unleashing on her.

With eyes heavy with lust, she glared at him, and pleaded, "Oh—God—no!"

"Are you sure, angel? I could just..." he said playfully and began to slowly pull his hand away.

In response, she wrapped her hand around the thick hardness of him and smiled as she applied pressure. "Two can play at that game."

He gasped. "It's hardly fair play."

"You started it." She nibbled his bottom lip and then moved along the line of his jaw as she caressed him. No, he would not relinquish control. He'd waited too long for this and wanted to focus on the one woman he never thought he'd have in his bed.

Moving out of her reach, he slid down her body until he could rest his mouth against her inner thigh. He kissed her there, occasionally thrusting his tongue across her center. She writhed as he continued his torture, alternating between kisses and slight sucking. Feeling her muscles begin to contract, he knew she was close. He slid his hands under her hips, ensuring she would remain where he wanted her.

"Levi!" she screamed out.

When he moved up alongside Sydney, caressing her as he settled in beside her, a seductive smile slid across the face of his temptress.

"My turn," she purred as she moved down his body. He let out a gasp as her hand slid over his shaft. A moan of pure pleasure soon followed as her tongue found the tip and her mouth encased him. Taking him in deeply, she slightly grazed her teeth along the length of him with each up and down movement. He moved his hips and met her halfway. With her hand preceding her mouth, she took her time and paid attention to every inch of him. He ached to be inside her, to feel the slick, wet heat between her thighs, and wasn't sure how much longer he would be able to hold out.

"Syd," his voice came out strained, but she continued the tantalizing movements of her mouth. He couldn't take any more. At this rate he would be spent before he made it to the final round. He sat up enough to slide his hands under her arms and drew her up the length of his body.

"Hey, I'm not done, cowboy." The sexy pout she wore would be his undoing.

"Don't worry, neither am I." With need riding him hard, he reached over to the nightstand, grabbed a condom and quickly sheathed himself. He rolled her over and pinned her beneath him. After brushing the hair from her face, he ran his hand gently along her cheek, enjoying the sight of her lying under him. Her eyes had darkened with passion. Levi slid into her slowly. With each controlled thrust, she arched her hips to meet him, allowed him to go deeper. They fell into a sensual rhythm. Heat began to build in him. Each moan and writhing movement that escaped her threatened to send him over the edge. He closed his mouth over hers, and they greedily took from each other. His thrusts came faster as he pounded harder into her. She wrapped her legs around his waist, ground her hips against him. Each breath was labored as he sank himself into her again and again.

"Levi," she screamed out, and he watched as orgasm claimed her. He continued his unrelenting pace, rocking inside her as he rode out her pleasure. One last forceful thrust and he let out a deep groan as he shuddered above her. Then he lowered his body to the bed, their limbs tangled together.

"I'll untangle myself from you when I can move again, angel. I promise." He reached up and caressed her face.

"I'm in no hurry. I couldn't move right now if I wanted to." She lay there, and he indulged in the sight of her nude and glistening with perspiration from their lovemaking.

As he got up from the bed, she rolled over onto her stomach. When he returned, he ran a finger over her moist skin and chuckled. "That, angel, is the sign of a job well done by both."

He lay beside her and she curled in against him, her head tucked tightly to his chest. If he died tonight, he would go a happy man. He pulled her closer, and drifted off to sleep.

Sydney woke the next morning with something very hard and masculine pressed against her ass. Ah, the male physique could be such a beautiful thing. Levi tightened his arm around her and pulled her back against him. A low moan reverberated along the base of her neck, and it sent a small spasm of pleasure rolling through her. She turned her body so she could face him.

He had a mischievous grin on his face. "Morning."

She studied his face, admired the feel of his muscles under her hand as she worked her way down his side, then back up, pushing gently against his shoulder. As he rolled to his back, he pulled her with him and then propped an arm behind his head. "Are you trying to take advantage of me, Miss Hart?"

"It's hard to take advantage of the willing." She slid down him a bit, the length of him hard against her stomach. Laying her arms across his chest, she rested her chin on the top of one hand while gently tracing the outline of his nipple with the other. Letting out a slow breath of air, she watched as his nipple puckered. He shuddered slightly.

"I think you might be the devil in disguise," he moaned.

She licked his chest.

"Oh God, you are the devil."

She lifted her head with a sigh. "And what exactly do you think you are, Mr. McKenna?"

"Famished. You are quite a workout." He winked at her.

"I could use a shower first." The bed creaked as she slid off and began gathering her clothes from the various spots they had ended up the night before.

"When I can muster enough energy to move, I'll join you."

*

The desire to grab Levi and have her way with him in the shower had been overwhelming, but she managed to behave herself, confident that this would not be their only time together. He sat with his hand across hers as they ate in the small dining area of the suite.

"What's your game plan?"

He looked up at her. "Game plan?"

"Yeah, don't you have a plan of attack when you go out there? Or do you just fly by the seat of your pants when you're in the ring with the bull?"

"Oh that plan—it's called trying my damnedest to make it to the next round."

"Good plan." She lifted the coffee mug and inhaled the rich aroma before taking a sip. She set the mug down and leaned back in the chair. Not usually one for breakfast, she couldn't think of a better way to spend a morning.

"Is that all you're going to eat?" He eyed her plate of fruit.

"Yeah." Contemplating her morning, she smiled. "Hey, why don't you ride with me to the dealership to pick up my truck? You can take my truck and just meet me at the bar later."

"Oh Dusty will love that." After taking the last bite of his omelet, he reached over and stuck his fork in the last piece of fruit on her plate.

"It's not like I'm offering his truck to you, though it's an idea." Dusty could be such a pain in the ass. One more hurdle she and her brother would have to overcome. Lord knew she had jumped over many in her life. Coffee cup in hand, she got up and went to the window. The glitz and glamour of the Vegas strip was non-existent during the day without the neon and didn't have the same impact, though it remained a sight unlike any other.

"Are you going home tonight?" He came up, wrapped his arms around her waist and rested his chin on her shoulder.

"I can hardly let Tyler run me out of my own house and I refuse to live in fear because of some asshole." She wished her confidence held the same steadiness as her words. Truth was she had no idea how far Tyler would go.

"Syd, don't worry. I hate hotels and I think I'll need another workout session later."

"Come on cowboy, let's get a move on." When she turned and grabbed her purse, he picked up the bag sitting by the door. "Planning on running if all doesn't go well tonight?"

"Ha-ha." He held the door. "Just don't want to come back if it's not necessary."

"Ah, a regular boy scout..." Ducking under his arm, she slipped past him. "Who knew?"

Chapter Eight

Sydney thought they would never escape the dealership. Levi could have stood there for hours signing autographs and bullshitting with every person who happened to stop in. His patience seemed limitless compared to hers. Price of fame, or so he said. Being a man who knew the value of his fans seemed more likely. If she wanted to continue a relationship with him, she would have to get used to it.

The Mustang was absent from the driveway when she arrived at her brother's house. Hopefully, it meant he had gone to the bar already. The front door opened and Dusty stepped out onto the porch. *Shit.* For a moment, she considered making a break for it. He didn't appear to have gotten much sleep, and his jaw held some nice coloring. Running would only postpone the inevitable, so she got out of the truck, sucked in a deep breath and headed to face the music.

"Hey, Syd." He held the door open for her. "I wanted to talk to you before we went to the bar."

A fight with Dusty never ranked high on her list of things to do. He looked out for her and she couldn't hold that against him, but she was turning twenty-five soon and she needed to take control of her life. She followed him into the kitchen, poured herself a cup of coffee and perched on the counter.

"Syd, I'm sorry. I really am. You're my sister and I should be happy for you. I just can't trust Levi though. Not when it comes to you."

"We both know my taste in men usually leads me down the wrong path, but living in fear or without love is a worse fate." She knew her brother wouldn't let it go.

"Levi's a good guy. Did you eat?"

And just like that the argument was done. "Yeah, just came by to grab a change of clothes and hoped you wouldn't be here."

For the first time that morning, he smiled at her. "Guess I spoiled that plan. Go change and we'll get your truck."

"Levi has it. He'll be by later to pick me up."

Her brother cringed at the statement.

"Look Dusty, you don't have to like the fact I won't continue seeing Levi, but you do need to realize I'm not going to let him go."

He accepted her declaration with a nod, and she headed back to the bedroom that had once been hers. She still kept a closet full of clothes there because she had nights where she couldn't stomach being alone in her house. Rifling through her clothes, she pulled out an outfit. Once dressed, she headed to the bathroom for the finishing touches and then headed back to the kitchen.

Dusty shook his head. "Why you wear tank tops in the middle of winter, I'll never know."

"It gets hot in the bar. I wear a jacket when I'm outside." She studied her brother for a moment. "Sometimes I think you forget you're not my father."

"You have a point. Let's go. I have some errands to run before we head in to work."

*

By the time they'd pulled into the parking lot of the bar it was late afternoon. Jerry walked out carrying a large bouquet of flowers, and then Becca followed with another. A sick feeling welled up in the pit of Sydney's stomach as they dumped the flowers into the dumpster.

"Where'd those come from?" Dusty glanced at the flowers, then to her and finally at Becca. "You've got to be shittin' me!"

"Hardly. Wait 'til you walk through the doors. I thought the delivery guys were smoking some heavy shit when they kept bringing them in." Jerry shook his head. "Damn gutsy if you ask me."

Panic seized her as she stepped into the familiar surroundings of the bar. Bouquets of roses, sunflowers and daisies sat around the bar. The only card on them advertised the flower shop where Tyler had bought the same bouquets while they were dating. Furious and shaking, she grabbed the nearest bouquet and hurled it at the wall, inches from where Dusty had stepped through the door. "Damn it!"

Her brother backed out of the bar and a few seconds later Becca appeared. "Come on, Syd, why don't we go back to the office? The guys will clean this up."

Not wanting to risk hurling another vase, she took her sister-in-law's suggestion and once in the confines of the office, sank into the couch. Still furious, she wanted to scream, or hit something, but being a somewhat rational person knew it would do nothing to make her feel better. Throwing the bouquet only managed to make her feel guilty for letting her emotions get the best of her. Becca came into the room with two beers, shot glasses and a bottle of Gran Patron. Watching as Becca poured the shots, she scooted forward on the couch and studied the label on the tequila bottle. "Expensive medicine."

Her sister-in-law laughed. "True, but well deserved, so shut up and take the shot."

While she was a straight shooter, her sister-in-law had to go with the whole lick, salt and lime routine, followed by the face pucker. Leave it to Becca to make her feel better.

"So, how is he?"

"What?" There were times when she couldn't keep up with where her sister-in-law's mind went. This happened to be one of those times.

Becca handed her another shot and tried again. "How's Levi in bed?"

The question caught Sydney off-guard and she snorted, the tequila burning her nose in the process. Smooth going down, yet not so smooth when inhaled. "Fuck, Becca, your timing sucks."

"Sorry, but you have to admit it served as a great distraction tactic." She handed her a beer and sank into the couch beside her. "So?"

"He rides bulls for a living, how do you think he is?" Not wanting to elaborate, she left it at that, because just thinking about it turned her insides to mush.

"Hmm, the visual is interesting." Becca winked. Boy, the girl had a dirty mind, all the more reason she loved her so much. Observing the video screen that displayed the front of the bar, she saw patrons had begun to straggle in.

"Guess we should head out." She downed the last of her beer and stood.

With a shrug her sister-in-law slid deeper into the couch. "I'd rather hang back here all night and get drunk."

Pulling Becca to her feet, she gave her a hug and they headed out to the floor. Dusty had the rodeo on the big screen and smiled half-heartedly when he saw her. "Your boy's coming up next. Pull up a stool."

"The place is a little busy. I should get to work."

The glare he sent her plainly said sit down and shut up, so she did. Her eyes did not leave the screen as Levi came out of the chute. Storm obviously had no intention of playing nice and she held her breath for those eight seconds, hoping Levi would hang on.

Becca leaned into her. "I can see where the bull riding skill would come in handy."

She ignored the taunt and her brother handed her a beer. "Outside of whatever torture session Becca and the band have planned for you tonight, you're taking the night off."

When she opened her mouth to protest, he shook his head. Unable to endure a night of simply sitting around the bar, she turned to Becca. "Well, let's begin the torture session then."

"I beg your pardon," her sister-in-law gasped. "Torture indeed."

"Hey, I only called it as your husband did."

"Wire yourself up then darlin', the crowd awaits."

∗

Levi managed to hold his own and stay in the game. A few more nights like this and the buckle just might be his. Thanks to Justin's evasion tactics, he ducked out on another media circus, but they would catch up to him sooner or later. For now, he would steal all the time he could. Sitting in Sydney's truck in the bar's parking lot, he hoped Dusty had calmed down. He held no desire to punch his friend again, but would if the need arose. He stepped into the bar and his eyes took a moment to adjust. Becca saw him and headed over.

"I have no issue with you and Syd as long as she doesn't

get hurt." The woman was petite, but fierce as she stared him down. Knowing the only way he would convince any of them would be through actions, he bit his tongue. Becca eased off a bit. "She's at the bar."

Surprised to see her sitting at the bar, he leaned in and kissed her cheek before taking the vacant seat next to her. "Evening, angel."

She glanced at him and for a brief moment his heart constricted at the fear in them. Sydney blinked and smiled, the fear disappearing as she leaned into him. "You looked a little tired out there tonight, cowboy."

"Yeah, I might need to limit my extracurricular activities." He winked. Jerry handed him a beer and Becca came over and placed a hand on Levi's back.

"I hate to break up the love fest, but the natives are getting restless. Ready for more torture, Sydney?"

"Depends on what we're singing."

"Bring the cowboy," Becca said as she headed towards the stage.

"Come on, you heard her and it's best not to tick her off." Sydney took his hand and they joined Becca on the stage. "Why am I dragging Levi up here?"

"Because, I'm making him come along for the ride."

Raising his eyebrows in disbelief he muttered, "Um, I don't sing."

"I know, but rumor has it you're quite a skilled guitar player."

Two stools were moved to the center of the stage. While Sydney propped herself on one, he settled onto the other and accepted the guitar one of the band members offered him.

Becca whispered into his ear. "*Cowboy Take me Away*—it's her favorite."

Thankfully, he knew the song quite well and Sydney began to sing while he played. When they finished, flashes erupted at the back of the bar and he spotted the photographers. Sydney grabbed his hand and she pulled him towards the office.

Sitting on the edge of the desk, he watched as Sydney paced around the office. "Sorry, Syd. I didn't know they followed me here."

"Why are you apologizing to me?"

Dusty came back into the office and made no attempt to acknowledge Levi's presence. "Syd, give me your keys. I'll pull the truck around back. You can leave that way."

Her purse sat beside Levi on the desk and she walked over and pulled the keys out. She tossed them to her brother, then turned and leaned into Levi, resting her head against his chest. "How can you stand them invading your life like that?"

"I can't. It's not easy to see all your flaws broadcast for the world to see, but it comes with the territory." Not everyone could adjust to having the media ever present in their lives and he knew this would be one obstacle they would have to overcome.

Jerry came in and handed him the keys. "Vultures are still out front."

So avoidance would be how Dusty handled this. Great. He took the keys from Jerry and escorted Sydney out through the back door.

$$*$$

The photographers were there because of Levi. She knew that, but being with Levi McKenna meant she would either have to get accustomed to being the subject of media interest or give him up. Neither option appealed to her.

Levi unlocked her front door and walked in behind her, keeping a protective hand against the small of her back. Few things in life held comfort anymore, but she would take comfort in this.

"Can I make a request?" Before she could answer, he turned her in his arms and captured her mouth with his. Heat spread through her body instantly with the contact. Breathing became more difficult and her heart felt as if it would burst through her chest.

"Sure," she managed.

"I want to sit in the swing tonight."

"Entirely doable." She walked into the kitchen and grabbed two glasses of tea. An evening of sitting in the swing with him sounded like a pleasurable way to pass the time. While he grabbed a quilt off the back of the couch, she turned the radio on and slid the front window open. When they were settled on the swing, Levi rested his head in her lap. She let her hands play with his curls as he gazed up at her.

"You remember prom?"

"I thought we discussed this already. What's not to remember?"

"You know why I agreed to take you?" There was a seriousness in his eyes.

"Yeah, because you are a good friend who didn't want to see your best friend's little sister cry."

"Nope, I thought I should take advantage of the situation because it would be the only time I would ever get Dusty's approval to take you out."

"What?"

"I was no different than the rest of the guys when we were growing up. You're beautiful, smart and you have a way of drawing people to you. But I'd stupidly made a promise to Dusty." He sighed. "That night at prom pretty much ruined me. I dated to take my mind off you and none of the girls could even come close to the one I really wanted."

She took in a deep breath and stared out over the front lawn. Here she sat with a man who truly wanted her. Hearing his declaration, one that mimicked her own thoughts, both delighted and scared her. When he reached up, he brushed a stray tear that she hadn't known was there.

"Nope, haven't found another out there like you."

Fear hit her hard. This was all too good to be true. She should end it. Stop it all before she was in over her head and wound up hurt yet again. But it was too late for all of that, because she'd given her heart away long before now.

Chapter Nine

The next night Sydney had to close the bar on her own. Becca hadn't been feeling well and Dusty had bowed out and taken her home. The bar had been eerily quiet since they had left. Though it had lessened, tension remained between her and her brother. Although she hoped it wouldn't last much longer, she knew stubbornness ran rampant in her family. She finished balancing the books and headed to the storage room to review their inventory. The front door buzzed and she looked to the security cameras. The dark Stetson made her heart leap, and she headed to unlock the door.

"Hey, babe." Tyler pushed past her. She stared at him in disbelief and took a minute to gather her thoughts.

"Tyler, you need to leave."

The smell of alcohol seeped through every pore as he grabbed her arm and pulled her close to him, holding her body against his. "I can be a cowboy for you, babe."

"Let go of me, Tyler." Memories of her mom came rushing to the forefront of her mind and she fought to repress the fear and try to keep her wits about her. She shoved her knee up to his groin, forcing him to release his hold on her as he dropped to the ground. When she turned to run for the office, he swiped his arm out and tripped her. The wood floor came up fast and her head smacked it with a loud thud. Pain surged through her. He crawled over to her and she desperately tried to move out of his reach.

"You are an ungrateful bitch." The back of his hand connected with her cheek. She regained her footing and made it to the office, but he was quick, moving right behind her before she could get the door open. Her head throbbed and her heart threatened to burst from her chest. Concentration eluded her. The rage in Tyler's eyes reminded her of her stepfather when he lost control.

Latching on to a fistful of hair, he slammed her head against the heavy wooden door of the office. She slid down to the floor, struggling to maintain consciousness. He straddled her, and she prayed it would end.

"You were always the best piece of ass I ever had. It's a shame the only way I can touch you now is by force."

There was no need to say anything. It wouldn't have made a difference. He tore at her clothes. Desperation took hold and she tried to focus on something other than the hell she found herself in. How stupid could she be? Her world began to swim into darkness. At least she wouldn't be awake for it.

✳

Tonight, Levi had made it through by the skin of his teeth. His mind had been occupied with things that had nothing to do with the rodeo. More like one thing—his future after the rodeo. Either way, his career would end this year. Unsure of what his future held, he knew whatever decision he made, it would be meaningless without Sydney. He pulled up to the bar and saw a single car he didn't recognize in the lot. The otherwise empty lot left him with a sudden feeling of unease.

The front door opened easily. Not a good sign. "Syd?"

No answer came, but he heard something back towards the office. Rage filled him as he spotted her lying on the floor, Tyler on top of her, tearing at her clothes. He moved quickly and pulled Tyler off. Her eyes were closed, but he didn't have the time to check on her, because Tyler rushed him. Moving purely on instinct, he threw a left hook, but the other man ducked and tackled him. He hit the floor with Tyler on top of him.

"Not so tough after all, are you, cowboy?"

Putting all he had into the movement, he sent another punch to the side of Tyler's head. It connected and knocked the bastard out cold. Shoving the man off, Levi pulled his phone out, headed over to Sydney and called the police. Then he sank to floor beside her and made the call to Dusty. Blood trickled from her head and her eyes remained closed. The rise and fall of her chest was his only indication she was still with him and he took it as a good sign. With the wail of sirens in the distance, he leaned in close, careful not to move her, and held her hand. "Hang in there, angel."

The police came through the door about the time Tyler began to come around. After explaining what he'd seen to the police, Levi stepped back enough to let the EMTs work, but refused to let her leave his sight. The media arrived, which only made matters worse. He didn't want her to see this on the news.

Dusty and Becca had to argue with the police to be let through. Her brother immediately rushed to Sydney's side. None of them wanted to part with her, but only one could ride in the ambulance with her. Levi needed to deal with the media and promised Dusty he would take Becca to the hospital. As the ambulance disappeared, he gave Becca a weak smile and then walked to the edge of the police tape.

Cameras flashed, microphones were shoved as the reporters threw questions at him. A police officer came up and advised him he did not need to speak with the press. What were his options, allow them to follow him to the hospital? He cleared his throat. "If you would give me just a minute, I'd appreciate it."

When Becca stepped up next to him and took his hand, he gave hers a slight squeeze. He greatly needed the support at the moment. The concern in her eyes surely mimicked his. With a deep breath, he looked to the reporters.

"I'm not going to answer questions. I ask that you give the Hart family and myself the space we need at this time. If Miss Hart would like for me to make a statement at a later time I will. Thank you."

A police escort led them to the hospital. When they stepped into the emergency room, they found Dusty waiting to hear from the doctor. Becca went and sat beside him. Knowing he and Dusty were still on uncertain ground, he sat across from his friend.

"After the flowers and the truck, it was stupid of me to let her close the bar tonight." The guilt in him was evident as he hung his head.

Levi watched the torment in him. No words he could offer would take away the remorse. Especially with him being a participant in the blame game as well. He'd been late picking her up.

Dusty looked up at him. "Good thing you got there when you did."

"Unfortunately, I wasn't there soon enough."

They all looked up when the doctor headed in their direction. "Mr. and Mrs. Hart, Mr. McKenna?"

"Yeah," The three of them stood and the worry on Dusty's face deepened, if it were at all possible, and Becca looked as though she might pass out. They took a collective deep breath.

"Sydney will be okay. There was no sexual assault. She has a slight concussion, bruising and she was in quite a bit of pain when she woke up. We gave her something, so she may be out of it for awhile. We'll keep her here tonight for observation. Given Mr. McKenna's tendency to draw attention, we're moving her to a private room. Once she is settled, I will let you see her."

"Thank you." Dusty said, and they all sank back into the chairs. Silence hung between them for a long while before Dusty finally looked at him. "I worry about her being with you."

"I know," he said. It wasn't an apology, more of a statement of fact. He didn't expect to hear words of remorse, as long as Dusty could live with him and Sydney being together. The doctor came to escort them to Sydney's room and the three of them followed in silence behind him. A slight chill ran over Levi as they walked the stark white corridors that smelled of disinfectant.

When they entered the room, Levi was thankful to see a nice reclining chair and a couch. They could all be comfortable if they had any desire for sleep, though he doubted sleep appealed to any of them. He stepped up alongside the bed. Bruising had already began to form on the side of Sydney's face. Even underneath it all, she was still beautiful.

"Dusty, I'm sorry." Now that he'd gotten a better look at her, he was kicking himself even more for not being on time.

"Hey, at least you got there when you did." The tone in his friend's voice spoke more than his words. Levi wanted to reach out to Sydney, but chose to exercise restraint in front of her brother. He allowed Dusty the time he needed with his sister, and went to sit beside Becca on the couch.

A forced smile crossed Becca's face. "Don't worry, she's a tough cookie."

"It doesn't make it any easier to see her lying there though."

The nurse came in to check on Sydney before the shift change and Dusty joined them to give her room.

"Are you going to stay with her tonight?"

"Not going back until she is comfortable somewhere I can have people wait on her hand and foot." The thought of not going back and finishing the rodeo didn't bother him as much as seeing the woman he loved lying in the hospital.

"I'm still not happy about the two of you, but I guess she could have done worse." Dusty sighed. "You know she won't let you miss the rodeo."

"Yeah, but I can be as stubborn as your sister if I need to be."

"True. Well, call me if something comes up. Otherwise, tell Syd I'll be by in the morning." Dusty stepped over to the bed and leaned in to kiss his sister's cheek. Before he escorted his wife from the room, he looked at Levi for a moment and unspoken words were shared between them.

Once the room had emptied out, he moved the chair closer to the bed. He took Sydney's hand and rested his head on the bed. Whispering to her, he talked about the rodeo and longed for her to look at him. The only thing in his life worth anything was in the bed in front of him. Titles and money couldn't change that. He drifted off to sleep with her hand in his.

Sydney woke up to the faint sounds of breathing when the nurse came in to check on her. The nurse whispered quietly to her. "Since you're awake, I'm going to remove the monitoring equipment. We'll check on you every hour until the doctor comes to release you."

"Thanks," she said quietly. The nurse left and her eyes drifted to the man at her bedside. Levi had fallen asleep with his head on the bed. God, he would pay for it when he woke up. He smiled, his eyes still closed, when she ran her hand through his hair.

"Hi, angel."

"You stayed here all night?" Her body felt stiff when she tried to move and a slight pain caused her to wince. Slowly, she eased back to the bed. "You'll be hurting later."

"Probably," he said as he sat up more. "Won't make much difference."

The implication in his words hurt her. "I will not be the reason you stop. You've worked too hard to get here." She let her hand rest across her stomach. Levi slid onto the bed beside her, gently moving her so he could slip his arm around her and she could rest her head against his chest.

"Syd, there are some things in life worth losing. You're not one of them. It's just a rodeo."

Tension crept into her body. He must have felt it too, because his hand slowly started to caress the bare skin of her arms. "Levi, I want you to go."

"You aren't going to get rid of me that easily." Propping himself up on an elbow, careful not to hurt her as he moved, he sat up in the bed enough to look down at her. "You don't really want me to go."

"No, but I'm asking you to."

"Why?" He turned her face and forced her to look at him.

"Please. I want this to work and I'm afraid that if you don't go out there and finish it will eat at you. I don't want to be the cause of regret in your life. " Tears threatened to break free of their prison and she knew it wouldn't take much more to cause their release.

"Go home with me, Syd."

"What?"

"Go back to Texas with me. Stay with me." Levi waited, but when she didn't answer he added, "I'm not leaving this bed until you say something."

"Can I have some time to think about it?"

"Of course." Bending down he kissed her forehead, then moved off the bed. "I really do love you more than the rodeo, Syd. In my heart I always have."

She didn't say anything as she watched him walk out the door. Wiping the tears from her face, she heard Dusty's voice, followed by some murmuring.

"Syd—"

"I don't want to talk about it, Dusty. Just get me out of here." With help, she climbed out of the bed and reached for the clothes Dusty had brought her. Fear kept her from blurting out an answer to Levi's proposition. The long awaited ride off into the sunset seemed within her grasp, but following the spontaneity of her heart never worked out in the past. Instead, it always ended with her broken and alone.

＊

Three days without seeing her or being able to touch her was beginning to wear on him. The few trips he'd made to the bar had helped to put his friendship with Dusty on the mend, but Syd was absent from the scene. The decision to move with him and make that level of commitment would be a huge leap of faith and wouldn't come easily, but the waiting was eating at him. His focus was shot. Sydney didn't realize it, but she could be the source of regret in more ways than one. Justin approached him, a bit apprehensively.

"You aren't going to turn into a girl and start crying on me now, are ya?"

"Real funny guy." He sighed. "Well, let's get this massacre over with."

"Oh, where's the positive thinking? You could still win this."

Yeah, he could, but what would be the point if he couldn't enjoy the win with Sydney. He knew he had acted irrationally at the hospital. She was right. He would have regretted not seeing this through, but it didn't seem to hold the same excitement without her there to share in the experience.

As they made their way through the arena towards the bull pen, Justin looked at him. "Who'd you draw?"

"Hannibal."

The man beside him let out a low whistle. "That's a bitch."

"Yeah." It figured his last ride would bring him face-to-face with the one bull notorious for being worse than Devil. "You?"

"Devil." Justin slapped his back hard. "I'm sure you'll do fine. If you need some reassurance, just glance towards the Gold Buckle seats."

＊

Sydney's nerves were in overdrive. Both her brother and sister-in-law had listened to her spill her heart out and without saying a word, they'd allowed her to rationalize her fears and accept that love was always a gamble. This time she truly felt like the odds were in her favor. Now it was a matter of waiting. Justin had been very helpful when she'd talked to him earlier in the afternoon and he'd assured her he planned on giving Levi a run for his money. God, she hoped so. What good would it do if Levi didn't earn it?

Her plan had been set into motion, now her cowboy just had to come through to make the pieces all fall into place.

"How are you holding up?" Her brother sat beside her, Becca on his other side.

"I'm okay," she said loud enough for him to hear.

"Good, because your boyfriend's in the bucking chute."

She snapped her head up. Sure enough, Levi was in the chute. He looked up and their gazes locked. Relief seemed to wash over his face. The announcer named the bull he'd drawn, her pulse began to race and fear racked her body. Hannibal was one of the toughest rides in NFR history. Injuries sustained by him were legendary.

This could end horribly. Holding her breath, she latched onto Dusty's hand when the bull exploded out of the chute. Levi's position looked good, but the bull's violent bucking made its dissatisfaction at having a rider on his back evident. Eight seconds. He just had to hold on for eight measly seconds. Dusty leaned into her.

"You aren't going to watch?"

She hadn't even realized her eyes were closed. "Um, I'm watching."

Forcing her eyes to remain opened, she counted. Five more seconds to go—four—three—two—one. The bull rope slipped from Levi's hand as he let it go and managed to quickly get away from the bull. Relief swelled though her. Justin was up, the last rider of the evening. Then they would know if Levi had scored well enough to take the win.

Devil burst out of the chute with Justin on board. He couldn't cover the bull and when Devil bucked, he was hung up in the bull rope. He broke free, but the bull managed to hook him as he dismounted. Moving to the edge of her seat, she felt every muscle in her body tense, but she relaxed when Justin scurried out of the arena.

It was done. She made her way down to the back section of

the arena. Justin hobbled his way over, holding an ice pack to his side, smiling when he saw her concern. "Just a scratch, darlin'. Don't worry."

"It looked pretty bad. May I?" Reaching for the edge of his shirt, she lifted it up enough to see the swelling and the blood.

"It looks worse than it is. He just caught the edge of my vest. Like I said, just a scratch. Come on. You might have competition for his attention. Everyone wants to talk to the new champ." He winked at her and then led her back to where the riders were milling around. She spotted Levi talking with a reporter.

✳

"No, this is my last rodeo. I'm retiring and going home to my ranch," Levi said, glancing up to see Sydney walking towards him with Justin at her side. Politely excusing himself from the reporters, he walked over to her, fighting the need to wrap his arms around her. "Hi, angel."

"That's all you have to say to the girl you're taking home with you? What would your father say?"

"He'd tell me to get my shit together and kiss her."

"So what's stopping you?" The invitation and smile were all he needed to spur him into motion. He leaned in and pressed his lips to hers. Pulling her close, he lifted her off the ground and she wrapped her legs around him. Cameras flashed all around them. Sydney smiled and he threaded his hands through her hair, keeping her face close to his.

"You know I'm gonna want more than just a live-in girlfriend."

"I refuse to be your maid. Everything else is open for discussion."

"I'm going to hold you to that." He smiled. Who knew the ride would end up being so sweet.

About the Author

To learn more about Moira Keith, please visit http://moirakeith.com. Send an email to Moira at moira@moirakeith.com or visit her at her blog http://moirakeith.com/blog.

Strong, Silent Type

Lorelei James

Dedication

For all couples who've held on through the bumpy spots in marriage...

Chapter One

"Get your goddamn hands off my wife."

Quinn McKay was in a rage. A red rage. An aneurysm-inducing rage. A going-postal rage.

And the worst part? His wife, his helpmate, his lover, his partner, his...everything—goddammit, Libby *was* his everything—didn't give two shits about his foul mood.

Not. Two. Hot. Shits.

Which enraged him further.

"Walk it off, Quinn," Libby McKay tossed over her shoulder, letting the young buck lead her deeper into the crowd on the dance floor. The last thing Quinn saw was the sassy head shake of her sassy new hairdo.

"I'm gonna fuckin' kill him. See how goddamn happy his hands are after I break 'em off at the wrists."

"Jesus, Q, will you sit the hell down? People are starin' at you."

"Let 'em look."

His brother Ben hissed, "Screw that. Get your dumb ass back to the table or I'm leavin' and you can hoof it home."

"Be worth it to punch that sonuvabitch in the face."

"I ain't bailin' you outta jail neither."

Quinn scowled, reluctantly following Ben back to the booth. He drained his cup of beer and poured another from the pitcher. Mostly foam. Didn't it just figure even the beer wasn't cooperating with him tonight?

"You gotta stop doin' this, man."

"Doin' what? Drinkin'?"

"No."

"Oh, you mean quit comin' to Ziggy's to watch my wife dance with every good-for-nuthin' loser in this place?"

"Bingo."

"Fuck that." Quinn slammed his empty cup down. "It's a free country. I live in this goddamned county. I got just as much right to be here as she does."

Ben jerked the pitcher away before Quinn dispensed a refill. "It's been three months since you and Libby separated, Q. Face it. Maybe it's time you moved on. Looks like she has."

"Wrong. If Libby is so all fired up to 'move on' then why the hell hasn't she hired a lawyer and filed for divorce?"

"Probably waitin' 'til school gets out and she has more time."

His answer resembled a growl.

"I don't know why you're so surprised." Ben poured himself a cup of foam. "You guys've been headed down this road for a while."

"The hell we have."

"You tellin' me you were just rollin' along, mindin' your own business and wham! Her demand of 'I want a trial separation' came from left field?"

Quinn hated—*hated*—talking about this kind of touchy feely crap with anyone. "All married couples hit rough patches. I thought it'd blow over. It always has before."

"*Before?*" Ben choked on his beer. "This ain't the first time?"

"It's the first time she's kicked me outta my own damn house." Three fucking months he'd been living in tin, eating out of tin and sleeping alone in absolute misery.

"So you been goin' to counseling and shit?"

"Nope."

"Why not? Did she ask you to?"

Sort of. Quinn knew he and Ben weren't talking about the same type of professional help Libby had suggested. He hedged. "Yeah."

"What'd ya say?"

"No."

"Jesus. You are one stubborn sonuvabitch. I can see why Libby is tired of it and booted your ass."

Stubborn sonuvabitch. A familiar phrase. His normally

sweet-tongued wife had hurled those words at him as she'd hurled a suitcase full of his dirty clothes on the front porch. "Fuckin' great. I'm glad you're takin' her side, bro."

"Quinn, man, no offense, but you suck as a husband."

Embarrassment flared. Libby'd said that much too. "How the hell do you know? You've been married what, *zero* times?"

"Don't mean I can't see when something ain't workin'," Ben countered. "Obviously your marriage ain't doin' so hot. I'd be more'n happy to offer you red-hot tips to fire it back up."

"Tips from the guy whose last relationship barely passed the one month mark? This oughta be interestin'."

"No skin off my nose if you're too proud to accept help. But even as a single guy, I'm aware bein' a good husband is more than bein' a good provider."

Yep. Quinn's spouse had also tossed that phrase at him. But the irony was that street ran both ways. Libby ought to realize there was more to being a good wife than having supper on the table, maintaining a spotless house, and cramming his dresser drawers with clean clothes. Not that he'd say that to her, knowing how much it'd hurt her feelings. Why hadn't Libby realized how deeply it'd cut him when she'd carelessly flung those same words in his face? He sighed. "Go ahead, Ben, wow me with your golden marriage tips."

"First of all, you have to stop takin' Libby for granted."

"I've never taken her for granted. Never."

"Fine then. You gotta show her how much she matters to you. You gotta...woo her."

"Woo her?" Baffled, Quinn stared at his brother. "How the hell am I supposed to do that?"

"Act like you did when you were dating. Bring her flowers, wine and dine her with candlelit dinners, take her to the movies. Spend time just makin' out and tryin' to cop a feel in the truck."

Quinn leaned forward. "I'm reminding you I've been with Libby for fourteen years. We started dating when we were sixteen. I married her the month after she graduated from college. We've been man and wife for nine years. So I'm a little rusty on my *wooin'* skills."

"Then it's past time to brush up on 'em, Q. Because if you don't use 'em on her, you're gonna need to use 'em on someone else."

Shame burned and he dropped his gaze to the table. "Then I'm doomed. I never done any of that romantic crap with her." Or any other woman. Libby was the first girl he'd dated. The first and only woman he'd had sex with. The only woman he'd ever wanted. The only woman he'd ever loved.

And I'm about to lose her.

"Never?" Ben prompted.

Quinn shook his head. "Libby's always been practical. That's one of the reasons I fell for her. She didn't need any of the superficial junk other girls did. She didn't expect me to be a rodeo star or go to trade school. She knew I'd never leave here because ranchin' is in my blood. She was fine with that. She wanted that life...or so I thought."

Things—no, *Libby* had changed in the last year. It had started out with small modifications. New furniture, repainting a room or two, hanging new draperies, trying out new recipes from faraway places. Then she'd started dropping hints about them doing "couple" activities.

When Libby had returned to her job as the school librarian after summer hiatus, she went on a diet and lost twenty-five pounds. He'd always loved her curvy body, but she seemed happier thinner. She'd tossed out her old duds and bought new ones. Gone were the long denim skirts, loose shirts, bulky sweaters, baggy sweats and oversized T-shirts she'd worn for years. Ditto for neutral colors.

No, Libby—his Libby—began wearing tight, low-cut jeans. Clingy blouses that accentuated her ample chest. Short skirts in vivid colors. Just as he was wrapping his head around those changes, she'd trotted off to Denver for a professional makeover. She'd chopped her long, honey-brown hair into a short, trendy cut and added blondish-red highlights. She'd never worn much makeup, so it'd shocked Quinn to see her freckles covered, her lips glossy red and black eyeliner emphasizing her blue eyes.

At that point he'd begun to worry, wondering if she'd met a man she was trying to impress.

When Libby asked him how he liked the "new" her, Quinn replied honestly: He'd liked the old her just fine.

A day later he was living in the horse trailer.

"Dammit. You aren't even listenin' to me, are you?" Ben demanded.

Quinn ignored the taunt and focused on Libby sashaying

off the dance floor. The smile she allotted her dance partner didn't reach her eyes like it did whenever she danced with him. Her shoulders were bunched up to her ears. Her normally graceful body movements were forced. Unnatural. She looked as if she were merely going through the motions.

Just like him.

The truth hit Quinn as viciously as a horse hoof to the head. He'd gone about dealing with this misstep in their marriage the wrong way, expecting Libby to come to him. *He* had to fix it, to man up, take the bull by the horns, grab the tiger by the tail, climb on the horse that threw him, reclaim what was rightfully his. Clichéd phrases, but truisms to lead him in the right direction—the only direction—straight back to her.

"Quinn? You okay?"

"Nah. I ain't been right since she kicked me out, Ben. Dammit. I miss her something fierce."

Ben froze. "Ah shit, Q, you ain't gonna start with that, *I love you man,* kinda drunk talk, are you?"

"Hell no." Quinn shoved the pitcher aside and propped his elbows on the table. "But I have been listenin' to you yammer on, and you're exactly right. I've gotta do something. And you're gonna help me."

"Help you do what?"

"Help me come up with a plan to win my wife back."

Chapter Two

"Second shelf on the bottom row."

The seven-year-old girl shook her head, bouncing her blonde corkscrew pigtails. "Huh-uh. I looked."

"Look again."

"But you're the librarian. You always help me."

"This time is different, sweetie, because your teacher wants you to find the book. It'll improve your alphabetizing skills." Libby resisted her impulse to smooth the girl's puckered brow.

"I wish you were my teacher, Mrs. McKay," she announced before flouncing away.

I wish I had a little girl just like you.

Libby briefly squeezed her eyes shut. *Don't go there.* She had enough issues and failures to deal with, thank you very much, starting with the demise of her marriage to Quinn McKay.

Damn stubborn man. What would spur him into action? To get across this wasn't a game? This was their life hanging in the balance.

Quinn hadn't balked at her demand of a trial separation. He'd taken it in stride and blithely continued his day-to-day life on the ranch, content to hole up in the horse trailer until she "came to her senses".

Three months had gone by and they were at an impasse.

It didn't help Libby hadn't spoken directly to her husband in that time frame. Her involvement with their ranching operation made their lack of daily communication a real dilemma. Being the efficient sort, she'd created a schedule for ranch business and bill paying, and for personal issues, such as when Quinn could use the shower and the washer and dryer in the house.

The system worked, but it forced them to leave each other notes. His were terse and to the point. Hers were polite and filled with detailed explanations. Which pretty much summed up their marriage in the last year or so.

But Libby still loved Quinn. She missed him like crazy. Yet after last night, she questioned whether love was enough. Why wouldn't he fight for her? For them? Why was it solely up to *her* to enact the changes they both so desperately needed?

If you're so eager for change, why haven't you signed the legal complaint paperwork the attorney gave you that's been in your desk for a month?

Good question.

But at least she'd made an effort to test her wings and gauge if walking away from him for good was a possibility. Bored and lonely, Libby had started hanging out with her single female coworkers at Ziggy's, a bar which catered to a younger crowd than the other honky-tonks in the area. Getting hit on by eager, hot cowboys did wonders for her self-esteem, even when she'd only flirted, danced and accepted the occasional free drink.

Then Quinn began showing up. He'd hunker down in a booth, drinking beer, sometimes alone, sometimes with his brother. Quinn never approached her. He just watched her.

Until last night.

Quinn's clipped, "Get your goddamn hands off my wife," had instilled a tiny seed of hope. Libby secretly wished for Quinn the Barbarian to hoist her over his shoulder and cart her out of the bar. She fantasized her he-man would be in such a lust-filled state to have her, he'd fuck her against his dirty pickup, not caring who might see him staking his claim.

Afterward, he'd race them home and make mad, passionate love to her for days on end. In their bed. On the kitchen table. In the shower. Up against the corral. All the while confessing his undying love for her. Profess he'd been a fool. He'd do anything to keep her and guarantee her happiness for the rest of their lives.

That hadn't happened. Libby had to face reality—it probably never would. Last night Quinn had simply muttered and walked away. Given up. Dashing her idiotic, girlish romantic dreams of reconciliation.

Tears fell as she reached for the file folder in the back of the drawer. She pulled out the sheaf of legal papers titled *Complaint.* Libby scrawled her name on the bottom line, dated it and crammed the whole works in a manila envelope.

The rest of Mrs. Rich's rambunctious second-grade class barreled into the library. Libby hastily set the envelope on her desk and put the whole thing out of her mind.

∗

A sage-scented breeze stirred Libby's hair as she exited the school hours later. Exhausted, she juggled a bag of books and her car keys, so she didn't notice the man leaning against her car until the tips of his boots were within view.

Libby raised her chin. Her heart *whomped* when her gaze caught familiar blue eyes.

Quinn.

Even after fourteen years together, just seeing him set her pulse racing. Quinn was the stereotypical Wyoming rancher, more rugged looking than classically handsome. He'd maintained the same stocky build as in his younger years, although it appeared he'd dropped weight since being forced to cook his own meals. But it looked good on him. Everything looked good on him.

His face was smoothly shaven. The fresh scent of his aftershave, mixed with the aroma of his sun-warmed skin, drifted toward her, swamping her with longing.

Damn him.

To top it off, Quinn had worn her favorite shirt, the one she'd bought him for Christmas, navy blue with pearl-snap buttons and white stitching around the pocket flaps. The cut of the material showcased his wide shoulders and broad chest. The sleeves hugged his muscled biceps, every bulge earned the hard way from manual labor required to run a ranch. The dark fabric emphasized his coloring, his blackish-brown hair, the long, thick, sooty lashes surrounding his mesmerizing blue eyes.

Those intense eyes locked onto hers. Quinn gave her the unsure smile she hadn't seen in ages. Her heart thumped harder.

"Hey, Libby. You, ah, look good. Real good."

"Thanks. What're you doing here?" A panicked thought crossed her mind. "Did someone die?"

"No." He paused. Frowned. Seemed highly flustered. "It's sorta sad you'd think that's what it'd take to get me to come around."

Libby shrugged. "You *haven't* come around."

"True enough. But last time I checked, the roads run both ways, darlin' wife."

She notched her chin higher. "What do you want?"

"You."

Her stomach did a swoopy roll. "Excuse me?"

He kept leaning against the driver's side door, hands jammed into the pockets of a new pair of dark blue Wrangler jeans, his going-to-town boots crossed at the ankles. "I'm here 'cause I'm waitin' for you."

"Why?"

For a second, his shoulders tensed. Then he pushed away from the car and ambled toward her. "Because I don't like you dancin' with other men."

Taunting him usually had no effect. No matter how pissed off he might be, Quinn McKay never caused a scene. Never acted improper or impulsive in public, which was why his outburst in the bar last night had thoroughly confused her. Hell, he rarely acted improper or impulsive in private. So, she couldn't help the flip, "Oh. Is that all?" to see if she could goad him into another heated reaction.

"No, that ain't all. I'm also here to remind you that you're my wife and I don't share what's mine."

A chill skittered through her at his possessive tone. "I didn't think you cared."

"You thought wrong. Now dump your stuff in the back of the truck and get in. We're goin' home."

Libby's jaw dropped. The book bag hit the dirt. Her temper skyrocketed and her voice escalated. "Just like that? You think after three months of ignoring me and our problems that you can just show up and...*command* me? I've got news for you buddy, not happening. Too little, too late."

A heavy pause lingered. She expected him to remind her to

lower her voice. She didn't expect him to lower his head until her face was shadowed beneath the brim of his ever-present cowboy hat.

"Wrong answer. Better late than never is my new creed." Quinn peered into her eyes so closely she felt his breath fanning her lips. "I agreed to give you the space you demanded, Libby. Now I can see that was a fool-headed mistake on my part. So you're gonna rectify it."

"Me? How?"

"By givin' me the second chance I deserve." Quinn lifted his hand to her face. It shocked her to see that strong, capable hand trembling. He dragged the back of his rough-skinned knuckles down her cheek. "Please."

Oh God. When was the last time Quinn said that simple word to her? And meant it?

Libby stared at him, puzzled, yet unable to squash that last bit of hope. Was she seeing new determination in the eyes of the man she'd loved most of her life? A man she swore she knew straight to the bone?

"Libby?"

The soft, gruff way he'd spoken her name as a question, not a demand, tore at her resistance. "What?"

"Spend the weekend with me. Just you and me."

"And what happens come Monday morning?"

"We'll take it one day at a time and see how it goes from there."

"If I agree to the weekend, you'll give me time to think it over next week? No matter what happens?"

"Yep. I promise. No pressure."

Perfect. She'd be in Cheyenne at the state librarian's conference next week. It'd allow her physical and emotional distance from him, and time to put it all in perspective, no matter how the weekend turned out.

You've got nothing to lose. This is the chance you never thought you'd have.

"Please. Come home. I, ah, managed to fix supper." A sheepish smile was there and gone again. "Nuthin' fancy, just fried potatoes and sausage. But I sure would like to share a meal with you tonight."

Libby kept her gaze steady and retorted, "Just as long as

you understand that sharing a meal doesn't mean we'll be sharing a bed, Quinn McKay."

Quinn's hand dropped and he stepped back. "I wasn't tryin' to... I never thought..." He smiled with deliberate slowness. "Hell, Libby, if I woulda wanted to be in our bed again, I woulda said so up front. You probably don't believe me, 'cause you seem to think the worst of me these days, but I didn't fix a quick supper in exchange for a quickie."

Heat climbed up her neck, setting her face aflame. She'd jumped to the wrong conclusion. Again. Not that Quinn pointed out her faults and failings like she'd freely done with his.

In his understated, gentle way, he said, "I'll see you back at the house." He hopped in his mud-covered truck and roared away.

*

Quinn had set the kitchen table with their wedding china before he'd left for town. He snagged a beer from the fridge, but hesitated before popping the top. Would Libby attribute his openness and willingness to talk to alcohol? Probably. He slid the Budweiser back on the top shelf.

Dishes washed, counters cleaned, he had nothing to do but wait. He'd gotten used to his own company in the evenings in recent months. Didn't mean he liked it.

After turning the burner to simmer, Quinn snuck upstairs and stood in the doorway to their bedroom. The same faded wedding ring quilt adorned the brass bed. The usual explosion of pillows were piled at the head and the extra wool blanket dangled off the foot.

The room smelled the same, Libby's cherry-almond hand lotion and a hint of wood from the cedar-lined closet. If Quinn peeled back the bedcovers, he'd catch a whiff of Libby's apple shampoo and the underlying musky-sweet fragrance of just Libby.

He stared mindlessly, trying to remember the last time he and Libby had made love in that bed. In the months prior to their separation, they may as well have been sleeping in separate rooms.

A memory came to him, leaving him as breathless and embarrassed as he'd been at the time. Missing his wife, feeling adrift and lonely, Quinn had mustered the guts to cross the invisible line running down the center of the mattress, only to have Libby literally give him the cold shoulder. Tired of being rejected, he hadn't bothered trying to touch her at all, in bed or out, for the next six months.

Initially, he'd blamed their lack of intimacy on a multitude of things, exhaustion, familiarity and laziness. It'd seemed weird to experiment with crazy new sexual positions when the old standbys worked so well. They both got off and wasn't that the point of sex? Besides, the red-hot-have-to-have-you-now passion had cooled into something more comfortable over the years. Which wasn't all bad until that comfort factor had turned into a sexual snooze-fest.

But Quinn refused to take all the blame for their fizzling— rather than sizzling—sex life. Heaven knew Libby rarely initiated lovemaking, but left the seducing up to him. Sure, once he'd stoked her fires she was a generous and enthusiastic lover, not particularly adventurous, but then again, he wasn't exactly the hanging-from-the-chandelier wild sex type either.

If he were completely honest, things had fallen apart on the sexual front when they'd decided to try for a baby. At first it'd been fun, the carefree let's-have-sex-all-the-time romps. But three years after Libby had stopped taking the pill, she still wasn't pregnant.

So his practical, organized wife had drawn elaborate fertility charts. Detailed lists of when they could—and couldn't—make love. First, she'd tossed his tighty whities and bought boxer shorts to keep his balls from getting overheated and inadvertently lowering his sperm count. Then, she'd purchased bottles of vitamins and cheerfully watched as he swallowed every blasted horse-sized pill. When that had no effect, she'd modified their diet and limited their alcohol intake. Finally, she'd insisted on sex in the missionary position only. After he ejaculated, she'd prop her hips under three pillows and stay in that pose for at least half an hour...while he wandered off to watch TV. Alone.

Eventually, sex had become just another one of his daily chores. Charts, cycles, basal temperatures, books and articles on conceiving a baby were the topics of discussion—but only at home. When another two years had passed and she hadn't filled the heirloom bassinet with a bundle of joy, Libby had suggested they schedule an appointment with a specialist dealing with infertility.

Quinn had flat-out refused. First, because they weren't that old. Making a baby could still happen the old-fashioned way, given time. Libby was just impatient. True, part of his refusal was masculine pride—no man wants to hear he's got problems with his Johnson. The other part of his refusal was personal. It seemed his relationship with his wife was no longer based on love, but on his capability, or incapability, as a breeder.

Quinn had told Libby he was perfectly content to spend his life with her, just her, and he wasn't basing his present or future happiness on whether the stick turned pink or blue every month.

That's when things had gone downhill.

So Quinn had lied to Ben when he claimed he hadn't seen the separation coming. He just hadn't known how to handle it, so he'd done nothing to prevent it. He'd been floating along, hoping like hell Libby would come around.

She hadn't. In fact, she hadn't been around at all.

Too little, too late.

Like hell. He might've been slow on the uptake, but he was good at playing catch-up. Damn good.

The sound of Libby's car crunching on the driveway brought Quinn out of his reverie and he headed downstairs.

Her arms were overloaded with bags and Quinn rushed forward. "Lemme help you."

"Thanks."

"Where you want me to put them?"

"Dining room table is fine."

Libby arranged her belongings to her liking before she looked at him.

God, she was pretty. Old hairstyle or new haircut, barefaced or all made up, it didn't matter. One glimpse into her eyes was all he needed to see the real Libby. His Libby.

She bristled. "What?"

"Can't a man admire his wife?" Quinn let his gaze roam over her sweet face and linger on her lips.

"I thought we were gonna eat."

Staring at her made her nervous. *Interesting.*

"We are. Go on in and have a seat. I'll dish up."

"This is odd, you waiting on me," she said.

"No more odd than you lettin' me do it."

That retort brought forth the cute wrinkle on her forehead and no additional comment.

Good.

Soon as Quinn sat across from Libby, she frowned and started to get up. Quickly, but gently, Quinn placed his hand on her forearm. "What do you need? I'll get it."

"A napkin."

He reached behind him for the wicker container and kept hold of her arm. "Here."

"Thank you."

"No problem. So what's been happenin' in the world of books?"

Libby clutched her fork. "You really interested or are you just making conversation?"

"I'm interested, Lib, I've always cared about what you do at the school."

Satisfied with his answer, she said, "I'm gearing up for the summer reading program."

"Betcha already got quite a few kids signed up for that."

"Yes, actually I do. How'd you know?"

Quinn gave her a noncommittal shoulder hitch. "Because you're you. You never do anything half-assed."

"My, my, aren't you full of compliments tonight?"

"I reckon I owe you more than three months' worth so I'd better start makin' up for lost time." He swept his thumb over the smooth skin on the back of her wrist. "That okay with you, darlin' wife?"

She squirmed at his term of endearment but didn't try and shake off his hand, much to his surprise.

"I'm not used to you acting this way."

"Maybe you oughta get used to it. Maybe I've realized the error of my ways and I'm a changed man."

"Is that why you behaved like that last night at Ziggy's?"

"Like what?"

"You know how you behaved."

Quinn chewed slowly and swallowed. "You lookin' for an apology?"

"Maybe."

"Okay. I'm sorry that sonuvabitch who had his paws all over you didn't spend all goddamn night pickin' his teeth up off the floor after I knocked 'em clean outta his mouth."

Libby stammered, "B-but, you didn't do anything! You just left."

"Huh-uh. Ben said he wouldn't post bond if I beat the snot outta that snot-nosed punk. With you and me on the outs, I figured I couldn't count on you for bail money either, so I let Ben drag me away, against my will, I might add."

"So you're not apologizing?"

Quinn flashed his teeth. "For actin' like a man and for protecting what's mine? Hell no." He leaned closer. "Does that shock you?"

"A little. Lord, Quinn, that was completely out of character for you, cussing, threatening a guy and causing a public scene."

He shrugged. "That's because I keep that side of myself to myself."

"Why?"

Should he answer? Could he?

Yes. No more hiding. Balls to the wall.

"Quinn?"

"Because it'd scare you worse than it does me."

"I'm not exactly a delicate flower," she retorted. "And I've known you all my life."

"Yeah? Then did ya think I'd go with my original impulse of draggin' you back home by the hair and provin' to you just who has the right to put his hands all over you?"

Libby's amazing blue eyes widened, not with reproach but with...interest.

Goddamn if his cock didn't take notice.

Quinn grinned at her. "Eat your supper 'fore it gets cold."

They managed normal conversation for the remainder of the meal. Afterward, they even washed the dishes together, something they hadn't done since the first year they were married. Over coffee and cake, Quinn said, "I have plans for us for tomorrow afternoon."

"Plans to do what?"

"It's a surprise." He sipped the last of his coffee and added, "A romantic surprise."

Quinn read the emotions warring on Libby's face. The need

105

to question him further. The disbelief of his casual use of the word "romantic". But mostly he saw a response that'd been a long time coming—hopeful curiosity.

"What time?"

Thank you, Jesus. "I'll come get ya at twelve-thirty. It starts at one o'clock. We can ride together."

"You aren't telling me where you're taking me, are you?"

"Nope."

Libby smiled. "You know it's gonna drive me crazy."

"Yep."

"Why are you doing this?"

"What? Drivin' you crazy?"

"No. Acting so unlike you."

"Because, you don't believe I can change, so it's up to me to convince you otherwise."

Her smile dimmed. "But what if it doesn't change anything?"

"What if it does?" he countered.

Silence.

Might as well get it all out in the open. "It hasn't always been like this between us. We were good together, weren't we?"

"Quinn—"

"Has every year of our marriage been pure hell for you, Libby?"

"God. No. Not even close." Libby started to say something else but snapped her mouth shut, choosing instead to fiddle with the lace edging on the placemat.

"Good to know." Quinn stood. He ached to stay, but he'd left her enough to mull over for one night.

On the porch, he paused to absorb the beauty of the place they called home. Dusk had fallen, turning the sky purple-gray and dusting the tree line in the distance with fluffy pink clouds. A brisk breeze rattled the bird feeders. The dark, ripe scent of wet earth filled his lungs. It seemed as if he'd taken his first real breath in months.

The heat of Libby's body behind his made him turn around very slowly, even when his heart raced like a snared rabbit's. With forced casualness, Quinn said, "Oh, one other thing."

"What?"

"This." Quinn cupped her face in his hands. He pressed his

mouth down, allowing his lips to reacquaint themselves with the softness and shape of hers beneath his. One smooth brush of his lips morphed into a dozen drugging kisses. At the insistent glide of his mouth, teasing nips of his teeth, tiny flicks of his tongue, Libby's lips parted on a soft sigh.

His tongue slipped inside and her flavor burst in his mouth, sweet coffee, sweet Libby and sweet temptation. It'd been an eternity since he'd kissed his wife this way, a slow seduction. A promise. A renewal of intent.

Quinn tilted her head, kicking the kiss from lazy exploration to undeniable hunger. For her. Only ever for her. A wet, wild reunion of dueling tongues, stuttered breaths and the powerful slide into passion they'd either forgotten or had denied themselves.

Despite the heat and the sense of yearning, he kept their bodies apart, because what was blossoming between them again was too important to rush.

Tonight. Tomorrow all bets were off.

He forced himself to break the kiss. His hands fell away and he buried his nose in her apple-scented hair. "I miss talkin' to you. Touchin' you." He kissed the start of her jawline beneath her ear. "I miss the way you smell. The way you taste. The way you feel. Goddamn, I miss the everything of you, Libby."

"Quinn, I..."

His body was primed for action and it took every bit of willpower to step back from her. "I ain't gonna apologize."

"I don't want you to."

Damn, if that admission didn't cause his cock to jerk with hope. Especially when he saw her gaze drop to the bulge beneath his zipper.

Double damn. Definitely time to go. "Good night, Libby. Sweet dreams." He smiled cagily and melted into the shadows.

Chapter Three

"You have no idea where he's taking you?"

"None." Libby peeked out the kitchen window, feeling silly for watching for Quinn's truck to barrel up the drive. She hadn't done that for years.

"And you just agreed?"

"Yep."

Jillian sighed. "Sis, no offense, but the last time Quinn surprised you, he brought you home a new crock pot."

Libby stuck her tongue out at the receiver. She loved that damn crock pot. Jilly didn't understand it'd been an incredibly sweet gesture on Quinn's part because he so rarely acted spontaneously. "He's trying, Jilly."

"Well, it's about damn time."

Usually Jillian's constant yakking was impossible to ignore, but today, Libby easily tuned her out. She had more important things to tune into. Like the steamy kiss that'd knocked her sideways last night.

Man. She'd forgotten Quinn could kiss like that. She'd forgotten she could kiss like that. She'd definitely forgotten how arousing a simple kiss could be, as evidenced by the soaking wet condition of her panties when she'd stumbled back into the house on wobbly knees.

And Libby couldn't help but notice Quinn's erection. Kissing her had the same effect on him—a good sign—since the man hadn't touched her for three months prior to their separation.

Six long months without physical intimacy. Half a year without her husband paying attention to her at all.

To cope with his apathy, she'd tried a few changes around the house, dropped some weight, updated her hairstyle, makeup and wardrobe. A confidence-boosting bonus she'd hoped would increase her physical attraction to her mate. But when she'd marshaled the courage to ask Quinn how he liked the "new" her, he'd responded he'd liked the old her just fine.

Quinn probably hadn't meant his remark in an unflattering way, but it'd stung nevertheless. In response, she'd lashed back at him like she'd never done, said hurtful things and then kicked him out.

And speak of the devil; the man was kicking up a cloud of dust as he zipped up the gravel driveway.

"Can I offer you some advice—"

She cut Jillian off mid-sentence. "Quinn is here."

"Libby, will you listen to me before you hang up?"

No. But Jillian would blather on anyway. "What?"

"Avoid talking about the baby issue. If you really want your relationship with Quinn to have a fair shot, it needs to only be about your relationship as man and wife."

"Meaning?"

"Don't bring up his refusal to take fertility tests or the years you've spent trying to get pregnant to the exclusion of everything else."

"That's unfair, Jilly. You make it sound like that's all I've cared about."

"It's certainly been all you've talked about for the last several years," Jilly gently chided. "I know I'm the only person you've trusted with your frustration about your inability to conceive, so my view might be skewed."

Libby opened her mouth to argue, but a teeny germ of guilt sprouted. Only in the last twelve months she hadn't been obsessing about babies because she'd been obsessing about what'd gone wrong between her and her husband. She'd figured by letting the big issue drop, they'd be able to focus on the smaller ones.

That hadn't happened either.

She let her disquiet build as she watched Quinn hurry into the horse trailer.

"Libs? You there?"

"Yeah. Sorry. I'm still here." Pause. "Was I really that bad?"

"It'll be hard for you to hear, but yeah, you were. Sometimes I understand why Quinn didn't protest too much about the separation. It's been a rough couple years on both of you."

Her stomach lurched. If she'd been so blatantly single-minded why hadn't Quinn said anything to her?

Because his unwillingness to talk about anything was the reason you asked for the separation.

But Quinn hadn't always been like that.

Maybe he's grown tired of discussing the same old things and silence was his only defense.

"I didn't say that to hurt you, Libs."

"I don't understand why you didn't mention it before now."

"Because it wasn't my place, honey. It was Quinn's. And we both know he wouldn't say shit if he had a mouthful."

Libby fought the urge to curl into a ball and weep. "Lord. How did everything get so screwed up?"

"I don't know. Good luck." Jillian hung up.

Quinn exited the horse trailer and Libby caught her first glimpse of his clothes. Gray sweatpants. A faded brown and gold University of Wyoming *Go Pokes!* T-shirt, tennis shoes and a "gimme" ball cap from the local Yamaha dealership.

Whoa. Quinn never dressed casually, especially if he planned on being seen in public. Some kind of proper public cowboy attire had been hardwired into the man's DNA. Did that mean he'd planned a private outing?

He bounded up the steps like an eager pup and barged right in. "Heya, Libby. You look great. Ready?"

A compliment right off the bat? The man really was trying. "Yeah. Just let me grab my purse."

Familiar warmth spread inside and outside her body from his hand caressing the small of her back as he followed her down the porch steps.

"Where are we going?"

Quinn smiled and opened the truck door. "You'll find out soon enough."

Inside the pickup, he patted the bench seat. "Scoot over. I wanna relive those times when we were first dating and you practically sat on my lap."

Touched by his request, she slid next to him until they

were matched thigh-to-thigh. "Is this a date?"

"As much as a man can be on a date with his wife of nine years."

Libby turned. His face was mere inches away.

"Bein's you *are* my wife, I'm entitled to steal a kiss." Quinn angled his head and gently brushed his lips over hers one time. Then he straightened up and started the truck.

"That's it?" burst out before she could stop it.

"You were expectin' something else?"

"I was hoping for a kiss like the one from last night."

"Libby, darlin', you can kiss me like that anytime you want. Any. Damn. Time. At all. And it don't gotta stop at kissin'."

Just like that, Quinn had gotten his point across in his usual low-key manner. She bumped him with her shoulder. "Maybe I will."

"I'll look forward to it." He kept his hand on her thigh during the drive to Sundance.

Quinn parked in front of the Sandstone Building. It housed three separate businesses, all run by women who'd married into the McKay family. Macie McKay ran Dewey's Delish Dish, Skylar McKay owned Sky Blue, and her sister, India, owned the tattoo shop, India's Ink, which were housed together in the same space, while AJ McKay operated Healing Touch Massage. It was too late to eat lunch so Libby couldn't fathom why they were here. A panicked thought struck her. "Are we getting a tattoo?"

He laughed. "You oughta see your look of horror."

She noticed he hadn't answered her question. "Are we?"

"No." Quinn offered a wicked smile. "Unless you've got a hankerin' to tattoo my initials on your sweet little ass?"

"Quinn!"

"What? It is a sweet little ass."

Married nine years and the man could still make her blush. "That's not what I meant."

He stroked the back of his knuckles down her heated cheek. "That's been part of the problem in recent years, ain't it? Neither one of us is sayin' what we really mean, or meanin' what we say."

Libby closed her eyes and basked in his tender touch.

"I wanna fix this between us, Libby."

Me too.

Two solid raps startled them both. Quinn rolled down his window. "Hey, Cord, what's up?"

"Just makin' sure you didn't get cold feet."

"Nope."

Cord grinned. "Good. Took a bit of finagling, but we made room. See you two in there."

"In where?" Libby asked.

"Healing Touch." Quinn rolled up the window. "AJ is offerin' a class on sensual massage."

"Are you serious?"

"Yep."

"You signed us up for a class so I could learn to give you a...sexy massage?"

"There you go jumpin' to conclusions again. I signed up so *I* could learn to give *you* a sexy massage."

Talk about being completely pole-axed. "When did you do this?"

"Yesterday. There was, ah, a last minute cancellation so I lucked out and they squeezed us in."

Last minute cancellation. Right. She'd bet a hundred bucks he'd strong-armed his way into getting a spot in that class—an example of McKay nepotism at its finest. But she couldn't help being impressed. "Why are you doing this?"

Quinn stayed quiet so long she was afraid he wouldn't answer. "In the last year or so you were pretty hell bent on us takin' some 'couples' classes together. I'll admit I was kinda a jerk about it, so I thought I'd make it up to you and learn a new skill to boot." He focused his gaze out the windshield. "Plus, I like touchin' you. Thought this'd be a good reminder for me. For both of us."

How had she forgotten the thoughtful side of this sweet, sweet man? Libby curled her fingers around Quinn's jaw, turning his face toward her. She smashed her lips to his, kissing him crazily, kissing him like he'd asked her to. Thrown off balance, she eased back and whispered, "Thank you."

Inside the massage studio, chairs were lined up in front of a projection screen. All the seats but two were occupied.

Good Lord. They knew everyone in the room.

The owner of the hardware store and his wife held court in

the front row. Dixie, proprietor of the Golden Boot, and her hubby of fifty years, sat next to Darnell Broken Nose, a board member of the Crow Agency and his wife, Leela. Libby expected Quinn to pull his ball cap down over his eyes out of embarrassment, but he nodded to the men and directed her to the two empty chairs.

Gorgeous, blonde and enormously pregnant AJ McKay stepped front and center. "Good to see everyone this afternoon. First we'll watch a twenty-minute film on basics of massage and then we'll get to the hands-on portion of the class." She smiled. "If anyone has questions at any point, don't hesitate to ask. And if you tend to be a little shy—" she looked directly at Quinn, "—I'll be happy to answer questions in private."

The lights dimmed. The movie rolled. Libby expected soft-core porn or worse, a thinly disguised instruction manual, but the video struck a good balance between sensuality and the how-to aspects of massage.

After the video ended, Cord unfolded four padded tables and four six-foot high privacy screens, positioning one in each corner of the narrow room.

AJ walked through the maze, stacking towels, and draping sheets over each screen. "Next, I'll demonstrate tricks and techniques on my guinea pig—I mean my helpful husband— before I turn you loose to experiment on your own." She directed them to a massage room at the back of the building.

A shirtless Cord was stretched out on a padded table. AJ affectionately swept her hand up his spine. "You ready?"

Cord grinned over his shoulder and focused on the swell of her belly. "It's obvious I'm always ready for you, baby doll."

AJ dribbled oil on Cord's naked back, but the look she leveled on him said she'd make him pay for that suggestive remark later, guaranteed.

Libby bit back a grin. The dynamics in the huge McKay family still fascinated her, even after being part of it for more than a decade. She got a huge kick out of how easily AJ led gruff Cord around by the nose.

The aroma of sandalwood and lemon filled the room. "First and foremost, there is a pronounced difference between giving your partner a sensual massage and a deep tissue massage." She dug her thumbs into the base of Cord's spine and followed the line up to his neck. "You don't want to cause your partner any discomfort. The amount of pressure used isn't as important as a strong and steady touch."

In order to see AJ, Quinn leaned over Libby's shoulder. Libby had a devil of a time focusing on AJ's instructions when Quinn plastered his male hardness against her backside. Her blood raced. Her face heated. Her palms sweat. She'd be a horny basket case by the time Quinn actually put his hands on her.

"The other aspect of sensual massage is setting the mood. If you have children, you'll want to plan this for when you have an hour of uninterrupted time. In most houses, the bed in the bedroom is the easiest place to set up. Music isn't necessary, but I've found it can be both relaxing and arousing. Candles are good. They provide light, scent and ambience. Plain white cotton sheets are a smart choice. They can be warm or cool to the skin. And if you get carried away with the oil they're easy to clean. But the single most important thing to bring is a positive attitude. Making your partner feel good shouldn't be a chore. It should be a sensual enjoyment for both of you."

When Quinn whispered, "Amen," in Libby's ear, a tremor of desire rippled through her.

AJ demonstrated a few more techniques and then dismissed everyone back to their areas.

"What do you suppose we're gonna do now?" Libby asked when they were alone behind the partition.

Quinn held up a sheet with a cat-who-ate-the-mouse grin. "You're supposed to strip."

"Down to nothing?"

"What else does strip mean?"

"But all those people are out there—"

He eliminated the distance until they were a breath apart. "It's just you and me. No one else matters."

"You wouldn't have a problem getting buck-ass nekkid with the family banker in the next cubicle?"

"Not if I knew it was gonna lead to you puttin' your hands all over me. Damn, do I love havin' your hands on me."

When had closed-mouthed Quinn McKay become such a silver-tongued devil? "You don't play fair."

"Because I'm playin' for keeps." Quinn smooched her nose. "You want my help gettin' undressed?"

"No!"

"If we were home I wouldn't allow you a choice. But I'll do the gentlemanly thing, just this one time, and step outside. Whistle when you're ready for me."

Whistle. Right. And what the heck did he mean by *doing the gentlemanly thing just this one time*? Did Quinn plan on showing her a more verbal, more commanding side?

Libby shivered and it had nothing to do with being naked.

∗

Quinn fought the urge to pace. He wasn't nervous so much as antsy, because after two steamy kisses, he was raring to crank up the sexual heat with his delectable wife.

AJ moved to the center of the room. "Once your partners are set, I'll come around with a bottle of oil. This'll be your last chance to ask questions before I shut off the lights, turn on the music and leave you to your own devices.

"Once everyone is settled, I'll be in the backroom for the duration of your massage experimentation time, so you'll have no interruptions from me—or anyone else—within your private areas. Remember, there is no right or wrong way. Sensual massage is highly personal and having a good technique isn't nearly as important as having fun and an open mind."

The table creaked and Libby swore.

Quinn spoke through the curtained panel. "You ready?"

"If you mean am I naked," she said in a hushed tone, "then yes. Throw me that extra sheet."

"Sure." He tossed it over the partition.

Loud instrumental music started and the lights clicked off. AJ sauntered up with her usual sunny smile. She popped her head around the partition and her smile slipped. "Oh. Umm. That's great, Libby. You're all set." AJ whirled on Quinn and hissed in his ear, "Didn't you tell her she only had to take off her shirt?"

"Nope."

AJ whapped him on the arm, but her eyes twinkled. "Typical McKay man. Here's your oil. Put it to good use."

"I intend to."

Quinn skirted the privacy panel and sucked in a harsh

Lorelei James

breath. Lordy, look at that. Libby's bare, toned arms were stretched above her head. Save for the sheet covering her lower half, her sexy, freckled back was completely exposed and his for the taking.

She lifted her head. Her eyes darted past the partition. "Quinn, I'm—"

"Just us, remember?" He uncapped the oil and drizzled a thin line across her shoulders and spine in a T-shape. "I'll start at the top and work my way down, is that all right with you?"

"This is your show."

"That it is. Keep that in mind later." When his hands touched her skin, his cock went hard as a brick. God, she was so feminine. So warm. So perfectly supple.

So his.

At first, Quinn feared he'd freeze up. But faced with Libby's naked body spread out in a sumptuous feast, when he'd been starving for her for months, something instinctual kicked in.

Lust.

He swept his fingertips through the oil, hoping it'd lessen the abrasiveness of his callused hands. He played connect the dots with her moles and freckles, promising himself he'd use his tongue next time. Once the oil glistened across her torso, he began to rub it in.

If her sighs and moans were any indication, he must've been doing something right.

Quinn worked his thumbs into the tensed muscles stretching across her back, rounding to the bottom of her shoulder blades. Then he gradually moved down her spine, a vertebra at a time. When he reached the sexy dimples above her ass, an area he remembered as highly sensitive, he decreased the pressure. His touches became playful. As Quinn drew ever-widening circles, she arched into his teasing caresses.

"Quinn—"

Instantly, his mouth was by her ear. "Something you need?"

"Yes. No. I...I wanted to tell you I love the way you're touching me."

"Good." He smiled against her damp neck and rained kisses along her nape, pleased as punch when gooseflesh broke out beneath his questing lips.

116

Quinn continued his sensual assault. His hands mapped her every tempting curve, his fingers soothed every quivering muscle. When he finished tormenting one area, he'd scatter openmouthed kisses over each inch of bared flesh before focusing his attention on the next trembling section.

When he completed his final pass to those alluring dimples, he caught a whiff of Libby's arousal. A primal male need slammed into him. His chance of tamping it down vanished, especially when he noticed her hips bumping up to meet his every touch.

Libby faced the screen, almost as if she was hiding her reaction from him.

Oh hell no. That wouldn't do at all.

As Quinn put his lips to her ear, he traced the crack of her ass down to where her body was warm and sticky. He groaned in her hair. "Lemme touch you here."

"No!" Libby's shoulders shot up.

Quinn pushed them back down. "Yes."

"But we aren't supposed to—"

"Aren't supposed to what? Ain't no rules but mine. This is my show, remember? Raise your hips higher so I can reach your sweet spot."

She had a moment of hesitation before she complied.

"That's my girl." Quinn slid his first and middle fingers through the sweet cream pouring from her sex, combining it with the oil, swirling the mixture up. After a few concentrated strokes, he slipped his fingers into her pussy, letting her clit rest on the bony section at the base of his thumb.

"Oh. That does feel really good."

He wiggled his fingers around the snug channel, satisfaction filled him at seeing her writhing and trying to force his fingers deeper.

"Please."

"What?" Quinn was in a fog of lust. His need to prove he could still satisfy his mate became a single-minded pursuit.

At her whispered plea, "Faster," Quinn lost it. Pumping his fingers inside her, he growled in her ear, "I wanna fuck you like this, darlin' wife. Face down on the dining room table, no foreplay, just hard, fast fucking. Poundin' into this pussy until you scream."

"Yes. God. *Yes.*"

"Give it to me, Libby. Come around my fingers. Prove to me you love the way only *I* can make you come."

Libby gasped.

"Ssh. When we're home you can cause a ruckus, but this time be quiet." He whispered, "And don't that just make our naughty little secret so much raunchier, knowin' you gotta be still when your whole body is buckin' for release?"

"Quinn...I'm gonna—"

"Come. Now."

Another gasp escaped Libby's sweet mouth as her orgasm exploded. Quinn felt it everywhere, a rhythmic pulling around his fingers, a steady throbbing where her clit pressed into his hand, even the skin on her back pulsed the same cadence. He stared greedily as her climax inundated her.

On a final sigh, Libby slumped to the table.

Quinn removed his hand from between her thighs and loomed over her. "Look at me."

She blinked at him.

"I love the way you taste." He placed his fingers inside his mouth and sucked noisily. Then he traced her lips with his wet fingers. "Taste yourself."

Heat flashed in Libby's eyes. Keeping their gazes locked, she parted her lips, sucking his fingers to the knuckles. Quinn growled at feeling her hot little tongue swirling around the rough skin. He withdrew his fingers, flipped her over, and took her mouth savagely.

The kiss was out of control from the start. After several blissful minutes, Quinn managed to find his sanity before they fucked right there in AJ's massage studio. He slipped his lips free from hers and placed them against her ear. "Get dressed."

"But—"

"We're done here, Libby. Get dressed. Fast." He drew in a deep breath. "Please."

In such close proximity, he felt—rather than saw—her nod. Unable to control his need for her or his raging hard-on, he presented his back to her, trying like hell to ignore the sexy sounds of her uneven breathing and the rustle of her clothing.

Libby cleared her throat. "I'm ready."

He clasped her hand and ushered her outside without another word.

Chapter Four

The wind whistled, blowing leaves and debris around their feet. Although Libby's mind was hazed with pleasure, she hated that Quinn was dragging her off like a disobedient child.

She dug her bootheels into the sidewalk and jerked them to a stop.

Quinn whirled around.

Everything feminine inside her cheered at his scorching look. His gorgeous blue eyes were nearly black, not from rage, but from passion, which increased her determination to set things straight before they took another step—literally or figuratively.

Testily, he said, "What?"

"Where are we going?"

"Home."

"Why did you haul me out of there so damn fast?"

"Guess."

Yippee, he was back to one-word answers. "Were you embarrassed about what just happened?"

"No. Were you?"

"No. It was hot as hell." Libby's gaze dropped to the front of Quinn's sweats. Bingo. Damn impressive tent. She smirked. "Are we leaving because you have a hard-on?"

"Yep."

"That's all?"

"Jesus, Libby, will you get in the goddamn truck so we can talk about this at home?"

"Nope."

Quinn stared at her as if she'd morphed into a three-eyed,

green-tentacled alien life form.

"So it's okay for *you* to get *me* off in public, but I can't return the favor?"

"What?"

Libby grabbed him by the shirtsleeve and towed him around the corner of the building. Luckily, this side of the two-story brick structure faced an empty lot. She pressed her back against the sandstone bricks and tugged him. Well, she tried to tug him, but the solidly built man wouldn't budge.

"What are you doin'?"

"Seducing you. Fair's fair, Quinn. I wanna get you off. Right here, right now."

"Good Lord, woman, what's gotten into you?"

"You've gotten into me, remember whose fingers were in who?" Libby wrapped her arms around his neck. "Hoist me against this wall and rub your cock on me until you come."

She could picture her husband mentally compiling a list of pros and cons. "We're outside. Anyone could see us."

"So?"

"Libby."

"What? Can you blame me for wanting more of the wild man I met behind the curtain?" Libby rubbed her lips over the baby-smooth line of his jaw and he angled his head, allowing her better access to all the tasty spots. "You've held back with me, Quinn. Sometimes you've shown me a glimpse of that beast inside you. If we're really going to try and make this work, no more secrets between us. No more politeness. No more PC behavior. No more hiding behind a mask."

He squinted at her. "If I lower my mask, you'd better be prepared to lower yours too."

"What do you mean?"

"That means I wanna see some of the shine worn off the perfect rancher's wife halo you wear like a tiara. Hell, I'd love to *knock* that crown right off your pretty, proper little head."

There was the opening she'd longed for. Masks off, gloves off, the real down and dirty side to each of them, squaring off with no rules. She said, "Deal."

Quinn's eyes took on a predatory look. "Make doubly sure you mean what you're sayin', 'cause once I let that cat outta the bag, it ain't *ever* goin' back in. I've got some dark edges I've never explored, Libby. Be one-hundred-percent sure you can handle 'em."

For a split second, Libby's determination wavered, seeing the steely glint of danger in her husband's eyes. But she'd loved him long enough to know he wouldn't physically hurt her. In fact, he'd probably hidden those rough edges to protect her. Silly man.

Meeting his gaze dead on, she gave him an unequivocal, "Yes, I'm sure. Now show me, dammit."

His answering snarl was decidedly feral. Quinn clamped his mouth to hers as he clapped his hands on her ass and boosted her against the building.

Libby circled her legs around his hips as he lined his cock to the top of her cleft, rocking his pelvis, so the length, from root to tip, rubbed perfectly on her pubic bone. He groaned in her mouth and kissed her harder.

Yes. This was what she'd wanted. His uninhibited response. A chance to crack the gentlemanly cowboy mantle that weighted him down like a yoke.

His every grinding stroke hit her clitoris. Her sex swelled and wept and gloried in the friction.

Quinn ripped his mouth free and nestled his cheek beside hers. "Been so long. God, Libby. I'm already there." His rhythm never faltered, even through his short and choppy breaths. "Lift your shirt. Pull my sweats down so I can come on your belly."

Those gruff words alone would've been enough to get her hot again, but she was already past the point of no return. Libby reached between them. The head of his cock poked up past the waistband of his sweatpants. He'd gone commando. Handy. She briefly touched the sleek maleness before aligning the weeping tip above her belly button. "Do it."

The thrusts were hard and fast. Quinn's head snapped back with enough force his hat fell to the dirt.

Libby shamelessly watched pleasure contort her husband's face as he came with a low moan. His pelvis kept pumping until warmth spurted across her stomach. With the constant abrasion to her clit, another quick orgasm erupted that left her gasping and selfishly wanting more.

Quinn stilled and slowly opened his eyes.

Rather than break the moment, Libby swirled her fingertips through the come dripping down her belly. She brought the slickly coated fingers to her mouth, licking at the salty offering. "Mmm."

His powerful gaze never wavered. Not even when she traced the seam of his lips with her wet fingers and demanded, "Taste."

Without hesitation Quinn drew her fingers deeply into his mouth and sucked.

Her sex clenched. Her blood seemed to sizzle and pop beneath her skin. Who was this wild man? She managed a raspy, "Quinn."

"I know, darlin' wife. Home. Now." He gently deposited her on the ground. Hat on, their clothes somewhat back in order, he guided her to the truck.

On the road home, Quinn reached for her hand, but didn't urge her to sit next to him. Nor did he speak, which caused a heightened sense of sexual awareness in the confines of the silent cab. Her stomach flipped whenever the coarse pad of Quinn's thumb stroked the pulse point on the inside of her wrist.

After he'd parked in front of the house, Quinn turned off the engine, but didn't attempt to get out of the pickup. He lounged against the door. Not in a relaxed manner, but tensed, like a coiled snake about to strike.

"What?"

His very hungry, very male gaze executed a methodical sweep of her body, from the tip of her nose to the toes of her boots. "Strip."

Not the response she'd expected. "Right here? In the truck?"

"Yep."

"But—"

"Huh-uh. Here's that darker edge, Libby. I ain't foolin' around when I say take off your damn clothes. Now."

"In a striptease?"

"If you like. I don't care just as long as you get nekkid. Fast."

The demand was so unlike Quinn.

Isn't this what you wanted? To witness the dark side of your lover you suspected he kept hidden from you?

Absolutely.

Libby tentatively unbuttoned her blouse. Once she'd taken

123

it off, she looked to him for further instruction.

"All of it. Bra, jeans, thong." He grinned. "Have I mentioned how much I love seein' nuthin' marring that sweet ass except a single string? Them bright pink ones are my favorite."

She swallowed hard. She'd assumed he hated the changes she'd made in the last year, since he hadn't said a word, good, bad or otherwise. Seemed she'd been mistaken.

What else had she been mistaken about when it came to her husband?

"Libby?"

"Fine. I'm doing it." First, she yanked at her boots. She'd been in such a hurry to leave the massage studio she'd pulled her boots on over her jeans. After peeling off her socks, Libby glanced over at him.

"Bra next. I wanna see your tits bouncin' and swayin' as you're wigglin' outta them skin-tight jeans."

Her face flamed at the mental picture he'd painted. "Quinn!"

"Don't act so surprised. You gotta remember how much I love your tits." He cocked an eyebrow. "Or am I gonna have to give you a very intensive refresher course? 'Cause I am *so* all over that."

Good Lord. She couldn't believe how hot his dirty talk and highhanded behavior made her. Her thong was soaked. She rubbed her thighs together as she sought the bra clasp in the middle of her back. Libby slipped the satin straps down her biceps. Once her arms were freed, she playfully flung the lacy bra in Quinn's face.

"God, I forgot how pretty your nipples are." Quinn licked his lips. "Get them britches off."

Libby rested her shoulders on the door and wiggled her hips. As her fingers made quick work of the button and zipper, she hoped her cottage-cheese thighs wouldn't jiggle as much as her boobs. She shimmied the denim and her underwear down her legs, past her knees and calves, kicking them to the floorboard.

Quinn didn't utter a peep. Libby stayed motionless, red-faced, heart pounding, blood racing, perched naked as the day she was born, on the front seat of his truck, in broad daylight.

"Libby. Darlin', look at me."

She slowly elevated her chin. Quinn's face glowed with pure male heat. And his eyes. Lord, his indigo eyes were filled with such love and need, that her soul nearly burst.

"You are beautiful. You've always been the most beautiful girl in the world to me. That hasn't changed in fourteen years. The way I feel about you hasn't changed. It never will."

"Quinn—"

"That said..." He distractedly adjusted his cock. When he realized she'd been staring at his crotch, his palm repeatedly stroked the bulge between his legs. "Oh, little wifey mine. I'm likin' this naughty side of you. I like it so much, in fact, that I'm gonna give you fair warnin'."

"About what?"

Instead of answering, Quinn removed his hat. Stripped off his T-shirt. Toed off his shoes and socks. But he left his sweatpants on.

"Fair warning about what?" she prompted.

"Fair warnin' that after you run into the house, I'm gonna be hot on your heels. And when I catch you, I'm gonna fuck you right where you stand."

Her heart thumped a whole lot faster.

"You wanted to let the cat outta the bag and here I am, more than ready to pounce."

Oh God.

"So if I'm the cat, I guess that makes you—" his gaze swept over her impatiently, "—the mouse."

Ah hell, she was so screwed.

And she loved every second of it.

Quinn showed his teeth in a ravenous smile. "Now's your chance. Run little mouse, run."

Libby opened the truck door just as Quinn lunged at her. Modesty forgotten, she raced up the walkway naked.

∗

Three. Two. One.

Quinn leapt out of the truck.

He ignored the burn and sting of the concrete on his bare feet. His focus was on one thing.

Libby.

Finding her. Fucking her. Marking her. A possessive, red haze, more animal than man, fogged his neural pathways. Every pounding footstep echoed in his head as a mantra: *mine mine mine.*

He tore up the porch steps and shouldered aside the front door. The kitchen zipped by in a blur. He sprinted past the dining room table into the front room.

No. Wait. He stopped. Backtracked in mind and body. There she was, trying to blend into the wall separating the three-season room from the living room.

Silly woman. She'd never been a wallflower in his eyes. She'd never blended. She'd always been the only one who'd stood out in every crowd. From the first moment he'd seen her.

Find her. Fuck her. Mark her.

Mine mine mine.

Quinn growled and advanced on her.

Libby remained utterly still. He ripped off his sweats and stood naked and fully aroused before her. He slapped his hands on the wall above her head, but she didn't flinch.

He planted his mouth next to her ear. "I found you."

"I see that."

"I want you." Quinn rubbed his cheek over hers, marking her with his scent.

"I know."

"You're mine. Only. Ever. Mine."

"I know that too, Quinn."

"Do you also know how I wanna fuck you, little mouse?" Quinn let his lips trail to where her pulse jumped frantically in her throat.

"Ah. No."

"Then I'll tell you. You're gonna be face-first against this wall. Me rammin' into that sweet, wet, hot, tight pussy from behind, takin' what belongs to me. And when I can't hold back another second?" He flicked his tongue across the hollow of her throat. "Then I'm gonna pull out and come all over your back. Just like I came all over your front."

She whimpered a sound of pure need.

Quinn spun Libby forward, positioning her arms above her head, flattening her palms to the wall. He curled his hands around her hips and angled her pelvis for easier, faster, deeper entry.

He slid his right hand over her swollen pussy lips and used the thick cream to stroke her clit. "You're drippin' wet thinkin' about what I'm gonna do to you."

Another moan. Louder.

"Gonna be fast, hard and dirty, darlin' wife."

"Do it."

Quinn kept his hold on the front of her body as his left hand aligned his cock. He thrust to the root with one sharp snap of his hips.

Tight. Hot. Wet. Damn. It was good to be inside her. It was damn good to be home.

"Oh. God. Yes." Her hoarsely spoken words shattered what little restraint he had left.

He slammed in. Withdrew quickly and rammed in again. Over and over. Setting a pace that robbed him of reason and the ability to do anything but sate his need for her by fucking her.

Sweat dampened his hair and trickled down his spine. Blood pounded in his head, his throat, his heart. His groin was on fire.

A familiar tightening at the base of his cock signaled he'd reached the end point. Four, five, six, ball-bruising thrusts and he withdrew from Libby in time to take himself in hand. He jacked his cock hard and aimed at her lower back, groaning at every hot burst of come exploding from his dick. He watched each spurt dotting her skin and a primal roar arose.

Soon as the final shot was over, he pressed his belly to her back, spreading his fluid between them.

"Quinn. I-I need—"

"I'll take care of you." Gripping her left hip in his left hand, he used his right fingers to rub her distended clit. No teasing touches. He focused every bit of attention on that pouting bundle of nerves.

Libby gasped. "Yes. Don't stop."

"I won't. Come for me. Show me you can still come undone at my touch."

Powerful contractions pulsed beneath his finger and Libby threw her head back. Quinn latched onto the sweet spot at the nape of her neck and suckled strongly, gifting her with a mark.

She bumped her pelvis in time to the throbbing pulses until

Lorelei James

they stopped. Then she sighed dreamily.

He whispered fiercely, "You're mine. Don't forget that."

After a minute or so, she wiggled her butt. "Good thing, because I think we're stuck together."

"Appears so." Lightly, he said, "You mind bein' stuck with me?"

She didn't respond right away.

Quinn waited, even though it damn near killed him.

Libby released another long sigh. "I'm finding the idea of being stuck with you more appealing than I imagined a day ago."

"I can work with that. Hang on." He turned her and slipped his right arm behind her knees, cradling her to his chest as he lifted her into his arms.

"Quinn! I'm too heavy for you to carry."

"No, you ain't. Now hush up."

"Where are you taking me?"

"To bed."

"Oh."

Sheer grit helped him scale the flight of stairs. He paused in front of their bedroom door.

"With you carrying me, I feel like a bride again."

"I'm gonna treat you like a new bride. 'Cept better, 'cause this time around I'll have the benefit of years of experience as a bridegroom."

"And what will you do with those years of experience?"

"Use them to please my darlin' wife." Quinn adjusted his stance. "Once we cross this threshold, it'll be like we're startin' over."

She wiped a bead of sweat from his temple. "Why, Quinn McKay. That was downright romantic."

"You sound surprised."

"I am."

He grinned. "I'm tryin'. So what say you, bride of mine? Shall we christen the marriage bed?" Then Quinn saw tears swimming in her pretty eyes. "Hey, now. None of that."

"I can't help it. You're so sweet."

"Sweet? Woman, it rips my guts out to see you cryin'."

"Even happy tears?"

"_Any_ kind of tears."

She kissed his Adam's apple. "Then take me to bed and see if you can't turn my tears into screams of pleasure."

"That, I can do."

Chapter Five

The instant Quinn deposited her on the bed, Libby yawned. Lord. She'd been through the wringer the last few hours. Emotionally. Physically. Her body was relaxed from the massage, as well as sated from the hot, fast orgasm. The cool sheets against her heated skin induced a strong wave of sleepiness.

"I saw that."

"Saw what?"

"Your yawn." Quinn propped a hip on the mattress next to hers. "Tired?"

"Huh-uh." She yawned again.

He laughed softly. "Liar. Why don't you take a little catnap?"

Libby allowed a quick smile. "Don't you mean a little *mouse* nap?"

"Is that a complaint about our game of cat and mouse?"

"God, no."

"Good. 'Cause that was the best time I've had in a long time."

"Me too."

They stared at each other in silence until Quinn tenderly swept a hank of hair from her forehead. He kept floating his knuckles up and down the side of her face.

Such serious eyes. "What?" she asked softly.

"Rest up. I ain't nearly done with you. Not even close. Not by half."

"If that's the case, maybe you oughta rest up too."

"You think I need a break so I can get it up later?"

"Maybe."

He grunted.

"Or maybe I just don't want to nap alone." Libby impishly nipped the inside of his wrist. "I miss how you used to hold me all night. Like you couldn't bear to be away from me for a single second, even in sleep."

"Seems a long time ago, huh?"

"A lifetime. Come to bed, Quinn. Remind us both of what we've been missing."

He stood and dove over her, almost bouncing her off the mattress.

Libby shrieked, thrilled by his playful side.

In one fell swoop, Quinn wrapped himself around her, tucking her head to his chest so their naked bodies were entwined. He pulled the quilt up and bussed her crown.

The steady *thump thump thump* of his heart lulled her into a sense of peace.

✳

An insistent circle drawn around the tip of her nipple woke her. Warm, supple lips drifted over hers in a seductive tease, bestowing fleeting kisses, interspersed with firm-lipped nips.

Libby opened her eyes. "That's a nice way to wake up."

"And I'm just gettin' started." Quinn kissed the corners of her mouth and traced the seam with the point of his tongue.

Libby parted her lips, an invitation for a more thorough kiss. He gently sank his teeth into her bottom lip and tugged. When a whimpering moan rumbled from her throat, Quinn didn't just kiss her, he inhaled her. His hands were on her breasts, his cock was slapping her belly, his tongue was thrusting against hers in a full-body kiss.

Then his mouth left a hot trail down her neck, straight to her cleavage. He glanced up at her from beneath lowered lashes. "I couldn't wait 'til you woke up so I could get my mouth all over these, because damn, do I love your tits. I'm gonna take my time refreshing my memory of them." He rubbed his face over the plumped mounds cupped in his hands. "It's been so long, Lib. God, I miss this."

"Miss sex?"

"Well, yeah, but I miss bein' with you, nekkid or otherwise."

She understood his difficulty in admitting the tiniest show of need. Softly, she said, "I know," and threaded her fingers through his silky hair.

He bent his head and lapped at her left nipple. Never using his whole mouth, never sucking, just licking in a delicate manner. The pad of his thumb swept the lower swell of the other breast in an erotic arc. He switched to her right nipple and did the exact same thing. Slowly. Sensually. Systematically.

No doubt, Quinn planned to torture her.

He placed his mouth on the top of her breast and sucked. Hard.

Libby gasped.

Quinn only broke the tight suction to apply the same stinging bite to the other side. A dark gleam of satisfaction filled his eyes when he angled back to admire the love-bruises.

That's when the real assault began. Quinn suckled and nipped and licked, using his teeth, his fingers, his breath until she writhed in abandon. "Please."

He ignored her plea and flicked his tongue rapidly over the right nipple, blowing on the wet tip until it puckered into a tight point.

Just when Libby couldn't take any more, that wickedly talented mouth traveled south. He paused to trace the indentation of her navel. He scattered kisses from hipbone to hipbone, letting his soft hair tickle her belly.

"Quinn."

"Right here." He lifted his head. "Hand me a pillow so I can prop your hips higher."

"Why?"

"I wanna see you. All of you."

It wasn't as if he hadn't seen her privates before. Yet her inborn sense of modesty caused her to waver.

He nuzzled her mound. "Don't you want me to eat my fill of your sweet pussy? You used to like it." His tongue wiggled an inch or so down her cleft. "Or has it been so long you don't remember?"

"I remember. I just..."

"Then grab a pillow. Now."

Another glimpse of that darker edge. She tossed him a

pillow and raised her hips while he placed it under her butt.

"Move your legs apart. I need room to work."

Libby hoped after he arranged her she'd feel less like she was getting a pelvic exam and more like she was about to receive the most amazing oral sex of her life.

"We seemed to have lost our momentum, darlin' wife." The bed jiggled as Quinn scooted down until his head disappeared between her legs.

After one long, wet lash of his tongue, Libby said, "I definitely remember."

He chuckled against the tender flesh and the vibration sent her belly muscles rippling.

With her hips propped up, Quinn's hands were free to roam. He stroked the inside of her thighs while his tongue drew feather-light circles around her clit. Then he'd back off, his growling noises heightened her excitement as he lapped at the juices dampening her entrance.

Quinn knew exactly how to make her body hum. So it surprised her when he asked, "Which feels better? This?" Using firmed lips, he opened and closed his mouth over her pussy lips and clit in little biting increments.

"Oh, I like that."

"How about this?" His fingers pulled back the hood covering her clitoris and he randomly flicked just the very tip of his tongue over the hot spot.

An electric tingle shot straight up her center. "Whoa. Where'd you learn that?"

"Figured maybe it was time for this old dog to learn new tricks." He paused. "If I did something you didn't like, or if you wanted more of something you did like, you'd tell me, right?"

Did he think his...technique was off? Lord. She'd never had any complaints about his oral talents. In fact, it'd always scared her that he instinctively could catapult her into pleasure in no time flat.

Had Quinn suffered a crisis of faith in his skills as a lover? Was that somehow her fault?

You've been so focused on the results of sex—creating a baby—you've forgotten the best part of sex is creating lifelong intimacy with the person you trust above all others.

Libby gazed at him. When had their marriage become only

about what she wanted and needed? What about Quinn's wants and needs?

"Lib? Darlin', what's wrong?"

She swallowed the lump of guilt stuck in her throat. Quinn deserved better than the little he'd been getting from her. Sobering, to consider she had just as much changing to do as she'd expected from him—maybe more. Those changes wouldn't happen overnight for either of them, but she'd do her part, starting right now.

"Nothing is wrong." Libby's voice dropped to a whisper. "I've missed you. Being with you like this. Whenever you put your mouth on me I can't think of anything else but how great you make me feel."

Quinn's eyes shone with male pride. He slapped his palms on the inside of her thighs and his dark head descended.

Libby held her breath. Every muscle in her body clenched in anticipation of the next swipe of his wet tongue.

"Relax."

"I am."

"Wrong. I can feel the tension vibrating off you."

"It's not tension, Quinn. It's lust. I don't need new tricks. I just need you."

An animalistic snarl was her only signal she'd pushed him to the brink.

No gentleness, just hunger. His single-minded, unyielding pursuit of her pleasure sent her body into overdrive. Dizzy from the sensations bombarding her, Libby closed her eyes, lost in the burning brand of his skilled mouth, the sweet suction, the bruising grip of his fingers. With her every shallow breath, Quinn's musky aroma filled her lungs.

Two fingers slipped into her sheath, curling behind her pubic bone, and she bowed off the bed.

He flickered his tongue over her clitoris in short, fast stabs as he rubbed her innermost tissues with his fingertips. Not in and out, but in the sweetest, erotic internal caress.

Before she'd gotten used to the feeling of fullness from those clever, fondling fingers, her blood gathered in the hot spot beneath his dancing tongue. "Quinn?"

"Tell me what'll get you there."

"Suck harder."

He did.

She clutched his hair. The orgasm flooded her, a throbbing, take-her-breath-away seizure of pulsing bliss. A drawn out, "Oh God," escaped as she arched hard into him, thrashing against the sheets and rolling her hips into his face.

He kept his mouth suctioned to her clit until the pulses slowed.

She flopped into the mattress with a final groan. Her body twitched as he gently lapped the super-sensitized areas of her sex, and she swore she felt him grin against the crease of her thigh when she sighed again.

Libby peeled her eyes open, pushing herself up on her elbows. "What other new tricks did you learn?"

Quinn laughed and gave her one last deliberate lick. "Now where's the fun in tellin' you? I'd rather show you. Later. First," he crawled up her body with an unholy gleam in his eyes, "you're gonna return the favor."

Libby licked her lips and looked at his cock.

"You can use that pretty little tongue on me later. I've got something else in mind right now. Something I've fantasized about doin' for a long time. The old me was too polite to ask. The new me, well...he's a bit more demandin'."

"What do you want to do?"

He straddled her belly and slid his knees next to her armpits. "I wanna feel these tits cushioning my cock as I'm slidin' it here." The tip of his index finger drew a line from the hollow of her throat down through her cleavage.

Libby wasn't gawking at him as if he were the biggest pervert on the planet, but frown lines appeared between her eyebrows, which meant she was thinking hard.

"Shocked?"

"No, just wondering if you thought I was so prissy that I wouldn't want to try it."

"Libby—"

"You brought it up, so answer the damn question."

The old Quinn would've clammed up. The new Quinn got right in her face. "What would you have said, darlin' wife, if I would've demanded to fuck these luscious tits? Not only that, I wanna come all over them. There's something mighty appealin' about seein' my sperm dotted all over your pretty freckled skin."

Her eyes narrowed. "So, you didn't ask me because you were waiting to fulfill that particular fantasy with another woman?"

"Hell no." Jesus. Was his even-keeled Libby acting all pissed off because he *hadn't* asked her?

"I'm your wife, Quinn. I've been your lover for fourteen years. Why couldn't you ask me or tell me what you want from me in bed?"

Frustrated, he snapped, "Because of the way I was raised. It ain't exactly easy for me to look my wife in the eyes and demand the sexual stuff that's out of the norm. Especially when we've been told that wantin' that kind of kink is just plain wrong."

What he didn't say—what he'd never say because it'd hurt her beyond repair—is in the last few years, when they were trying for a baby, the only place she wanted his sperm was in her baby channel. She'd stopped giving him handjobs or blowjobs, unless it led to him sticking his dick in her and filling her with his seed.

Libby stared at him. A dozen different expressions crossed her face. None of them good.

Ah crap. Sexual playtime was obviously over. His cock had gone soft. His hopes had gone south. He scooted back, but she clamped her fingers into the top of his thighs, keeping him in place.

Quinn heard a muttered *stupid* tumbling from her pursed lips. "What?"

"I said we've both been so stupid. Full of pride. Listening to other people's viewpoints, and not deciding our own." Her grip on his legs turned into a caress. "I've been so insistent on being a 'proper' wife to you that I've actually not been any kind of wife at all, least of all the kind of wife you need."

"Libby—"

"Hear me out. And you're so worried I'm gonna think you're a pervert that you're afraid to ask me to take a walk on the wild side of sex with you." Her gaze roamed his face. "Is that true?"

He nodded, half-worried, half-hopeful of where this conversation was headed.

"I don't want it to be like that between us any more. No more tiptoeing around what we want because it might be considered dirty. I want sex to be fun and raunchy and spontaneous like it's been today."

"As long as we're bein' honest, I don't always wanna be the one to get things goin' in the bedroom. It'd be good if you touched me without me havin' to ask."

Libby beamed a decidedly naughty smile. "Did you like me dragging you around the corner and demanding you get your rocks off on me?"

"Like you wouldn't believe."

"Then bring your cock closer so I can suck on it. Once that bad boy is hard, let's see how it feels sliding between my tits."

"Really?"

"Yes. I wanna fulfill your every fantasy, Quinn."

"Goddamn. Hearin' nasty talk comin' from that sweet mouth is a fuckin' turn on, Lib."

She'd slid her hands up until they were curled around his ass. She urged him forward. "Gimme."

Quinn leaned until he could grip the brass rails of the headboard. He kept enough space so he could look down and watch the show.

And what a show his sexy wife put on for him. His cock had already started to stir, but it was still soft enough she could get the whole thing in her mouth. The warmth and wetness of Libby's mouth surrounding his dick...nothing like it in the world. Nothing. It was sheer heaven.

Libby's little humming noises sent chills up his shaft and vibrating through his body. After teasing him to distraction, she released his erection. "It's been a long time since I did that."

"I missed it. You're as good at it as you ever were."

"I could get used to this sweet-talkin' side of you, darlin' husband." Libby stretched her arms above her head, fully aware he was watching how her breasts swayed with the sensual movement. "Now what? Do you wanna get right to it?"

"Probably be a good idea to use some lube." Quinn reached toward the nightstand drawer where they stashed the K-Y, and Libby nearly knocked him off the bed when she scrambled upright.

"Whoa. Careful."

"I'll get it."

"That's okay. I can reach it."

"Maybe we won't need any." She tugged him back on top of her. "Let's just do it like this."

His funny feeling intensified when he noticed the guilty expression his wife wore. "What's goin' on?"

"Don't you wanna get started? Since this has been a longtime fantasy?"

"Yeah. But I want the K-Y." He dodged her wandering hands and his fingers connected with the drawer handle.

"Quinn. Wait."

Stay calm.

"What's in the drawer, Libby?" He'd lose his fucking mind if he found an opened box of condoms. Absolutely lose his fucking mind.

"I can explain."

Keeping his eyes on his wife, Quinn jerked the drawer open.

She turned her head toward the opposite wall.

He inhaled deeply before he looked. He didn't move for the longest time. "When did you buy this?"

"I didn't. My sister did."

"Jilly thought this might come in handy?"

"Yes."

"Look at me."

Libby raised her chin to the level he deemed stubborn.

"Has it come in handy?"

No answer.

Rather than demand her response, Quinn picked it up and turned it on. A loud buzzing sound echoed in the room.

Libby's face was beet red.

"Tell me, have you used this vibrator?"

"Yes, damn you, I did, okay? I was curious and horny and I burned through an entire sixteen pack of batteries in the first week. Happy now?"

"Did it make *you* happy?" Quinn tossed the tube of K-Y on the bed and moved over her so they were face-to-face. "Is this piece of vibrating plastic better than the real thing?"

She shook her head. "It takes the edge off, but it's..."

"What?"

"Impersonal. Mechanical. Not you." She gave him a considering look. "Are you mad?"

"Hell no." The grin he'd been hiding bloomed. "I'd been tryin' to figure out a way to bring up sex toys to spice up our sex life long before our...break. I'm happy to see you're good with it." Quinn lowered his head, reviving their desire with a steamy kiss.

"Mmm." Libby whispered against his mouth, "You ready to fulfill your fantasy?"

Chapter Six

"Nope." Quinn rolled her so she was on top.

"What're you doing?"

"I want you to ride me so I can test out your new toy."

Libby blushed.

"You already know how much I love to see certain parts of you bouncin'."

Her whole body seemed to flame with embarrassment.

He brushed his finger over the hot spot on her cheekbone. "Interestin'."

"What?"

"I can still make you blush. I'll probably try to turn your cheeks bright red when you're an eighty-year-old lady."

"You think we'll still be together?"

"Yep. I can't imagine my life without you, Libby. These last few months have been pure hell."

Even though Libby was buck-ass nekkid, she seized the opportunity to talk, since it appeared Quinn was in a rare mood to do just that. "It didn't seem like you cared."

"Jesus. No. I cared, I was just..." Quinn frowned and a minute or so passed before he spoke again. "I can see where you'd get that idea, bein's I took off right after you kicked me out to help Ben and my cousins with calvin'."

"I thought after you returned from living at Ben's for three weeks you might've been ready to hash it out."

Quinn's eyes searched hers. "Wanna know the real truth?"

She nodded, even when her stomach pitched.

"I didn't know what to say to you. I ain't ever been good at sharin' my feelings and shit. I thought if I ignored it, maybe it'd work itself out." He scowled. "Stupid, huh?"

"Naïve, maybe. Our problems didn't happen overnight."

"Yeah, well, I guess those problems never seemed that bad to me."

That comment floored her. "Are you serious?"

"It ain't like one of us was cheatin'. Or one of us was drinkin' too much. Or we were bein' physically or verbally abusive. Or that we'd gotten in debt up to our eyeballs. Hell, I didn't think much beyond that our problem was us just bein' stuck in a rut."

"How'd you figure we'd get out of that rut?"

He shrugged.

"Or were we just supposed to sit and spin our wheels?"

"Better that than burnin' rubber tryin' to get away." He sighed. "I don't wanna fight with you, Libby."

"And I don't wanna sweep this under the rug anymore, Quinn."

He mumbled and looked away.

"What?"

"I said this is typical."

"Typical?" She braced her hands on his chest and got in his face. "Explain that."

His focus snapped back to her. "We're nekkid. In bed. I had a fuckin' hard-on to rival a fencepost, we were all set to have hot, fun, wild sex with toys, with extra lube and trying new positions...and now all you wanna do is talk, talk, talk."

Stung, she retorted, "Yeah? You think ignoring the important stuff and having wild, kinky sex is gonna fix it?"

"It sure as hell can't hurt, and at least we'd be havin' sex for once."

"For *once*?"

"Christ. You ain't gonna deny that in the last year, even before you demanded a separation, we weren't havin' sex on a regular basis."

"Sex on a regular basis?" she repeated inanely. "That's what's so all-fired important to you?"

"Sex is a big part of the important stuff we need to discuss. At least it is to me. You're all for talkin' about what's bothering you, and yet, whenever I tried to bring up what's bothering me, you changed the damn subject."

When she froze in shock, he moved her off his body.

"That's not fair. My unwillingness to talk about sex was in the past."

"You're right. Forget it." He rolled sideways and perched on the edge of the bed with his back to her.

What'd just happened? Everything had been going so well. "Quinn?"

No answer.

Libby forged ahead anyway. "What makes you think that sex isn't important to me?"

"For the last several years sex is important to you as long as you're gettin' what you want out of it, and out of me."

"Which is what?"

"A baby." He stood. Without looking at her, he said, "I need to check cattle," and booked it out of the room, apparently not caring that he was completely naked.

Stunned, and a little heartsick, Libby slipped on her robe. She went to the window and opened the blinds.

A few minutes later, a bare-chested Quinn exited the house and plopped on the porch steps. He yanked his old boots over his gray sweatpants in angry, jerky movements. He stalked to the truck, grabbed his T-shirt from inside the cab and pulled it on over his head. Then he slapped on his ball cap, climbed in and roared off.

Needing something to do besides pace, or wait to see if Quinn returned to the house, or if he preferred the cramped horse trailer to her lousy company, Libby went downstairs.

Darkness enveloped the big, bold Wyoming sky by the time Libby heard the porch screen slam. The table was set and ready, but supper had gone cold. Would Quinn fight with her? Or pull that silent macho crap and ignore her? At this point she didn't know which she'd prefer.

Wrong. She wanted his fire. His anger. His honest reaction. Because his words spurred her to take a longer, deeper look at her actions and inactions over the last few years and she hadn't liked what she'd seen.

Consequently, she'd been staring out the kitchen window,

nursing a glass of whiskey for the better part of an hour. She didn't turn around when he entered the kitchen.

The silence between them was absolute.

Who would be the first to break it?

Quinn said, "I'm—" at the same time she said, "I didn't—"

They both laughed, but it was forced laughter.

Quinn approached her. Her heart sped up.

Slipping his arms around her waist, he rubbed his face in her hair. "Sorry."

"I'm sorry too."

"We probably oughta talk about it, huh?"

"Or we could just get drunk."

He chuckled. "There is that option. Might be less painful initially, but guaranteed we'd pay for it in the mornin'."

"True."

"Where do we start?"

"Where we left off." Libby drained the last of her whiskey. "Where the problems began. Jilly warned me about bringing up the baby issue, or lack thereof."

"Jilly? What's she have to do with it?"

"She called and offered me some free advice."

"Then take it for what it's worth. Nuthin'. Besides, I'm the one who brought it up. And not in a nice way neither."

"I don't think there is a nice way to tell me that I seriously screwed up everything with my quest for a baby."

"Libby—"

"Just let me get this out, okay?" Would this confession be easier if she wasn't looking into his all-knowing eyes? Probably not.

"I'm not gonna pretend that I was aware that I was driving you away when I became obsessed with getting pregnant. After you stormed away a couple hours ago, it was like a light bulb went off in my head and I saw everything in a whole different light. I didn't like what I saw.

"It was all about me. My body. What I wanted. What I needed." Tears gathered in her eyes when she considered how selfish she'd been. How much she'd hurt him and without knowing it.

"And?" he prompted.

Suck it up. You made the bed, you can lie in it.

"And the truth is you were one hundred percent right when you said I cared only about your sperm, not about sex. Making love with you or to you didn't cross my mind if it didn't have...purpose. Sad to admit that mindset would've stayed even if I *had* gotten pregnant, because I would've focused all my attention on the baby. You suffered either way. God, Quinn, what kind of horrible, self-centered wife does that make me? And yet, I justified my attitude because I blamed you for not being interested in whether we got pregnant or not."

"I just didn't see the big rush, Libby. It wasn't like we were too old then or even now. It's just...well..."

"What?"

"Part of me wondered if you were in some sort of competition with your sister. She popped out four babies with no trouble. Then every time she came over with the kids, it was like she was rubbing them in your face. Jilly always was hinting around maybe one or both of us had problems with our, um, plumbing, so to speak."

How much weight had Libby given to Jilly's suggestions regarding fertility issues? A lot. After all, with four pregnancies under her belt, Jilly was an expert. She just wanted to help. Why had Libby confided her fears to her sister instead of her husband? God. She'd been such an idiot on so many levels.

"Libby?"

She couldn't face him when she blurted, "I spent years feeling like a failure as a woman because I couldn't pop out a little McKay."

"It ain't like the McKay name is gonna die out with the way my cousins are reproducing like rabbits."

"True. But I was constantly fielding questions from relatives about when you and I were going to start a family since we've been married a while. If I hedged, then they asked if we were having marriage problems or reproductive issues. It was a stick poking an open wound you didn't even know I had."

Libby felt him wince.

"I'm so damn sorry. To be honest, it hurt that you wanted a kid more than you wanted me. Part of the reason I refused the fertility tests was I was afraid you'd leave me if I was the reason you weren't pregnant. Sounds selfish, don't it?"

No more selfish than what she'd done.

He sighed. "Jesus, Libby. I'm such a prick. Not talkin' to

you. Lettin' you think the worst of yourself, makin' you handle all that family shit alone, when I didn't know the half of it. No wonder you booted my ass."

The resentment she should've felt was strangely absent. It felt good—freeing—to be brutally honest, to air all their dirty laundry. They had nothing else to lose, because they were damn close to losing it all.

"Look. We both were wrong. We both made mistakes. We both closed down and dealt with our issues separately, rather than together. We didn't have fidelity, financial or substance abuse issues, but our issues were big enough to cause a rift in our marriage."

Quinn didn't say anything, which wasn't surprising. He'd said more than she'd expected.

Still, she'd been carrying the burden for quite some time, so she might as well get it all off her chest. "When I realized I probably wouldn't ever get pregnant, I created a new me—Libby McKay 2.0. I fixed up the house, jazzed up the meals, pursued new interests and stopped thinking about babies entirely. I thought if I wasn't a frumpy, chubby, boring ranch wife, you'd want me again."

Quinn spun her around so fast spots danced in front of her eyes. "Want you again? I've always wanted you. Jesus. You think *that's* how I see you? Frumpy? Chubby? Boring?" He shook her slightly. "Dammit. I see *you*, Libby, not a fuckin' brood mare! You are the smart, funny, sexy, hard-workin' girl that knocked me for a loop when I was a dumb kid of sixteen. A woman I've always known is too good for the likes of me. A woman I pledged my life, heart and soul to. A woman I love with every goddamn bone and breath in my body. What don't you understand about that?"

"Quinn—"

"Just shut up. We're done talkin'." His mouth crashed down on hers and he kissed the living daylights out of her.

Arms, legs, hands, fingers clashed and collided as they tried to touch each other everywhere, all at once. The wet, hot kiss overwhelmed her until she could only cling to him and experience the spectacle of her calm, cool and collected husband totally out of control.

Quinn ripped his lips from hers. "Now. Goddammit. I need to prove...to show you how much I—"

"It's okay."

"I want you right now."

"Where?"

"Table." He untied the belt on her robe, pushed it to the floor and groaned satisfaction she was still naked.

"But the dishes—"

"Fuck the dishes." Quinn turned, jerked the corners of the tablecloth until all the plates and silverware crashed together and rolled to the opposite end of the table. "Problem solved."

Libby grabbed his face in her hands and kissed him, needing that connection as he lifted her on the kitchen table.

∗

The woman absolutely pushed his limits of restraint today...and he'd never been happier in his frustration.

Quinn needed to get inside her. *Now now now* pounded in cadence with the blood throbbing in his cock.

Libby twisted her hand in his T-shirt, stopping him. "This gone. I wanna feel your skin on mine."

Yank. Off it went. He latched onto her hips and pulled until her legs hung off the table. He jerked his sweatpants to the tops of his boots and his cock went *sproing* like it was spring-loaded. He circled the opening to her pussy once and plunged inside to the root.

She hissed. Her upper body bowed up and she slid up half a foot from the force of his thrusts.

He scooted her back down. "Grab onto the edge. Hands above your head. Like that. Oh hell, yeah, exactly like that."

"You're watching my tits bounce, aren't you?"

Quinn laughed and drove into her hard. "Uh-huh. Goddamn that's sexy."

"Just as long as you aren't so busy watching you forget what you're supposed to be doing."

"And what is that, darlin' wife?"

"Fucking me until I scream."

The noise leaving his throat was half-grunt, half-snarl and all possessive male. He obliged her with thrusts that rocked the table and his legs quaked from the strain.

"Yes. Don't stop."

He gave her everything he had. A heart-thumping, sweat-inducing, hip-pounding, teeth-grinding, primal mating. As he anchored her hips, his avid gaze moved from the steady bounce of her breasts to where they were joined. It was hot as sin to see the wet proof of her excitement coating his dick as he pulled out, then feeling the tight clasp as he slammed home. Again and again and again. Every thrust seemed to bring him deeper into her.

When he noticed Libby biting her lip, he leaned over her. "You okay? Too much?"

"No." She arched into him. "Your chest hair on my nipples drives me crazy. And God, you're hitting the exact spot pressed against me like that."

"Like this?"

"Yes."

"Harder?"

"No."

"Faster?"

"Yeah."

Quinn clasped their hands together so they were matched palm to palm. "Fly apart for me." He added a little grind at the end of his upstroke and she gasped.

"Good?"

"Uh-huh, more—*yes!*"

His hips began to piston, each stroke brought forth more sweat and more labored breaths and a more desperate race to the finish. When Libby squeezed his hands and cried out, Quinn felt that deep, rhythmic pulsing of her body sucking at his cock like a separate mouth.

Closing his eyes, he let himself fall into the moment. As his cock emptied, he was reminded how perfect it felt being with Libby, naked in body and soul. Quinn buried his face in her neck and clutched her tightly, silently swearing to never let her get so far out of his reach again. "God, I love you. Don't ever leave me...I can't..."

"Ssh. I know. It's okay. I'm here. We're both here."

After they'd leveled their breathing and their heart rates returned to normal, she shuddered beneath him. He raised his head to peer into her eyes. "Cold?"

"With two hundred pounds of hot rancher on top of me?

Hardly."

"Am I too heavy?"

Libby shook her head.

He kissed each nipple and pushed upright. Studying her face for signs of pain, he slowly pulled out. "Sore?"

"No. And even if I was, I wouldn't mind. Because you just fulfilled one of my fantasies."

"Really? On the kitchen table?"

"Mmm-hmm."

"Well, hot damn." After Quinn tugged his sweatpants in place, he helped her sit up and noticed her eyes darted to the pile of dishes beneath the rumpled tablecloth. "Sorry I ruined supper."

"Don't be. Being with you, having you look at me like that..."

"Like what?"

"Like you used to. Like I was everything."

Quinn rested his forehead to hers. "You are everything to me. You always have been. I'm sorry it got to the point where you ever doubted that."

"Me too."

The moment, while brief, seemed to reinforce a connection between them Quinn hadn't realized was broken.

Libby's stomach rumbled.

"Since I wrecked supper, and you're clearly starving, can I take you out?"

"Good Lord, I'm a mess. By the time I get myself cleaned up, every place within thirty miles will be closed."

"You do look kinda mussed. But it's a well-fucked, well-kissed kinda mussed."

"Quinn McKay!"

He loved that indignant tone, mostly because it was all for show. "Tell you what. Let's go to the Tasty Treat Drive-in. We don't have to get out. I can sneak a couple kisses between feeding you curly fries. Like we used to." He nibbled on her lips. "And we might finally christen the damn truck after six years."

Libby leaned back. "We've had sex in your truck."

"No, we haven't."

"Yes, we have."

"When?"

She appeared to be thinking. "Shoot. I thought after some big McKay bash you and I..." Libby looked him expectantly.

"We did. But that was my old red Dodge years ago, not this one."

"Huh."

"What?"

"Just remembering the first time we had sex in your pickup."

He cringed. "I'm surprised you ever had sex with me again."

"It wasn't *that* horrible."

"Well, it sure as hell wasn't romantic. Woulda been better if we'd waited and done it in my bed rather than on a pickup bench seat in the middle of a damn pasture. You deserved better."

"I didn't care. I just wanted to be with you." A wistful look crossed her face. "Sometimes I think we've come so far...and then I look at you and still feel like that unsure sixteen-year-old girl."

That jarred him. "Unsure about me?"

"No, unsure on why you picked *me*."

"Why?"

"The McKay boys' reputation for preferring wild girls. I've never been wild."

"I ain't ever been like my cousins when it comes to skirt chasin'. Didn't interest me." He allowed a small grin. "On the other hand, I'm likin' that you're finally gettin' wild with me."

"But, you could've had any girl."

"Don't matter. I didn't want any other girl besides you, Libby. Then or now."

Libby's gaze roamed his face. "What are we doing?"

Quinn knew she wasn't referring to their supper plans. A temporary break from the issues would do them both good, so he deliberately misunderstood her. "Soon as you slip on some clothes, we're headed to the Tasty Treat."

Her mouth opened. Closed.

"Come on, it'll be fun."

"Fine." She hopped off the table. "But I'm not sharing my chocolate malt with you."

Chapter Seven

"Wanna another bite?"

"No. I'm stuffed. I shouldn't have eaten all those mozzarella sticks."

"It's good to indulge once in a while."

Libby stirred the dregs of her shake. "I worked damn hard to lose weight. Overindulgence will pack those pounds right back on."

"If I haven't said so, you look good. Real good. Damn good."

She snorted. "You weren't very complimentary when I asked you that same question three months ago."

"You can apply my earlier 'I was a prick' comment to that response too."

"So why *did* you say that?"

Quinn sighed. "I thought you were fancyin' yourself up because you were fixin' to dump me."

Her hand froze on the straw. "And then I—"

"Told me you wanted a trial separation."

"Oh Quinn, oh damn. That's not why I..." Good Lord. With all the mixed signals they'd been sending each other it was a miracle they'd managed to stay married as long as they had.

When he didn't add anything else, Libby shoved the empty cup on the dash and scooted closer. "I'm sorry."

"I get that now. It's over and done with." Quinn slapped his thighs. "Climb on over here and sit on my lap."

"We gonna kiss and make up?"

"Maybe. Or maybe I just wanna cop a feel in the truck."

"I guess we'll see if you get to second base, buddy."

"I'm hopin' for a grand slam." Grinning, he adjusted the

seat.

Libby balanced on one knee and swung the other over his left leg, placing her hands on his shoulders as she lowered onto his lap. Then she took his hat off.

Quinn flexed those scarred, callused hands she loved so much across her upper back and slowly pulled her toward him.

Eyes locked, bodies pressed together, each inch they moved closer built anticipation higher. Heated breath mingled, lips softened, hearts raced.

A whisper apart, Quinn cocked his head and let his mouth sink into hers. He teased, tempted, nibbled, drawing out the kiss until Libby shook with need.

The moment was as erotic as it was familiar.

She allowed her hand to wander over his jaw, cheeks, temple and forehead. She raked her fingers through his hair. Gently biting at his mouth, dipping her tongue between his parted lips and slicking it across his teeth. When he opened wider, she dove in, offering him the same reckless passion he'd shown her.

A satisfied groan rumbled from Quinn's throat.

Giddy, feeling freer than she had in ages, she touched, stroked and rubbed against her husband until they were both panting. Frantic. Aroused.

Three raps on the passenger side jolted them out of the moment and the crotch-grinding kiss. They squinted at the interloper through the steamed-up windows.

Vaudette Dickens. President of the Presbyterian Ladies Guild, neighbor to the Charles McKay family for years...and Quinn's mother's best friend.

Quinn swore under his breath.

Libby began to slide back, but Quinn stopped her retreat with a terse, "Stay put."

He offered Vaudette a smile and leaned sideways to roll down the window. "Miz Dickens. I'm surprised to see you."

"I'll just bet you are, Quinn McKay." Her eyes narrowed behind thick-lensed glasses. "Who's that with you? Libby?"

Libby wanted to snap, "Who else were you expecting?" but she managed a civilized, "Yes, it's me, Miz Dickens."

"Goodness. I thought you two were separated."

"We are. Were. Anyway, we're workin' it out," Quinn said.

"That's wonderful. Does your mother know?"

"Ah. No, ma'am."

"Honey, with the way you two are carrying on, by tomorrow morning everyone will know you were fogging up your truck windows at the Tasty Treat."

Mostly courtesy of Vaudette's lips, Libby thought.

"And your point is?" Quinn drawled.

Vaudette's shoulders snapped straight. "I was looking out for your best interests. I popped over here because I was certain some wild teenagers were out joy riding in your truck and I wanted to give them what-for before I called the sheriff."

"Now why on earth would you think something like that?"

She motioned to Libby still perched on Quinn's lap. "Because I expected such behavior from hormonal teenagers, not from a longtime married couple. Goodness, aren't you two a little old to be necking in the Tasty Treat parking lot at ten o'clock on a Saturday night?"

Quinn smirked at Libby. He smoothed a piece of hair behind her ear. "God, I hope not. A man's entitled to kiss his wife, whenever and wherever he pleases."

Libby bit her lip to keep from laughing at Quinn's double meaning.

Vaudette let out a gasp that managed to be both indignant and chiding.

"But we appreciate your concern, Miz Dickens. And you're right. I reckon we oughta take this someplace more private." He looked at Vaudette and winked. "Tell my mother I said hello," and he cranked up the window.

Libby lost it. She buried her face in Quinn's neck to muffle her laughter.

"Damn busybody."

She lifted her head. "The gossip won't bother you?"

"Let 'em gossip. I could give a damn." He frowned. "This ain't gonna affect your job at the library, is it?"

"Kissing my husband in public is hardly a firing offense." She brushed her lips over his. "But fucking my husband in public is a different story."

"You wanna fuck me?"

"Uh-huh. You got me all hot and bothered. I'm thinking about the positions we didn't try today because we were too busy talking." Libby traced the inside of his ear with her tongue and gently blew across it. "I don't wanna talk anymore."

He started the truck with her still on his lap.

"Quinn! You can't drive like this."

"Like what? Bein' horny as hell with a hot woman bouncin' on my pole as we hit every damn pothole on Main Street?" He grinned. "Sounds good to me."

She whapped him on the chest before returning to the passenger side.

He wiggled his hat back on his head and threw the gearshift in reverse.

When they hit the outskirts of town, Libby casually asked, "So, since you didn't get to fulfill your fantasy earlier today, do you have any others you wanna share with me?"

Quinn shot her a sideways glance. "What's good for the goose is good for the gander."

"I've got no problem sharing a fantasy, but you go first."

"Okay." He shifted in the seat. "I wanna fuck you while you're wearin' nuthin' but them tight, black suede chaps with the long fringe runnin' down the sides."

"That's it?"

"I'm a simple man. Your turn."

Libby wondered how he'd react to her fantasy. Would he get angry? Go along with it? Think it was weird? Or stupid?

"Lib?" he prompted. "No more secrets, remember?"

She blurted, "Let's pretend we're strangers. You picked me up in a bar after we slow danced and shared a couple of smokin' kisses. You're taking me back to your place to have your wicked way with me."

"You wanna do this now? Tonight?"

"Yeah. And when we get home—I mean there—I wanna spend the night in the horse trailer."

"Deal. But if we were strangers and so hot to have each other, I bet you'd be sittin' closer to me."

Relieved at his willingness to play along, she slid next to him. She flipped the radio on low and Dwight Yoakam crooned a mournful song about love gone wrong. Quinn wrapped his arm around her shoulder and lazily rubbed her bicep.

Libby stroked the corded muscle of his thigh beneath his soft sweatpants. With every sweeping pass her fingers drifted higher, lingered longer. She'd forgotten how much she loved touching him and hearing the soft catch of his breath whenever she did something he liked.

She glanced at him. Quinn's knuckles on the steering wheel shone white in the dashboard lights.

Talk about tense. What could she do to relax him?

A naughty idea popped up. Smiling, she hid her face in his neck. "Mmm. You smell good."

His answer was a low groan.

Encouraged, Libby continued nuzzling his throat, letting her fingers wander until they reached the swelling between his thighs. She traced the length of his erection. The only barrier between his cock and her hand was a thin piece of fleece.

Dragging openmouthed kisses to his ear, she whispered, "Help me slide these down so I can touch you bare."

Immediately, Quinn gripped the back of the seat with his right hand and lifted his hips.

Libby hooked her fingers in the waistband and pulled the sweatpants down to his knees. She curled her hand around the girth of his cock and squeezed.

He hissed. Loudly.

Hmmm. What other noises could she elicit from her normally silent cowboy?

Still kissing his neck, she played with his cock. Feathering touches from tip to root, circling her thumb through the pre-come to tease the sweet spot below the head.

After giving his jawline one last nip, she lowered her face into his lap and replaced her hand with her mouth.

"Sweet Jesus, woman, what are you doin'?"

Libby scooted back slightly for a better angle and cranked her head around. "If you don't know I must be doing it wrong. You want me to stop?"

"No!"

"Thought you might say that."

"It's just, I never thought you'd..." He looked down at her. "You're a wild one, eh?"

"Yep." When Quinn kept staring at her, she reminded him, "Eyes on the road, buddy."

"Ah, shit. Sorry."

She worked him over. Licking the head with little whips of

her tongue, then pulling him into her mouth an inch at a time until her lips were against the base. She breathed through her nose, filling her lungs with the musky scent that was uniquely Quinn. Then Libby released all that male hardness, loving the sleek feel of his tight skin moving backward across her tongue.

A muttering curse sounded above her, but she paid no attention. She kept the deep-throating rhythm, letting her saliva coat the shaft. The darkness, the heat rolling from his body, the constant wet glide of her mouth on his rock-hard cock, soaked her panties to the point she knew Quinn smelled her arousal.

She loved this. His sense of surprise. The confidence she could please him. But mostly she reveled in the knowledge that passion this intense still existed between them.

Quinn's hand had somehow landed on her head. His hips were bumping up, a signal he was close to blowing.

Libby switched to shallow strokes. Lightly holding his dick at the root, her hand moved up to meet her mouth moving down. She applied more suction to the head.

"Goddamn, that feels so fuckin' good."

She hummed around his cock as her head bobbed faster.

"Oh hell yeah, baby, almost there."

Sexual power raced through her. Libby wanted his climax. She wanted to taste it, to bathe in it, to glory in it, because goddammit, she'd *earned* it.

"Uh. Fuck. There it is." Quinn groaned, his fingers increasing the grip on her hair.

His cock throbbed against her tongue with each hot spurt. She swallowed, keeping her lips wrapped tightly around the head until the very last pulse.

He sighed. His body went slack against the seat. After a bit, he said, "That was amazin'. 'Cept, I almost wrecked the truck. Twice."

Flush with success of pleasing her man, she gave his cock one last kiss and lifted her head. She gazed out the window and noticed they were about a mile from the turnoff home.

Quinn reached for her hand. He opened his mouth. Snapped it shut. Apparently he was too stunned to talk.

Good. That was the type of silence she preferred from him.

They parked alongside the horse trailer. In the darkened truck, Quinn stayed still. Libby wanted to crawl out of her skin at the renewed tension.

"I want you like crazy."

A shiver raced up her spine at his husky tone.

"But I want you on my terms. So if you get outta this truck and follow me into that trailer, we're gonna do things my way. Everything. No arguin'. If you wanna back out, say so now."

Practical Libby would demand to know the parameters. But tonight, she wasn't Libby. She was a temptress who'd given a stranger a blowjob in his pickup. Plus, she was damn curious to know what Quinn meant by his "terms".

"I put myself in your capable hands."

The wicked smile that'd charmed her since high school lit up Quinn's face. He opened the glove box and snagged a folded red bandana.

"What're you using that for?"

"A blindfold."

✳

"Turn toward the window. Might feel a slight pinch." He knotted the material at the back of her head. "There. Can you see?"

"Not at all."

"I'll come around and help you out." Quinn aimed to keep her off balance, so he didn't kiss her, talk to her, as he piloted her into the trailer.

Once they were inside, he plastered his body to hers so completely that a single grain of wheat wouldn't have fit between them. His kiss was a flat-out, I-love-you, I-need-you, I'm-gonna-fuck-your-brains-out mark of passion and possession.

Her whimper was his sign to move to the next stage. While unbuttoning her blouse, he spoke just below her ear. "Kick off them shoes, ditch the britches. I want you naked."

She stripped in record time.

"You're gettin' good at that." Quinn balled her clothes up and whipped them in the corner. He let his hands meander down her neck, across her collarbones, over those incredible breasts and sweetly rounded belly to her curvaceous hips. She looked damn fine. Felt damn fine too.

Gooseflesh broke out across Libby's skin.

He stroked the area between her hipbones. A leisurely caress of his rough flesh against the suppleness of hers. Gradually, he allowed his fingertips to brush the hair covering her mound. He trailed nibbling kisses from the bottom of her earlobe to her shoulder as his fingers traced her cleft. "You taste so sweet here. And I've got a hankerin' to feel nuthin' but your velvety-soft, bare skin against my mouth."

"What are you talking about?"

"I'm gonna shave you. Every bit of hair gone so you're smooth as a ripe peach."

"Oh my." She swallowed hard. "But, I-I—"

"You were the adventurous type in the truck. I'll be extra careful."

"You promise?"

"I swear."

"Then okay."

Quinn unfolded a chair and situated Libby with a pillow behind her upper back, close enough to the small table and counter that she could hold on. "Be right back."

In the small bathroom, he soaked two washcloths in hot water and grabbed a new razor. Shame he didn't have an old-fashioned barber's kit with a lathering brush. The tickle of the bristles on her naked sex would heighten her senses. With shaving cream, razor and towels in hand, he returned to his naked wife.

She hadn't budged.

"Don't jump, this is just a hot towel." Quinn laid the steaming cloth across her mound. He filled a plastic bowl with warm water and dropped to his knees.

"Spread your legs more. Scoot down. That's it. You comfortable?"

"As comfortable as I can be, naked, blindfolded, with my privates flapping in the breeze and a man wielding a razor staring at me."

Quinn laughed and slathered on shaving cream. "Don't look that way to me. You look sexy as all get out." He held the razor aloft and said, "Ready?"

"I guess."

"Don't flinch." He made the first pass of the razor down the outside of the left side of her sex. A quick rinse and he shaved the next section.

"That tickles."

He glanced up at her. "Is it makin' you hot?"

"I was already hot from what happened in the truck."

"You liked havin' my cock in your mouth?"

Libby blushed. "Yeah. I liked surprising you."

"That you did." Quinn swished the razor and bent closer. "You also fulfilled another one of my longtime fantasies."

"Really?"

"Yep."

"Why didn't you tell me?"

"Thought we was only sharin' one."

"No. I mean, why didn't you tell me that was your fantasy before tonight?"

"If I woulda said, 'Libby, I want you to suck me off some night while we're zipping down the road in my truck' you'd have said yes?"

"Maybe. You never know unless you ask. Hey, we're not supposed to be using names. We're strangers, remember?"

"My mistake. Hang tight, I wanna wipe you down before I get to the delicate parts."

"I'm actually really glad I'm blindfolded."

Quinn smiled. "I am too, because I'm drooling like a fool, seein' all this pretty pink flesh that's gonna be mine for the takin'."

They didn't say anything for a while. Quinn wanted to be done so he could bury his face in her. So he could lick and lap at the cream he saw welling in the opening to her sex, but he forced himself to stay slow and steady.

She said, "I can feel your breath on my delicate parts."

"Pretty soon it's gonna be my tongue on those parts. All of 'em."

"I like it when you talk dirty."

"Then I'll make sure to whisper naughty sweet-nuthin's in your ear as I'm fuckin' you. Almost done. Scoot down a little more and tilt your hips so I can see your ass crack."

A tiny gasp. "You aren't going to shave me...there?"

"Sure am. You get the whole treatment."

"Lucky me."

"Indeed, 'cause darlin', you ain't seen nuthin' yet."

"And yet, you've seen everything," she muttered.

"What I'm seein' is makin' my mouth water and my dick hard."

He rinsed the washcloth and cleaned her until not a bit of hair or shaving cream remained. After the last swipe, he washed his hands and dumped everything in the sink.

Quinn crouched in front of her. He rubbed his cheek over the top of her cleft, losing himself in her softness and warmth.

Libby made a surprised noise.

"Do you like that?"

"Yes. It feels...Bare. Super-sensitive. Put your mouth on me. All over me. God. Everywhere. Like you promised."

"I ain't lettin' you outta my bed until mornin'. We clear on that?"

"Uh-huh."

He helped her to her feet and they shuffled to the single bed inset into the wall. "Step up."

She stretched out flat on her back. Quinn ditched his clothes and turned off the lights before climbing in.

After giving her a quick peck on the mouth, he kissed straight down her torso. Quinn used the tip of his tongue to trace her silky smooth pussy lips. He burrowed his tongue inside that hot, clenching channel then retreated to lick every hairless inch of her pussy. Damn. He could stay there for hours, coaxing the sticky sweetness from her body and gorging himself on her juices. On just her. His lover. His best friend. His wife. His everything. Not a stranger, his Libby.

"That feels so... Oh, don't stop."

He used his thumbs to hold her open as he focused on her clit. His tongue strokes were fast, relentless and accurate.

She gasped, "Yes!" and held his head in place as she orgasmed against his mouth, making those sexy little squeaking moans that ratcheted his lust to a whole new level.

Soon as Libby settled down, he growled, "Again. Come for me like that again."

"I can't."

"Wrong. And this time, you're gonna scream."

A sense of sexual power consumed Quinn, as she did just that.

As Libby was coming down from another climax, he untied the blindfold and flipped her on her belly. "My turn. Get up on your hands and knees."

Quinn followed the arc of her spine with his tongue from her nape to her tailbone. He parted those sweet cheeks and kept going down the downy crack of her ass. His wandering tongue met the bud of her anus and he painted it with wet swirls.

"Oh. My. God." Her whole body shook.

He'd never done that before, but damn if she didn't like it. So he did it again. He ventured past merely licking the sweet rosette and wiggled his tongue inside the pucker.

Goddamn, he wanted in there, the one place she'd balked at allowing him access. No more. He'd marked her everywhere else; he'd mark her there too. He'd fuck that virgin channel with his fingers, his tongue and his cock.

Keeping his finger pressed to that tight hole, Quinn warned, "I'm gonna take you here, darlin' wife. Not tonight, but soon. You want that, don't you. Wanna experience my cock slidin' into your ass."

Libby just moaned.

"Right now I'm gonna fuck you like this." He yanked her hips back and impaled her.

Jesus. She was so wet and hot and making such sexy sounds, greedily pushing her body back into his. He gritted his teeth and attempted some semblance of control.

"Quinn, don't you dare hold back. You're not gonna break me. More. Harder."

Her plea cut his last thread of restraint. Quinn fucked her without pause. Fucked her through another orgasm. Fucked her hard enough that she'd have bruises on her backside from the grip he maintained to keep her from skidding across the sheets. The sheer force of his thrusts set his knees on fire.

And he didn't stop. He couldn't stop.

Sweating, shaking, Quinn was helpless in the haze of passion, indebted to the woman who gave herself over to him so freely, the woman who still had the power—and the desire—to rock his world.

When Libby looked at him over her shoulder and said, "Baby, let go," he did, saying her name as a benediction as he came until his balls were empty.

She collapsed face-first on the bed, dislodging his cock.

Quinn's dizziness subsided after he braced his hand on the wall and took several deep breaths. He lowered himself next to her.

Libby turned her head and blinked at him.

No smile. No flip remark. Maybe he had been too rough with her. He smoothed his hand down her damp, naked back. "What?"

"I can't be what you need if you don't let me see all sides of you."

"Libby—"

"You know what scares me?"

Being married to a man who fucked you until your elbows and knees were raw with sheet burns? "What?"

"That after this weekend we'll revert to the way it was between us before."

"It won't—I won't. We won't. But havin' wild sex a coupla times a day ain't gonna be the norm for us either."

"I know." Her eyes searched his. "Do you think we've accomplished anything besides proving that sex between us can be fantastic?"

"We've talked more in the last twenty-four hours than we have in the last twenty-four months. Is every little thing ironed out? No. But I reckon there's lots of stuff we ain't gonna see eye-to-eye on, even if we talk about it for the next fifty years. As long as we have open discussions, no accusations, no holdin' back, no ignorin' the problem, then I think we'll be okay."

"Just okay?"

"Better than okay. We're gonna be better than we've ever been. And that's a promise." Quinn wrapped her in his arms and kissed her forehead. "You plum wore me out today. Let's get some sleep. We'll talk more in the mornin'."

Chapter Eight

Libby tried to roll over but a warm, dry hand on her stomach held her in place.

"Whoa, darlin'. Ain't a lotta room on a twin bed to be thrashin' around. I gotta say, I much prefer it crowded with you."

"So last night and yesterday wasn't a dream? I won't open my eyes and wake up in my queen-sized bed alone?"

"Not a dream." Quinn's lips brushed her ear. "I'm hopin' to make yesterday's events a new reality in *our* queen-sized bed."

"Mmm." She stretched, loving the feel of his legs tangled with hers and their bodies pressed together. "Does my 'night with a stranger' fantasy include breakfast?"

"Sure, if you don't mind blueberry Pop-Tarts, 'cause that's about all I've got."

"Yuck."

"After we shower and get dressed up at the house, I could cook us up eggs and toast. I think there's deer sausage left in the deep freeze."

"Are you offering to wash my back?"

"And your front." Quinn's hands slid up to cup her breasts. "And every place in between."

He started biting her neck and she squealed, so they only heard the last couple rings of his cell phone.

"Thought I left that damn thing in the truck," Quinn muttered. He climbed over Libby and snatched the phone from the tiny table where it'd started ringing again.

"Hello? Hey, Ma. Nah. Because I didn't feel like goin' to church, that's why."

Libby withheld a groan. As much as she liked Quinn's mother, Violet McKay had a tendency to forget Quinn wasn't a teenager but a grown man. Since she and Quinn had been together since their teen years, she treated Libby the same way.

Quinn said, "Nope, Ben's takin' care of it this weekend. Because Libby and me are spendin' time together. What's that? I didn't tell you because it ain't your concern." He sighed. "Sorry."

Ooh, pissing off Mama McKay? That was a first. Libby heard the woman's rapid fire reprimand on the other end of the phone from five feet away.

"I don't know. We're workin' on it." Pause. "I don't give a damn what Vaudette Dickens told you. It ain't none of her concern neither."

Good Lord. Vaudette had been a busy bee; it was only nine-thirty in the morning.

"Ma. Ma! Look, I know you think you mean well... Butt out. This is between me and my wife." Pause. The floorboards squeaked as Quinn paced. "Jesus. Please tell me you didn't take it upon yourself to ask her that." Pause. "Because it ain't none of your goddamn business. I don't care if it's the Lord's Day; you had no right. No right." Pause. "Fine. Put him on the damn phone."

Libby's stomach cartwheeled. She'd never heard Quinn speak to his mother so harshly. Never. She crawled out of bed and laid her cheek between his shoulder blades, wrapping her arms around him. His body shook, not from cold but with fury.

"Dad? No, you listen. I don't give a good goddamn if she claims she meant no harm." Pause. "Huh-uh. This is your first and only warning. Back off. Both of you." Quinn clicked the phone shut and threw it on the floor.

His breathing was rapid and shallow. His body both hot and cold. He didn't say anything or move to dislodge her arms, so Libby clutched him tightly, hoping it might calm him down.

"I didn't know. I swear to God, I didn't know. What kinda husband does that make me? Dammit, how could I not have seen it?"

Libby stepped back. "What was that phone call about?"

"My mother chewed me out for not bein' in church. She demanded to know why Vaudette Dickens found out we were back together and why I hadn't bothered to tell her first. She expected me to deny the rumor we were acting 'obscene' in public last night. Then she asked if we were done bein' separated and when she could expect grandkids, 'cause she'd been waitin' a long time and she was tired of nagging you about quittin' your job and us startin' a family."

He spun around. His eyes were black with rage and his lips were drawn into a thin white line. "I didn't know she'd been hounding you about grandkids because she ain't said a single word to me. Not one word. Ever." His eyes frantically searched hers. "She makes a big deal about it to you, doesn't she?"

Libby nodded.

"Why didn't you tell me?"

"She's your mother."

"So?"

"So, if I would've said, 'Quinn, your mama's been demanding answers on why I'm not pregnant yet', we both know you would have brushed it off. If I had complained every damn time she did it, you would've thought I was being overly sensitive and brushed it off too."

Guilt flashed across his face.

"It wasn't bad at first. But as the years wore on, her comments became a little sharper. I didn't want to cause family problems or make waves so I didn't tell you."

"Dammit, Libby, I didn't know. I'm sorry. So damn sorry."

"You can't control her. I'll admit I was jealous when your cousins started having babies. It embarrassed me at McKay functions hearing your mother complaining to the other women in the family that she didn't have a grandchild to spoil yet."

"And yet, she never said a fucking word to me. Sayin' sorry doesn't seem like enough. No wonder you resented me. No wonder you wanted to rid yourself of me and this overbearing family."

"Your mother didn't cause our marital problems."

"I realize that, but her behavior, coupled with my ostrich-like mentality, didn't help matters." He blew out a frustrated breath. "Enough."

"We still have a lot to talk about, but you're right. Let's take a break. No more discussions about babies, fertility tests, mixed signals, meddling mothers and sisters."

"For how long?"

"A while. Look, we can't solve anything in two days, and with the resentment and confusion on both our parts, some issues we weren't even aware we had...frankly, I'm too emotionally raw to deal with any of it right now."

"Amen. And I ain't sayin' that because I'm hopin' you'll forget about it. I know we have to talk about this. Sooner, rather than later. But when we're ready...well, I ain't opposed to talkin' to a fertility doctor to see if there is something wrong, if that's still what you want."

Feeling a little misty eyed, Libby walked straight into Quinn's arms.

"You all right?"

"No. My head is spinning."

"You wanna go up to the house and lay down?"

"Maybe for a bit. Then can we just hang out at home today? Screw around. Take the four wheelers out, maybe snuggle up and watch a little TV?"

"You sure?"

"Yeah, why?"

"I thought you'd wanna do something more exciting."

She pushed back and looked at him. "Is that what you think? I have to be doing something new and exciting all the time? I find being on the ranch with you...boring?"

Quinn gave her a half-shrug and ducked his head.

Another truth hit her. "I've hurt you by letting you believe you and our home weren't enough for me anymore." Libby rubbed the tips of her fingers over his morning whiskers. "Oh Quinn. Oh, honey, that's not why I wanted the separation. I'd hoped if we were apart we'd miss each other. We'd be forced to communicate beyond 'What's for supper?' and 'I washed your coveralls' and we'd work harder to stay together."

"Has it worked? Us spendin' the weekend together?"

Libby laid her head on his chest and listened to his heartbeat. So strong. So steady. "We're off to a damn fine start."

Quinn stayed silent a beat too long and Libby knew she hadn't given him the answer he wanted.

"Whatcha doin'?"

She shuffled the papers as the printer spat them out. "Research."

Why did she look so guilty? "Can I see?"

"What time is it?" Libby asked, avoiding his question.

"Almost eight. Why?"

She unplugged the printer cable and powered down her laptop. "I thought it'd be fun to play cards."

"I'd be up for a game of strip poker." Quinn waggled his eyebrows.

"I was thinking a game of hearts and you were thinking with a hard-on."

"I can't help it. All the smokin' hot sex yesterday, in the shower this mornin', and my mind is runnin' on one track."

"Hold that thought. And get your money out. After I've finished packing I'm gonna whip your butt in poker."

Quinn froze. "Finished packing for what?"

"I'm going to Cheyenne tomorrow for the state library conference, remember?"

"First I've heard of it."

"I thought I'd told you." She shrugged. "Must've slipped my mind."

"How long you gonna be gone?"

"All week. There's two days of training and then the actual conference. I'll be back Friday afternoon."

He flipped the station to an outdoor hunting channel and stared at the screen without seeing it. "Maybe I oughta go with you."

Libby kissed his forehead. "Don't scowl, it'll give you wrinkles. Besides, Cheyenne wouldn't be fun for you, stuck in the hotel all day."

"But the nights of hot motel sex would make up for it."

"I'm assigned a roommate."

Quinn hated when she went to conferences. She was too damn busy during the day to call him and too tired at night. He was lucky if they talked one time.

"Speaking of... I have to leave at the crack of dawn, so I'd better get going." She flounced out of the room.

That sucked. He dropped his head back on the couch and gazed at the ceiling. Had Libby deliberately misled him?

You two weren't exactly talking before last Friday.

True, but they'd done a helluva lot of talking since then. Then he remembered her insistence they not make promises for the future beyond the weekend, because she might need more time to think it over.

Evidently, Libby always intended on taking that time, in Cheyenne—whether he liked it or not.

Quinn didn't like it one little bit.

But he'd damn sure give her something to remember him by before she left. He managed to cool his heels for ten minutes before he went upstairs.

The suitcase was open on the floor. The suit bag was spread out across the bed. Both were almost full. Quinn leaned against the doorjamb and watched Libby scurrying around.

She finally noticed him. "Why are you skulking in the doorway?"

"Can't a man appreciate his wife?"

"Sweet-talker."

"I'm tryin'. How much packing you got left?"

"Almost done. Just have to pick shoes, but I'm tempted to take one pair."

"Need help?" He ambled toward the closet.

"Nah. I'm good."

Libby paid no attention to him as she mumbled and pawed through her dresser drawers.

Her side of the closet contained fewer clothes. It was easy to find what he wanted. Quinn unhooked the heavy material from the metal hanger. After she'd zipped up the suit bag and set it next to the suitcase on the floor, he tossed the pair of black suede fringed chaps on the bed.

She slowly turned around with an odd look in her eyes. "Umm. I think those are inappropriate for a librarian's conference, don't you?"

"Good thing you ain't wearin' 'em for nobody but me."

"Quinn—"

He loomed over her in a half a heartbeat. "Put them on. No arguin'. No panties. No shirt. No bra. No socks. No boots. Just the chaps. I'll be back in five minutes. You'd better be undressed and ready."

"Ready for what?"

"Ready for whatever I tell you to do."

Libby blinked at him. A few seconds passed and she nodded.

Quinn retreated to the bathroom. Seemed an eternity before he trekked back down the hallway to their bedroom.

She was sitting on the bed and jumped up the instant she saw him. "Was I supposed to be standing?"

"You're fine." Quinn shut and locked the door. He closed the blinds. Turned off the overhead light and flipped on the bedside lamp. Rolled back the quilt, exposing the sheets. Then he faced her. Crowded her, really. "Hands by your sides."

She dropped the arms she'd crossed over her chest.

"Lord almighty, lookit you." And what an eyeful Quinn got. His wife made his pulse race and his cock hard. "Turn and let me see the view from the back."

It appeared Libby might argue, but she swiveled her hips, tossed her head and twirled around.

"Holy mother. That's the sexiest damn sight I've ever seen." The leather hugged her legs. The cut of the chaps highlighted her rounded, naked ass. The thick strap spanned the curve of her lower back and brought to mind bondage games he'd salivated over in porn flicks, but hadn't thought he'd ever get the chance to try. He'd like to tie her up. Bind her hands in all sorts of tempting ways—above her head, behind her back, in front where the ropes would rub against her—

"Quinn?"

His gaze whipped to hers. Another time he'd remind her of his expertise with ropes. A small smile crept up. "Lemme see you shakin' that badonkadonk."

"What?"

"I wanna see your ass swingin' and the fringe flappin'."

"But—"

"Do it, Lib. Make me wild to get my hands and mouth all over you."

"For being a man of few words you sure do use them well."

"I'm a new man, darlin' wife."

At first, her hands were clutched into fists by her side, but eventually she hitched her shoulders back and raised her arms. Cupping each elbow, her arms created a square above her head. Libby twitched her hips side-to-side, adding a quick snap at the end, causing the fringe to slap against the leather and her skin.

Quinn groaned at the erotic *swish-swish-snap* sound. "Keep goin'. I'm gettin' all kinds of worked up."

Libby widened her stance, performing a bump-and-grind routine that'd cause a stripper envy. She rolled her pelvis as she shimmied forward and peeped at him upside down from between her legs. She cooed, "How'm I doing, cowboy?"

"Definitely makin' me wild. Stand up and face me."

She spun around. "What now?"

"You'll see. Be still." He idly dragged his index finger from the tip of her chin, down the flushed skin of her throat, through the valley of her cleavage, zigzagging over her ribs and stomach. He traced the leather strap between her hipbones and her flesh quivered.

Libby trembled when he fell to his knees.

Quinn admired his handiwork from the previous night—her completely bare-shaven pussy. He passed his palms down the outside of her thighs. The fringe tickled her legs as he followed the sensuous curves to her ankles.

When he allowed his hands the same leisurely journey back up, she emitted a soft moan. Brushing his lips across the swell of her belly, he murmured, "Tell me what you want. I'll do anything you ask."

"You know what I want."

His let his hair tease the underside of her breasts, knowing it drove her crazy as he feathered butterfly kisses over her lower torso. "Say the words, Libby."

"Put your mouth on my...sex. Suck my clit. Use your hands and your tongue, just...make me come."

"Sit on the edge of the bed. Lay back. Close your eyes."

The bed bounced she hit it so fast.

He withheld a smile as he grabbed the lube and her vibrator out of the nightstand drawer. He scooted between her legs, bent his head and tasted her.

"Oh. Yeah."

Another pass of his tongue. Quinn licked and teased, rubbing his face all over her smooth skin. Evidently the sensation of his wet mouth and cooling breaths across her hot flesh, coupled with soft tongue flicks and the rough scrape of his evening beard, quickly drove Libby to the edge.

"Quinn. Please."

As he zeroed in on her clit, he began to lightly massage her anus. She tensed up, like she always did. This time instead of backing off, he said, "Relax. Lemme make you feel good."

Surprisingly, she did relax.

With every suck and lick, Quinn swirled his finger a little deeper inside her back channel, while he thrust his thumb in and out of her wet pussy. When Libby began pushing down on his hand, he suctioned his lips around her clit and slid his middle finger in her ass as she started to come.

It was hot as hell, feeling her throb against his tongue as her interior muscles contracted around his finger and thumb.

After the pulses subsided, Libby opened her eyes. "Wow."

He took his time tasting the dips and hollows of her body, steeping his taste buds in the sweet and salty flavor of her skin. Against her throat, he said, "Did you like that?"

"God, yes."

"Do you want more?"

"Mmm. You could probably persuade me."

"Flip onto your belly." Once Quinn had her stretched out at an angle across the bed, he followed her spine with his tongue. "You got what you wanted. Now it's my turn. I wanna slide my cock in that virgin hole and fuck you."

She sucked in a harsh breath. "Are you giving me a choice?"

"Nope. I'm claimin' this part of you I've waited for, for years." His teeth tugged on her earlobe. "Admit it. You liked my finger."

"Well, yeah, but there's a difference between one finger and your cock."

"I ain't exactly hung like a bull."

"I don't think—"

"So don't think. I'll make sure you're ready, and when you are, I'll go slow." He kept kissing everywhere his lips could reach, brushing his clothed body against her bare skin. "Come on, darlin', I'm dyin' here. And if you were honest with yourself, you'd admit you're just as curious as I am."

Libby lifted her head to look at him. "I swear to God, if it hurts—"

The rest of Libby's protest was lost in Quinn's demanding kiss. He seduced her, inflamed her, brought her back to the magical place where desire ruled.

She ripped her mouth free with a gasp. "Do it before I change my mind."

Didn't have to tell him twice. He hopped up and stripped. He liberally coated his fingers, staring greedily at the rounded globes of her ass and the hidden pink hole as he greased up his cock.

When she attempted to push to her hands and knees, he hiked her hips into the air and pressed her chest against the mattress. "Stretch your arms above your head."

Quinn climbed on the bed and squirted a dollop of lube on the rose-colored pucker. He swirled his index finger around, waiting for her to clench.

She didn't.

While stroking the expanse of her naked back with his free hand, he inserted his finger deep, to the webbing.

Libby hissed.

"You okay?"

"Yeah, it just feels...different from this angle."

After squeezing out more lube, he added a second finger.

Her body stiffened slightly but the muscles surrounding his fingers remained loose.

"So sexy, so hot, so damn tight." Quinn leaned forward and nibbled on her shoulder blades as he carefully stretched her. When she rocked her ass back onto his fingers, he knew she was ready. "Give me your right hand." She slid her arm down and he placed the vibrator in her palm. He turned it on. "I wanna see you usin' this as I'm fuckin' you."

Libby made a sound that was half-moan, half-gasp as her hand disappeared between her legs.

Quinn pressed his cock against the opening and gently pushed the head past the ring of muscle. Despite his need to pound into her, he stopped. Took a breath. As a man of few words, Libby wouldn't expect a play-by-play and he was too far gone with lust to indulge in dirty talk.

Holding her soft butt cheeks in his hands, he watched his cock disappear into her ass an inch at a time.

Oh sweet Jesus, that was good. He waited a minute to savor claiming the last piece of his wife's virginity and giving her the last of his.

Vibrations inched closer to his balls as Libby stroked the vibrator over her slit. The buzzing sensation sent tingles up his spine. Straight up his dick. He pulled out little by little, leaving just the tip of his cock hugged by her flexing muscles. Then he slid deep until her anus was snug against the wider base of his shaft.

Two, three more times, he drove in and out, the warning *slow slow slow* screamed in his head, warring with the ever louder *harder harder harder*. Quinn managed to keep the pace steady even when sweat dripped into his eyes. He clenched his teeth, his fingers and his ass cheeks against the need to pound into that tight channel with everything he had.

"Quinn?"

"Uh-huh?"

"You're holding back, aren't you?"

"Uh-huh."

"You aren't hurting me."

"You sure?"

"Positive. Take me how you want."

With a noise similar to a snarl, Quinn unleashed the beast inside him. He withdrew and slammed into her with enough force to send her grasping for purchase on the slippery sheets. Over and over. Without pause. "Fuck, that's so good."

Each pounding thrust had Quinn climbing the precipice to that elusive point of pleasure. The tight clasp of her untried passage, the buzz of the vibrator, the visual of Libby's body stretched out before him as he'd always dreamed. He fucked her hard enough the bed shook.

Libby's orgasm hit. She screamed.

The high-pitched feminine wail was one of the sexiest sounds Quinn had ever heard.

When she bore down on his cock, and her body attempted to suck his pulsing sex deeper, Quinn lost his thin grip on control. He rammed in to the hilt as his balls lifted and he bathed her channel with his seed. He squeezed his eyes shut as her body milked every hot spurt, each blast of heat burst from his cock like a pipeline of liquid fire.

Eventually, the primitive roar in his head lessened. Even when he could think and breathe again, his heart kept a rapid *thud-dunk-adunk* as he eased out of her.

After kissing the back of her head and murmuring sweet nonsense, Quinn retreated to the bathroom, cleaned himself up, and brought back a warm washcloth to do the same for her.

She didn't move much. She didn't look at him. He didn't know whether that was a bad or a good sign. After he'd tossed the washcloth aside, he rolled her over. Finally, she opened her eyes.

"Hey. You all right?"

"Tired." Her jaw cracked as she yawned. "Man. I'm not used to two days of raunchy sex."

"Complaints?"

"Not a single one. I liked that. I didn't think I would."

"Good."

Silence.

Libby sat up and reached for the covers. "I've gotta be up early tomorrow. You coming to bed?"

Quinn toyed with the lace on the pillowcase. "I didn't know if I'd be sleepin' in the horse trailer again."

"Why would you think that?"

"Because I was rough with you."

"I asked you to be rough with me."

"But—"

"No buts, silly man. Of course I want you here. No more regrets, no more holding back." She touched his face. "I want to be everything you need, Quinn. Everything. In bed and out."

"You are."

"Good. Now come in here and warm me up."

He slid between the sheets and spooned behind her. "I missed sleepin' with you, Lib."

"Is that all you missed?" she teased.

"No. But I don't got time to tell you everything I missed. It'd take hours." He let his lips follow the outside shell of her ear. "Days maybe."

"You're so sweet."

After a bit, he whispered, "I love you like crazy, Libby McKay. I ain't ever lettin' you get away from me again."

Chapter Nine

Late Thursday morning, Quinn was wrenching on an old tractor outside the barn when a Crook County sheriff's car pulled up. He wiped his hands on a rag and squinted at the familiar driver.

His cousin, Cam McKay, had signed on as a deputy after his return from Iraq. The door opened and all six-foot-five inches of Cam unfolded from the vehicle.

"Mornin'," Quinn said.

"Mornin', Q," Cam replied, slamming the door.

Cam's limp was noticeable as he ambled over. Quinn focused his attention on Cam's face rather than his disability. "Out makin' the rounds today, Deputy McKay?"

"I wish. Is Libby around?"

"Nah. She's at a conference in Cheyenne all week."

"That explains it."

"Explains what?"

"This." Cam held up an envelope. "Why I'm serving you with papers from Ginger Paulson, Attorney-at-Law."

Quinn's stomach pitched. "You're shittin' me."

"Nope. Sorry." Cam passed over the envelope. "This part of my job sucks worse than dodging bullets."

"When did you get this?" Quinn asked as he ripped the flap open.

"First thing this morning. I grabbed it soon as it was dropped off. I figured you'd rather get it from me than from Sheriff Turnbull." Pause. "Unless you plan on shooting the messenger?"

"Not hardly. Ain't your fault and my gun is in my truck."

Quinn didn't know squat about legal procedure, but he had a pretty good idea what kind of papers were inside the envelope. The rag fell to the ground as he scanned the document.

A Summons and Complaint, filed by Ginger A. Paulson, Attorney-at-Law, on behalf of Libby Adams McKay, Complaint. Dated...Tuesday morning.

Son of a bitch.

Quinn's face grew hot, his eyes smarted. He felt like he'd been bucked off a bull—breathless, blindsided and stupid.

"Q? Buddy, you okay?"

He couldn't look at his cousin. The pity in Cam's eyes would do him in. "No. I'm about as far from fine as a man can get." Spilling his guts. Nice. Maybe he oughta throw himself in the dirt and start bawling too.

"Look, I ain't tryin' to be a dick, or to stick my nose in, but Ben made it sound like you and Libby had gotten back together last weekend."

"I thought we had."

Silence.

Finally, Quinn glanced up and waved the paper. "This ain't some kinda mistake?"

Cam shook his head.

"Fuck."

"Have you talked to Libby since she's been in Cheyenne?"

"Once. She's always so damn busy at those conferences she don't have time to call." Come to think of it, when he'd called her Tuesday night, she had acted more distracted than usual.

Why?

Because you showed her your darker side. It scared her and she's rethinking whether she wants to spend her life with you.

No. Libby had wanted to see it. Hell, she'd demanded to see it.

Then why with all your sharing of feelings and hours of lovemaking didn't she tell you she loved you?

His heart nearly stopped.

Surely Libby had uttered those three little words at some point over the weekend.

Hadn't she?

He'd said them to her, but now that he really thought about it...his wife hadn't reciprocated. Not one time. Why not? Was

175

this past weekend a way to get him to open up before she leveled the killing blow to their marriage?

No. Libby wasn't a cold, vindictive woman—even when the divorce petition clutched in hand suggested otherwise. So what in tarnation was going on with her?

Only one way to find out.

Quinn's boots kicked up dust as he raced to his pickup.

Cam called out, "Hey! Where you going?"

"Cheyenne." Within two seconds, his cousin jerked him around and got right in his face. Damn. Cam was scary fast and stealthy, even sporting a fake leg. "What?"

"I can't let you go, Q, if you're planning on doing something stupid."

"Jesus, Cam, you think I'd ever hurt her? I love her. She's everything in the damn world to me."

His younger cousin gave him a hard cop stare.

"I've hurt her enough. Only stupid thing I'm doin' is standin' here, tellin' you what I oughta be tellin' her."

Cam grinned. "That's all I wanted to hear. Drive safe."

$$*$$

Four hours later, Quinn hit the state capital. The parking lot of the Sheraton was jam-packed. He rolled the papers up and shoved them in his back pocket.

Inside the convention center, he checked the electronic display board listing class times and rooms. Librarians roamed the halls. Mostly females. Luckily in Wyoming no one paid attention to just another man in a cowboy hat.

He paused outside the door to Conference Room B and took a deep breath. Rounding the corner, he scanned the women congregated around the beverage station and scattered in groups of twos and threes. Bingo. There she was, looking pretty as a picture in a clingy purple pantsuit, chatting with a lady twice her age and half as tall.

Quinn strode toward her.

Libby glanced up when ten feet separated them. Her eyes widened. "Quinn? What on earth?"

"I'm happy to see you too, darlin' wife."

The older woman tittered.

Color rose in Libby's cheeks. "Why are you here?"

"Because I got hold of some interestin' papers today and I wanted to talk to you about them." He slipped his arm around Libby's stiff shoulders and smiled at her companion. "Ma'am. If you'll excuse us."

"Certainly."

He sensed Libby fuming as he attempted to steer her out of the room. She dug in her heels. "I'm busy. This is not the place to discuss this."

Quinn placed his lips near her temple. "Wrong. Unless you want me to hoist you into a fireman's hold and drag you outta this room, you'd better keep movin'."

She jerked back. "You wouldn't dare."

"Try me." After a couple seconds of her indecision, Quinn flashed his teeth at her. "Fine. If that's the way you wanna play this." He bent down, intending to throw her over his shoulder.

"No! Wait." Libby grabbed his hand and hustled him out the side door. She kept dragging him along at a good clip until they reached a deserted corridor. She whirled around, hands on hips. But he could tell she wasn't really mad, just...worried.

"What happened between us last weekend?" Quinn asked. "Was it only about sex?"

She shook her head.

"It wasn't one last tumble before you moved on?"

"Moved on? Why in the world would you say that? You were there, Quinn. You know how everything changed between us."

"Yeah, but I thought it was a change for the better."

"It was. It is."

Quinn reached into his back pocket and held out the rolled-up papers. "Then how in the hell can you possibly explain this?"

Libby's eyes darted away. "It was supposed to be a surprise."

"A surprise?"

"We've never done anything like that. I thought it'd be fun."

"Fun?" he repeated. "Since when is a surprise divorce fun?"

"What are you talking about?"

"This." Quinn waved the papers. "A signed document from Ginger Paulson, Attorney-at-Law, starting the divorce proceedings at your request."

177

"Gimme that." Libby snatched the papers and unrolled them. All the blood drained from her face and she wilted against the wall as she flipped through the pages. "No. No. No! This wasn't supposed to happen."

"Then how did it?"

Silence.

"Libby?"

"Last Friday, I'd given up hope. I thought you didn't care—"

"I remember that conversation. We've been through this."

"You don't know this part. Earlier that day I signed the Complaint paperwork. I put it in my outbox, intending to mail it...and then you were waiting for me in the parking lot. Since I was out of town this week, someone at the school must've thought they were doing me a favor and sent it off."

"Some favor."

"This wasn't what I wanted." Libby looked at him beseechingly. "You have to believe me. I forgot all about it. Especially after we spent the weekend trying to work things out."

"Did we work things out, Libby?"

"Yes!"

Relief like he'd never felt swept through him. "So if you would've gone into the library on Monday?"

"I'd have ripped this into shreds." Her chin wobbled. "God, Quinn, I'm so sorry. You probably were thinking all sorts of horrible thoughts about me."

Quinn pulled her into his arms. "Never. I was just mighty confused and needed to get to the bottom of it straightaway, since we talked about not keepin' things from each other."

"So you...?"

"I hopped in my truck and headed for Cheyenne right after Cam dropped it off this mornin'."

"Your cousin delivered this to you?" She cringed. "That oughta be fodder for the McKay gossipmongers."

"Since it was official business, I doubt he'll say anything." He swallowed his pride. "But I wouldn't mind reassurance from you that it ain't gonna be grist for the mill."

She tipped her face up to look at him. "Like?"

"Like...do you still love me?"

"Of course I still love you. I never stopped loving you."

"Say it again."

Libby stood on her tiptoes and peppered his face with kisses. "I love you. Love, love, love you, with my heart, my soul, my everything. Quinn McKay, you are my everything, and if you think for one moment I'm ever letting you go, after all we've been through—"

Quinn dipped his head and kissed her. For a good long time.

When they broke apart, she murmured, "My roommate is in a class right now. Wouldn't it be fun to mess around? Especially when there's a chance we'll get caught?"

"Sounds like my kinda fun." *Fun.* That reminded him. "What did you mean when you said you thought it'd be a fun surprise and we'd never done anything like it?"

Color tinged her cheeks. "Oh. When I saw those papers, I thought you'd found the tropical island 'couples only' getaway packages I'd printed out on Sunday. I wanted to tempt you into taking a real vacation, just you and me, the sand and the sea."

Quinn brought her hand to his mouth and kissed her knuckles. "Is that another one of your untold fantasies? Jetting off to a tropical island?"

"Only if it's jetting off with you."

"Then the week after you get outta school for the summer, we'll hop on a plane and be sippin' drinks on the beach by sunset. You can call it a fantasy. I'll call it our second honeymoon."

"Really? You'd do that for me? Even though you hate to fly?"

Quinn touched her, the woman he'd loved most his life, the woman who was his everything, the woman who loved him enough to give him a second chance. "Libby, I love you. I'd do anything for you. I wanna make you happy. I want us both to be happy. Not just for a week, or for a weekend, but for the rest of our lives. Let's go home."

Libby stepped back and gave him a wicked grin. "Right after we test the bounce factor of the mattress in my room."

Yep, he was really grateful for second chances.

Epilogue

Six months later

Libby barely made it to the toilet before she threw up.

Again.

Damn flu.

She managed a sip of water. The liquid stayed down for a change. Good. She wiped her mouth and let the sink cabinet hold her up, hoping she could climb back in bed before Quinn returned home from checking cattle.

Yeah, she'd pop to her feet and walk those twenty steps to their bedroom. In a second. She just needed to rest her eyes for a minute or two.

"Nappin' in the bathroom again?"

Her eyes flew open, giving her an instant case of vertigo. Dammit. She'd dozed off. Worse, he'd *caught* her dozing off.

Quinn crouched down, his face lined with concern. "Libby—"

"I'm fine."

"No, you ain't. You need to go to the doctor."

"It's the flu, Quinn." When he scowled, she added, "It's flu season. I work with coughing, hacking, feverish kids every damn day. Do the math. I'm bound to get sick a lot."

"I have done the math, which is why I know it ain't the damn flu." He stood and stalked out of the bathroom.

Libby yelled, "I am *not* going to the doctor."

No answer.

Crap. She hated arguing with him. It'd been a rarity since their reconciliation, but not because they weren't communicating. They talked all the time. In fact, her formerly strong, silent type of husband had become downright chatty. Libby wasn't complaining. She'd never been happier and Quinn felt the same. Their life wasn't perfect, but it was damn close.

Now, if she could just get over the flu that'd been hanging on for the last month.

Paper rustled and she looked up at Quinn leaning in the doorway. A white pharmacy bag dangled from his hand. She managed a wan smile. "You went to town and got me medicine? That's so sweet."

"No, I went to town and got you a pregnancy test."

Her stomach lurched. She crawled to the toilet and threw up again.

Quinn held her hair back and wiped her face. After he situated her on the floor, he stretched out across from her. "Better?"

When the queasiness subsided, she said, "I'm not pregnant. I'm never pregnant."

"This time is different."

"How do you know?"

"Pregnant is pregnant. I recognize the signs."

Indignantly, she snapped, "I am not a heifer! You cannot judge me by the way I twitch my backside or behave erratically whether or not I'm pregnant for the first time." To Libby's utter dismay, she began to cry.

"Ah hell. Take a deep breath or else you'll be right back hangin' over that toilet after gettin' so worked up."

"Shit. Shit. Shit. I hate to bawl. I hate to whine. I hate to throw up. I hate that I'm sitting on the damn bathroom floor again doing all three."

"I know you do." He ripped off a chunk of toilet paper and handed it to her. "Lib, what's really goin' on?"

She sniffled and blew her nose. "I'm scared."

"Me too." He paused, but his silences no longer made her nervous.

"It's just...things are so good between us now. I don't want anything to wreck it."

"You think havin' a baby could do that?"

"Me wanting one so badly did before."

"Yeah, but it wasn't the only thing that caused our problems. We're different now. We're probably better prepared to deal with all the issues involving a baby. So maybe there was a reason we didn't get this gift until we were both ready to handle it."

Libby stared at him. "You really think I could be pregnant?"

Quinn took her hand. "Come on. Indulge me. I believe in my gut and in my heart we'll be fine no matter what the stick says."

She did too. "All right."

"Good." Quinn cracked open the pregnancy test kit, read the directions a billion times and watched her like a hawk so she didn't screw it up. In all the years she'd locked herself in the bathroom and conducted multitudes of pregnancy tests, this was the first time she'd involved Quinn in the process.

They left the urine-soaked stick on the back of the toilet and Quinn set his watch.

Holding her close, he gave her a reassuring kiss on the top of her head and murmured, "I love you. Nothin'll ever change that. Baby. No baby. Don't matter as long as I have you."

"I feel the same. I love you. God, I love you so much."

The watch beeped.

"Ready?" he asked.

"Ready," she answered.

They held hands as they peered at the indicator.

Finally, Quinn said softly, "I'll be damned."

The results window read...a plus sign in big, bold type.

Not the flu after all.

Libby didn't know whether to laugh or cry.

"You okay?" he said.

"Uh-huh. I'll probably freak out once it sinks in."

"That'll make two of us, darlin'."

"Don't you mean, three of us?"

"Three. Right. God. A baby. We're havin' a baby." His body went ironing board rigid. "Now that we know, get your butt back in bed, pretty mama. I'm callin' Doc Monroe and you're goin' to see her first thing tomorrow. But today you need to rest."

"But—"

"No buts. I'm gonna make sure you don't move, even if I hafta hogtie you to the headboard. 'Cept I know how much you love bein' tied up."

"Quinn—"

"No arguin', Lib, I mean it."

She sighed. "Are you gonna be one of those hovering, overbearing husbands who obsesses about every little thing during this pregnancy?"

A beat passed. "I reckon so."

Libby leaned into him, grateful to have him standing behind her, holding her up, in every possible way. "I can live with that."

About the Author

To learn more about Lorelei James please visit www.loreleijames.com. Send an email to lorelei@loreleijames.com or join her Yahoo! group to join in the fun with other readers as well as Lorelei! http://groups.yahoo.com/group/LoreleiJamesgang

Look for these titles by
Lorelei James

Now Available:
Rough Riders Series
Long Hard Ride
Cowgirl Up and Ride
Tied Up, Tied Down
Rode Hard, Put Up Wet
Rough, Raw, and Ready
Branded As Trouble
Shoulda Been A Cowboy
All Jacked Up
Raising Kane

Wild West Boys Series
Mistress Christmas
Miss Firecracker

Beginnings Anthology: Babe in the Woods
Three's Company Anthology: Wicked Garden
Wild Ride Anthology: Strong, Silent Type

Dirty Deeds
Running With the Devil

Coming Soon:

Rough Riders Series
Cowgirls Don't Cry

The Real Deal

Niki Green

Dedication

To my mother. For giving me the best advice in the world on writing—I didn't take it, but you know that already.

Chapter One

The Garden was located just a few miles south of Dallas, Texas and an hour and a half from the Kiel ranch. Rumor was that a hundred years ago it had been a brothel—a profitable one. But that was long ago. The Garden was now a gentlemen's club. A modern-day burlesque show reminiscent of Gypsy Rose Lee or even Dita Von Teese. It abided by the rule that less was more. Less skin showed, more tease available, was the golden rule of The Garden. A strip club it wasn't, a haven of seduction it was, and for Nick and Hayden Kiel it was a young man's dream come to life.

Nick stood just inside the doorway of the place tapping the brochure he'd received against his leg and taking in his surroundings. The lighting was low, most of it radiating from the enormous stage that took up the center of the club.

The stage had two separate platforms separated by wide glowing stairs. Nick watched as two of the dancers on stage made their way back and forth, up and down the steps as their erotic dance captured the audience's attention. Less was more, Nick reminded himself as he watched the dancers glide along to the tempo of a recently popular rock song. The beat of the music made his insides thump just as the dancers were making his pants throb.

"Can you believe this? I'm horny already!" Nick had almost forgotten his brother's presence. Hayden Kiel had graduated high school three months ago and the trip to The Garden was a late graduation present Nick bestowed upon him. He should have given him money instead. It would have been safer that way.

At eighteen, Hayden was hell on wheels, literally. In the

past two years he had wrecked and destroyed countless vehicles, spent more than one night in the county lockup for being what the Millbrook sheriff called, "a danger to himself and others", and had succeeded in breaking the heart of almost every young girl the small town of Millbrook had to offer. Hayden was a regular menace to himself and to society, and therefore needed a babysitter from time to time, which is where Nick came in.

Being the two youngest of the five "Kiel boys", as they were called, bonded them closer together. Nick glanced in his brother's direction, feeling relief that the younger man was still close by and hadn't ventured off. Venturing off in The Garden, a place they weren't supposed to be in the first place, was not a good idea. Just getting through the doors had been nerve-racking enough.

The large man guarding the gates to the club had held onto Nick and Hayden's IDs longer than Nick would have liked. The man, who could have played strong tackle for the Cowboys once upon a time, had studied the two plastic-covered rectangles and then studied the two young fellows standing before him. Nick had felt some sense of relief when the giant had started to hand the cards back and then Hayden had opened his big mouth and said, "Dammit man, you cramming for a test or something?"

Nick was a pacifist, generally, but at that moment had seriously considered doing his baby brother major bodily harm. Hayden just didn't know when to keep his fucking mouth shut. He had explained on the ride up to The Garden that they needed to keep a low profile and draw little, if no, attention to themselves. But if Hayden had heard him, he'd never acknowledged it.

Nick turned to his brother, tapped him on the shoulder and motioned him to an empty table on the far side of the stage. Holding up a hand, he summoned one of the traveling waitresses and quickly ordered a round of beers. After doing so, he noticed Hayden already held a bottle in each hand. Just like Hayden, he thought, never wasting time.

"You know what my two favorite things in the whole world are?" Nick leaned closer to hear his brother's question. Even though Hayden's voice was raised the music drowned out most of the words.

Shaking his head at the question Nick asked, "What's

that?" Nick caught the flash of his brother's straight, white teeth and then heard him say, "Hot pussy and cold beer." Nick rolled his eyes and laughed a bit.

"Man, this place has them both. I've had a hard-on since we walked through the door." Hayden's eyes were locked on the stage and Nick noticed that the music stopped. Applause started, then ended with whistles and yells from various tables and a new act was about to begin.

Two more dancers occupied the stage now. The lights dimmed in between performances leaving The Garden in almost complete darkness. Steadily, the lights began to come up reveling two dancers sitting center stage facing each other. Separating the two was a vanity and mirror of sorts, but there was no glass. The girls were the mirror images of each other. From their cropped, glossy wigs to their knee-high boots, they were identical.

Hoots, hollers, yells and whistles again became deafening. Evidently most of the crowd knew what was about to come. Nick had to admit he couldn't wait to see for himself.

The music began roaring its way through the speakers filling the club. Nick recognized the song. It was popular and played on nearly every radio station numerous times a day. He couldn't remember most of the words but he knew the overall theme, someone had kissed a girl and she had seemed to like it, or so he thought. He couldn't remember. All he could think about was the pressure his zipper was putting on his increasing erection. Never in his life was he so grateful for a table cloth.

Hayden on the other hand didn't seem to care if his arousal was evident to the rest of the patrons or not. There he sat an elbow's length away laid back in the opposite chair, beer bottle lifted halfway to his mouth, eyes roving over the eye candy moving before the crowd. Nick shook his head at his captivated brother and returned his undivided attention to the stage and to the ones who occupied it.

After the first few beats introduced the song a throaty, ultra feminine voice rang out the lyrics that propelled the dancers along. Each movement from the two was synchronized. What one did, the other mimicked.

They moved with the beat of the music, at first only watching each other through the faux mirror in front of them. Black fishnet gloves traced an eyebrow and moved seductively to the sets of cherry-red lips. Material ran gracefully and without pause over the glistening pair. Their fingertips stroked the top first, then bottom and then back to the top before blowing a kiss to one another via the mirror.

Without faltering, breaking their timing or rhythm, the pair removed the gloves slowly and let them fly into the crowd. With bare hands placed on the vanity top, the dancers rose and inched closer to each other, inspecting the reflection that should have been there. Closer and closer the pair drew to each other until only a breath separated them from each other.

When the crescendo proclaimed that the chorus had arrived the two stepped away from the prop and twirled and stomped their way around the stage. Each and every step they took was determined and full of intent—the intent being to arouse and seduce every man at their feet.

Little black pleated skirts barely reached the top of the thigh. Nick swallowed numerous times as he watched them both move closer and closer. Black garters ran the length of each leg, connecting the striped, sheer stockings under the skirt. Connected them to what, Nick wondered and then realized he didn't care.

His knowledge of lingerie ran as far as the occasional Victoria Secret catalog placed in their mailbox by mistake. Those were good months.

Stiletto boots sheathed the long, trim legs that descended the stairs in time with the music. Those black patent encasements laced all the way to the knee looked both sexy and dangerous at the same time. An image of the dancer in nothing but the boots flashed before Nick's eyes and he felt his cock jump beneath his zipper. If this was any clue as to how the rest of the night was going to continue, he was in for a few hours of heaven and hell, either one welcome.

As the two made their way to their respective side of the stage, Nick was grateful they'd found an open seat near the stage. The long-legged, raven-haired goddess, with the fuck-me mouth, fuck-me eyes, fuck-me everything was right on top of them. Nick found that the garters connected underneath a pair of ruffled, red boy shorts that barely covered the firm little bottom peeking out from beneath the skirt.

Nick watched her transfixed. She swayed, dipped and thrust to the beat as did the dancer behind her. He noticed that even though their backs were to each other the synchronization never ended.

He held his breath as she ran her hands down the front of the tight bustier top, releasing each clasp one by one on her way back to the top. Holding the top together with both hands she teased to the right of Nick's seat and then to the left only revealing a flash of caramel torso here and a hint of round breast there.

In the next instant, both dancers crouched down balancing on the stiletto heels of their boots and exposed what the red camisole has concealed. Covering most of the breast and the entire nipple was a red pasty shaped like a pair of lips. And they were right in Nick Kiel's face. He thought at that moment he could die a happy man. And in the next second wished he was a dead man. Then the realization came that he may in fact be a dead man come morning.

"Holy shit!" The words were out of his mouth before he could stop them. Even with the music blaring, the crowd's screams and Hayden whistling, she heard him. Her midnight bob swiveled toward him and those eyes her bangs tried to hide met his. Her mouth gaped open, her hands pulled the sides of the bustier together and she repeated his sentiment, "Holy shit."

Her voice was low and strangled and jumped a little. She kept staring at him. Nick wished he could disappear, and from the look on her face she wished the same thing. He felt Hayden's hands grasp his shoulders and shake him a bit. He couldn't pay attention to his brother. He couldn't take his eyes off her.

His brother must have realized, finally, that he was the only one at the table for two who was still enjoying themselves. Out of the corner of his eye, Nick saw Hayden's face sober a bit and then turn toward where his brother gazed.

Never having much tact and lacking the filter that most people had between their brains and their mouths, Hayden's exclamation was louder and higher pitched than either brother would have liked, "Holy fucking shit!"

Nick saw the girl jerk her eyes from brother to brother. She paled more, if it was possible. She risked a quick peek back at Nick and then inch by inch rose from her crouched, exposed position on the stage to her full height. Nick would pay for his next thought soon enough, but all he could think about was her encased legs, that seemed miles and miles long, wrapped tightly around his waist, clenching her to him. Those dewy, painted lips, even though set firm and unsmiling now, held promises of deep kisses that would run the length of a man's body over and over again. Yep, he was going to hell.

Quickly and with style, she turned on the stiletto heel and made her way, with her partner, back to where the whole thing had started. The lights dimmed once more, a cheer resounded and yells for more filled the area.

The only thing Nick heard was the sound of his own heartbeat and the rush of his blood from his jeans back to his head where it belonged. It took a minute. Hayden's words finally busted their way through Nick's frantic thoughts and he turned in his seat.

"Tell me that was not who I think it was. Tell me this is all some fucked up nightmare and we both are going to wake up any minute. Tell me. Lie to me if you have to. I can take it." Watching Hayden down the contents of the three beer bottles on the table made Nick's throat drier than it already was. He swallowed a few times and then made the decision to tell his brother, "You're right about one thing."

"What's that?" Hayden asked as he wiped his arm across his mouth.

"We're in a fucking nightmare."

"No shit." Hayden chuckled a bit but there was nothing funny about the situation. Nick knew that the wry laugh was Hayden's way of showing that he was nervous, and he had good reason to be. "What are we gonna do now?"

Nick shook his head. He didn't know what to do. She'd seen them. They'd seen her. There was no changing that.

"It was her, right? I mean," Hayden pulled his seat closer to his brother's and rested his arms on his thighs, whispering, as if anyone could hear him, "my brain didn't just make that up, did it?"

"No, that was her all right. Every last inch of her." Shit, he thought. *Shit, shit, shit, shit, shit!*

"Well shit!" Hayden said, throwing his hands over his head in frustration and what looked like defeat.

"My thoughts exactly."

"Willa?" Hayden inquired.

"Willa." Nodding his head and studying the table top, Nick Kiel gave his brother the one conformation in the world he did not want.

"Willa." As her name passed his lips, Hayden let his head drop to the table with a resounding thud. Nick glanced at him and felt the need to do the same. Who knew? Who knew that a simple, harmless night of beer, half-naked women and good-natured fun could turn into hell on Earth? It was just their luck.

Nick rolled his eyes toward the ceiling, rolled them back to his brother, who still had not lifted his head and then rolled them back into his head and closed his eyes.

I should have stayed at home, Nick chanted silently to himself over and over again. But he hadn't, and now he was screwed like nobody's business.

Chapter Two

After the stage was cast in shadows, Willa Tate, or Willow Reed as she was known to the patrons of The Garden, rushed off and pressed her body to the closest wall. Her breath came in short pants, her chest heaved and her heart rate escalated. Inhaling slowly, she did all she could to restore her breathing to normal.

As soon as she could easily take a breath and expel it, she darted past the curtains and down the narrow hallway that led to the dressing rooms. On her way she passed Little Red Riding Hood, two naughty nurses, a cheerleader complete with pompoms and an overly large man called Babe.

Babe called out a greeting and a compliment and all Willa could do in reply was throw up a hand. She was on a mission. A mission to bounce two cowboys out of The Garden faster than anyone could pass the ammunition. But to do that, she needed help. She needed Raven.

Reaching her dressing room, she turned the knob and forced the door open with more momentum than she would have liked. The door bounced against the wall and threatened to come back and smack her in the face.

Raven stood at one of the two vanities and visibly jumped at Willa's entrance. Standing there in nothing more than black leather and lace was the solution to Willa's problem.

"You need to come with me." Without further explanation, she grabbed one of Raven's arms and ran back toward the stage.

"Could you slow down a little? Neither one of us can afford a broken ankle at this point in time. Loved the new set by the way, the boots too." Raven was rambling, Willa paid her no attention. The warning about the shoes stuck in her mind though. She knew that running in stilettos was a no-no but desperate times called for desperate measures. Reaching the sheer curtains that hid backstage from the audience, Willa pulled the material to the side just enough so that she and Raven could clearly see the few tables lining the side of the stage.

"You see those two cowboys sitting right there?" Pointing a finger Willa indicated the table where Nick and Hayden were. *Dammit*, she thought. When Raven didn't reply to her question, she looked at her friend to urge the response along. Raven was squinting in the direction of the table. Willa rolled her eyes then grabbed the glasses that were hanging from the bodice of Raven's black corset. "Are you ever going to get contacts?"

Raven only shrugged and put on the glasses. Willa watched her scan the audience and then heard her ask, "Who am I looking at again?"

"The two cowboys sitting down front by the stage." Turning her head in the general direction, she saw that Hayden now sat with his head flat on the tabletop. She hoped he wasn't passed out drunk. She wanted both of them to be good and sober when she laid into them. Nick looked no worse for wear, a little pale, but gorgeous nonetheless.

"You're going to have to be a little more specific. We are in Texas. Everyone thinks they're a cowboy and dresses for the part." Willa couldn't argue with her affirmation. Many men liked to wear the hat but only a handful could claim to be the honest to goodness real thing.

"The two sitting at table eight." Jabbing her finger toward the table, she indicated a wide-eyed Nick and faceless Hayden. "As for the cowboy part, those two are the real deal. I don't think you can get any closer to real than them." The real deal Kiels. That is what they were called in her hometown, the "real deal".

"Nice." Raven said as she continued to stare at Nick's profile and what little of Hayden's face that was visible now from the chin up. "Friends of yours?"

"Hardly." Willa chewed her bottom lip after she answered. Were they friends? They used to be. Gone were the boys she'd left behind and in their places where two drop-dead-sexy men. Frayed blue jeans, work-worn boots and T-shirts that molded every bump and plain of their chests reaffirmed that they were no longer the two boys who had dogged her steps and bent to her every whim. They were men, sexy men. They both looked just like their brother. From the chocolate hair to the long, muscular legs, they looked just like him. *Dammit.*

"Too bad." Raven held the curtains now and was in the middle of drinking in the attributes the two held. After further evaluation she said, "What's wrong with that one right there? Is he sick or something?" Hayden's head was still more on the table than not and he looked as pale as Nick had a moment ago.

"He's not sick. I think he may be in shock." Willa left Raven at the curtain and paced. She needed to do something. They needed to leave. She had three more sets to do and come hell or high water, she was not doing them in front of those two.

"In shock? You don't think they have ever seen a half-naked woman before?"

"I'm sure they have." Willa took her place next to Raven again and stared. "But I'm sure this is the first time they have ever seen the girl who, at one point in time, was supposed to be their sister-in-law in nothing more than a couple of pasties and a nice pair of ruffled shorts."

"Uh-oh." The "uh-oh" was muttered with little or no feeling behind it. It seemed like an afterthought or something said for lack of a better word, then reality set in. "Uh-oh!"

Her eyes were wide when they met Willa's. She started to say something, looked back at the table, started to speak again and then bit her bottom lip when there was nothing else to do.

"What are you going to do?"

"I've got to get them out of here." Willa walked away from the curtains, leaving Raven to drool and stare a little more. She couldn't blame her. It was a nice way to pass the time. She was halfway to the stage's side door when Raven caught her.

"How are you going to do that?"

Willa stopped. Turing slowly on her six-inch stilettos, she smiled at her friend. "I'm not going to. You are."

"Uh-oh." Was all Raven could reply.

✳

Nick should have been impressed with the tall blonde cheerleader shaking her pompoms in his general direction. Hell, he loved cheerleaders. Long, tan legs, breasts large, full and threatening to burst from her tiny top and a bow that barely covered the tanned globes of a great ass. But impressed Nick was not.

Each and every time he closed his eyes he saw her. Her standing in front of him with nothing on but those boots. He shook his head and tried to clear the thoughts that lingered. He reminded himself time after time, "It's Willa. Chase's Willa. Your brother's Willa." No matter how many times he repeated those words, they did nothing to relieve the massive hardening he felt beneath his zipper. At this rate he would bust his fly before ever leaving The Garden.

Nick ran a shaky hand over his face, picked up one of the forgotten beer bottles from the table and took a healthy swallow. Two more long gulps and the drink was gone and Nick was in desperate need of another one. Maybe with enough alcohol the images traveling through his mind would dim and his cock would relax.

"I need a beer." Hayden lifted his head from where it had been lying and scratched his overly long hair, causing it to shift and stand on top of his head.

"My thoughts exactly." Raising a hand, Nick caught the eye of the cute little waitress who had been more than attentive the entire night. She caught his gesture, smiled and made her way to one of the bars that lined the club.

He watched her stroll to the bar, prop one flared hip against it and wait patiently for her order to be filled. She looked in his and Hayden's direction and smiled. It was a warm smile, one without seduction or sensuality attached to it. Her smile had the same effect on Nick that Willa's image had. There was something wrong with him. Every female in here was causing him to nearly bust the seams of his pants.

He squirmed a bit in his seat, smiled back at her and tried to watch the show that was going on close by. Easier said than done. Bored once again by the cheerleader, he scanned the audience hoping to see the woman who would torment his mind for days, if not weeks to come.

Several dancers mingled with the crowd. They laughed with some of the customers, flirted with the others, but all in all seemed to enjoy what the night had to offer. A movement from the left caught Nick's eye and he twisted in his chair to get a better look.

What he saw made his mouth go dry and his Adam's apple bob uncontrollably. Walking in even, long, sultry strides was a vision decked out from head to toe in nothing more than black leather, a little bit of lace and a whole lot of skin. From her high-heeled boots that laced up her calves to the demi-mask that concealed half her face, she was a walking wet dream. If anyone could take his mind off Willa, this one could. And she was coming their way.

When Nick realized her destination his throat closed a bit and his pants tightened painfully. As she came closer, he took in more of her appearance as it became visible. A mass of ebony curls sat upon her head and draped down her narrow back. The mask hid most of her face, but the part it didn't hide revealed lush, pink lips and a smile that could drop a man to his knees.

A black corset showed off a slim waist and breasts that slightly swayed beneath the tight material as she walked. Fingerless, lace gloves ended at her wrist and emphasized her sun-kissed arms. Her shoulders were bare and Nick noticed a dusting of freckles along them. He was a sucker for freckles, he wondered where else on her body the dusting appeared.

She stopped for a brief second, spoke to one of the other girls but never took her eyes off of him. Her smile increased as she talked and watched him. She whispered something to the Indian princess she spoke to and the girl turned. She smiled at them also.

The vision in black wrapped her arm around the princess's waist and led her away from the party of men she was entertaining. Both were now headed right in Nick and Hayden's direction. Nick popped his brother with the back of his hand, connecting with a firm, hard shoulder that made a smacking sound under the material of his shirt.

"What!" Hayden said, rubbing the sting from his flesh. Nick couldn't speak. He couldn't put two sounds together. All he could do was nod. He hoped his brother would follow the nod's direction. He did. Nick saw Hayden stiffen in his seat and heard his intake of breath. Before he could release the breath both of the beauties stood before them. The princess spoke first.

"Mind if we sit down?" Her voice was as sweet as honey and

Nick wondered if she tasted as sweet as she sounded. At her request, Hayden pushed a chair from the table with his booted foot then jumped from his own offering it to Pocahontas. The vacant chair closest to Nick was now occupied by the vixen in black. He couldn't take his eyes off of her. She was giving him the same attention he was giving her. Her mouth was set in a slight grin. A knowing grin. A grin that told Nick she knew what the tablecloth hid.

"Which one of you..." The sound of her voice made Nick's body tense. It was low and husky, a voice a man wanted to hear in bed—morning, noon or night. It didn't matter which as long as he heard it, "...is Nick?"

If she had slapped him in the face he wouldn't have been more surprised. He cleared his throat, prayed he could speak and then uttered, "I am."

She smiled. "Then that makes you..." she pointed a red nail at his brother, "...Hayden." Nick saw Hayden's eyes widen and his throat work before he nodded his chocolate-colored head.

"Yes, ma'am."

Nick rolled his eyes. What a time for his brother to develop manners.

"I'm Raven." *Raven.* It suited her, almost as well as the leather did. "I have a message for you two."

"From who?" Hayden asked the question before Nick had a chance.

"From my friend and yours."

"Willa?" Nick asked, hoping. Raven nodded once in acknowledgment and then continued.

"There is a diner down the road. Two miles down on the left. You can't miss it. You two need to be there in half an hour. You may want to think about making your way out of here as soon as you can." With her errand complete, Raven rose from the chair and took Pocahontas with her. The cryptic message only produced more questions for Nick's already spinning head. He called out to her as she turned to leave and grabbed one of her silky arms.

She glanced down at his grip and shook his arm off as easily as she would have a drop of water.

"Is Willa going to be there?" He saw her eyes narrow then become round and slightly dreamy again. She leaned down to him, her face hovering just above his. To anyone observing the two it would look like she might kiss him. But she didn't. She moved those swollen lips to his ear and whispered, "Why wouldn't she be?"

Nick thought he felt the brush of velvet against his earlobe. It was there and then it was gone just as she was. Without another word or explanation, she left, the Indian princess following in her wake. He sat and stared for long moments after she had disappeared.

"What'd she say?" Hayden pressed. Nick shook his head, lifted his tall frame from the chair and maneuvered himself around the rest of the tables toward the front entrance. He never looked to see if Hayden followed. He could feel him there.

Making their way to the large Chevrolet truck, both brothers jerked open their respective doors and slid into the cab. With a roar of pipes and a quick turn of the wheel, Nick angled the vehicle toward the diner they had seen on the way in. Neither brother spoke during the short drive. What was there to say? Nick hoped that she would be waiting when they arrived, though he highly doubted it. If he knew one thing about Willa it was that she waited on no one and everyone waited on her.

Chapter Three

"What in the hell are you two doing here?" Willa smacked the top of the table as she asked her question. Two sets of eyes flew to hers but neither responded. They just stared. "What? Cat got your tongue?" When the two still didn't reply, she slid into the booth next to Hayden and faced Nick.

"We could ask you the same question."

Willa jerked her head to the "boy" who sat beside her. She used the term *boy* very loosely when referring to Hayden Kiel. She was pressed hip to hip with him in the tiny booth and she could feel that he was no longer a "boy". That had been apparent in the club not an hour ago. Willa hated to admit it, but she had caught sight of the bulge that sat in the front of his pants. Nope, he was not a boy.

"I guess you could." Willa propped her elbows on the table and covered her eyes. It wasn't until her fingertips grazed the blunt tips of her bangs that she realized she still wore the black flapper style wig from her last set. With the practiced grace of a person who wore a wig regularly, she pulled the shiny bob from her head, revealing her natural blonde locks beneath it.

Her long, wheat-color hair was braided and pinned tightly to her head so that each wig would sit smoothly and look as if it were her own hair. She caught Hayden staring as she removed pin after pin from the tight mass.

"What?" She stopped momentarily to ask her question and then released the braided mass and shook it out with a hand. Long waves reached her shoulders and drifted down her back. Hayden looked stunned and a question looked to be on the tip of his tongue. "What?"

"How do you get all that under there?"

Willa set her mouth in a thin line, huffed a bit and said, "Do you really want me to go over the fundamentals of hair binding with you?"

"Have you been here the whole time?" Nick's voice sounded haunted to Willa's ears. It had changed over the years, just like everything else. She thought at first that everything might have gone back to the way it had once been, but she knew better now. The look in Nick's eyes, the low voice he spoke in and the stare he penetrated her with were all awful reminders of the distance between them.

"Here? As in The Garden?" Willa watched as he nodded his head. "No. I got the job there about a year after I left."

"You mean ran away." His voice was deliberate and accusing. She couldn't blame him. Truth be told, that is what she had done. She had run away, hard and fast as she could.

"Runaway, left, took off...they're all the same." Running her hands through her hair, massaging the aching scalp, she watched him. He was looking at her the way Chase used to look at her. All knowing, all seeing. He could read her. He could anticipate her. It was time for her to change tactics.

"What the hell made you two decide to honor The Garden with a grand Kiel appearance anyway?" She knew she sounded snooty and snide but she didn't care, staying one step ahead of these two was just like just like staying one step ahead of their brother all those years before.

"We thought it would be fun?"

Willa glanced at Hayden and saw that he stared at Nick.

"Well? Did you have fun? Did I earn my paycheck?"

"Hell yeah." Hayden supplied a little too enthusiastically. It earned him a hard look and a kick under the table from his brother. "That was until you showed up." He cleared his throat and dropped his gaze to the scarred Formica.

"Until I showed up? I work there. I get paid to show up. And unlike you two, it's legal for me to be there." She crossed her arms over her breasts and leaned back into the cushion the booth held, what little was still there after forty years of truckers, dancers and late night travelers. "How did you two get in anyway? I did the math. You," she indicated Nick, "may be old enough by a day or two, but you," she jabbed Hayden in the bulky biceps with her cotton-candy fingernail, "are barely this side of jailbait."

Nick's eyes never left hers. He meant to intimidate her, but it wasn't going to work. If she'd learned anything in the past few years it was how not to be intimidated. Hayden on the other hand, couldn't look her in the face. He could however look her straight in the breasts.

"Are you going to answer my question or not?"

"You going to answer ours?"

Willa shot Nick a look telling him with her eyes that she didn't like his tone and he needed to change it. The better side of three years ago, the look would have worked. It wasn't working today though.

"I want to know how you got into The Garden. When you answer my question I'll answer yours."

"We have IDs." Hayden supplied.

"Whose IDs?" Willa replied.

"Ours."

"Liar." The comment came from her mouth in a low whisper. She mouthed the word more than she said it.

"We kind of borrowed a couple for the night." Hayden worried a place on the table as he made his confession.

"You mean stole," Willa said with a laugh behind her words.

"I mean borrowed. They'll have them back before we hit the range tomorrow." The second he spoke he looked as if he had swallowed his tongue. Willa did laugh then.

"You stole *their* driver's licenses. Oh, I'll tell you what, I didn't think you had it in you." She couldn't stop herself from laughing. It had taken guts for these two to steal or borrow anything from Brent and Jason. "If they find out they will have your balls in a vice."

"They'll never find out. Hopefully." Hayden looked nervous when he finally spoke. Evidently he knew the penalty that would be inflicted if they were caught.

"He was worried about you. We all were."

Willa heart contracted at the mention of *him*.

"You could have called and told us you were okay."

She could have but she hadn't.

"Would that have made it any better?"

"It would have helped."

"It would have been like dangling a red flag in front of a

raging bull." The bull being Chase Kiel. If she had ever called or written Chase would have been on her trail quicker than lightening, for a while anyway. Willa couldn't stop the next question from passing her lips. "How is he?" She didn't have the guts to ask the question to their faces so she spoke to her hands instead.

Moments passed while they each seemed to weigh their responses. When they came Willa wished for more.

"Good."

"Fine."

"You going to tell him you saw me?" Again, a period of silence followed her question. She cut her downcast eyes in Nick's direction and saw that he was weighing his response carefully. When he finally gave his answer, twin pains of relief and remorse filled her body.

"No."

Willa felt Hayden tense a bit and then watched him relax under his brother's glare.

"Thank you." What else could she say? Why not? How come? She didn't want him to find her, did she? The thought of seeing Chase again frightened and excited a part in Willa, as it always did. There were nights when she wished he would come for her. Times when she wished she could touch him once more. Nights that she wished she could feel his touch again. But they were only wishes, wishes that would never be granted.

"On one condition." Nick's statement pulled Willa from her thoughts of Chase. Chase's face. Chase's lips. Chase's tongue and of all the promises it had made. Her body shook a bit with the faint memory then she regained herself.

"What condition?"

"I...We want to know that you're okay. I want to hear from your mouth that you're okay and don't need anything." He was sweet. Nick had always been her protector. From the first night Chase had brought her home to meet the entire Kiel brood, until the night she slipped out of Millbrook under the cover of darkness, Nick was always ready to fight for her.

"How exactly do you plan on doing that?" Willa's mind raced. She had to be careful, or did she? Enough time had passed now that it probably didn't matter if Chase knew where she was or wasn't. But Willa, being cautious, didn't feel like testing the waters just yet.

"I want you to call."

"Not going to happen. I'm not about to call your house and risk your brother, any brother, answering that phone. No way. Try again."

"You can call my phone." Nick leaned back in the booth and retrieved a cell phone from his pocket. "I'll give you my number and when you get ready to call I'll be ready to talk. I don't care if you talk for a minute or an hour; I just want to know that everything is alright and that you're alright." His eyes were as sincere as his voice. Willa chewed her lip a bit and took her own phone from her pocket.

"Give me the number." Nick gave her the digits and she entered them into her phone's log. She closed the flip of the phone, looked at both of them once more, trying to etch the new faces into her memory and scooted from the booth. She started to leave, paused, and turned. She couldn't stop her next action. Even if she could have stopped herself she wouldn't have. Leaning over the table, she placed a kiss on Hayden's cheek then on Nick's. She then let her hand linger in Nick's hair, loving the feel of the silky smooth texture as it glided across her fingers. "You need a haircut."

She placed another kiss on his forehead, smiled and winked at Hayden and walked out of the diner. It was the second time in her life she had left the Kiels behind. On her way back to The Garden, she realized that the second time was just as hard as the first.

She kept her tears at bay as long as she could. Turing into her driveway, well after four the morning, feeling drained and heavy limbed, Willa Tate let her heavy head fall to the steering wheel and cried just as she had one night years ago.

Her tears came easily and heaving sobs of regret came with them. Opening the car door allowed the wind to nip at her tear-streaked face. She didn't remember walking into her house or collapsing into bed. She didn't know how long she cried before drifting off into a dreamless sleep. All she knew was that her heart was breaking and she didn't know how to fix it or if it had ever been fixed before.

Chapter Four

The dream was always the same. It hadn't changed. He tossed and turned as the images became clearer in his sleepy mind.

It was summer. The air was hot and carried only a whisper of wind, but that wind had caught her hair and swept it across her face. She laughed a whimsical distant laugh of youth and innocence. Then she looked at him and her eyes darkened.

She came willingly into his arms, pressing herself comfortably into his body and allowing him to lay her gently into the grass. They were beneath the large oak tree in the west pasture. The lake a few feet away rippled and played with the air. He brushed her face with his fingertips and she followed his movements. Her eyes closed and a soft moan passed her lips. Those lips. He saw her tongue dart across the puffy plains of her lips as she waited for him. She was always waiting for him.

He lowered his head and gave her mouth what it wanted. His. He was tender at first with the flesh, but bit by bit his control slipped and he devoured. After a few seconds of savoring her lips, he let his tongue move past the seam they created and into the warm, sweet depths of her mouth.

She tempted him with her tongue. She repeated her motions time after time. She would lick his bottom lip, nip it with her teeth and then draw it into hers and suck lightly as her body arched toward his.

She wanted him. As badly as he wanted her. He moved his hand to her stomach, under the flimsy material of her shirt and flirted with the flesh. She moaned into his mouth and moved her lower body against his thigh. He felt the heat and the dampness even through the denim they both wore.

In the next instant they were skin to skin, body to body, hardness to softness. Her nipples were puckered and begged for attention. He obliged them. He let his tongue sweep the first one, coating it with moisture and then pulled it into his mouth and sucked greedily at the tip. She arched and moaned and pushed the peak deeper. He moaned.

With one nipple in his mouth and the other being rolled between a finger and a thumb, he teased and teased until she was writhing beneath him. Satisfied he had paid ample attention to the swollen flesh of her breasts, he made his way down her damp body.

Reaching his destination, he spread her long, honey-colored legs and found the spot that he fantasized about. Her taste was addictive. It lingered on the tongue and in the senses for days. It made him hard and ready. He was ready now, but he had to be patient. He had to take care. He had to make her wet. Wetter than ever so that she could take him. Take all of him.

He let his tongue flirt with her inner thighs, inching higher with each stroke. Her fingertips grazed the stubble on his face and he turned his head slightly and took one into his mouth. He licked the tip, lapped the length and then nipped at it as she had his lips. She gasped and her hips bucked and he returned his attention to the flesh inbetween her thighs.

She was wet. So wet. Her lips were coated with moisture, moisture he caused. A sense of pride and possessiveness swelled inside him. She was his. After today there would be no question of it. He blew a quick breath over her dewy flesh and saw the cream between her lips increase. He was a man possessed.

He lowered his head and traced his tongue along her slit. She brought her hips to meet his mouth. She moaned with encouragement. His tongue dipped, glided, plunged into the sweet nectar of her body. His fingers parted the flesh beneath his hungry mouth and found the swollen piece of flesh he hunted.

He took it into his mouth. On contact, her body tightened, her legs squeezed and the muscles of her pussy contracted. She was close. He backed away and kissed her thighs again. She gripped his shoulders, painfully digging her short nails into muscle. He heard a word cross the barrier of her lips, "More." He smiled and caressed her flesh with his tongue. She pulled at his shoulders, drawing the length of his body against hers. They both groaned when their lips connected. This kiss was not gentle or teasing. They fed off each other.

"Can you taste yourself on my mouth?"

Her eyes, still dreaming and at half–mast, flared at his words and then she nodded.

"Do you like the taste?" She seemed shy for a moment and he took the opportunity to ease a finger into her slick, tight, waiting pussy. So tight, he thought. She could kill him. Squeeze him to death, milk the life out of him. What a way to go, buried balls deep inside of her.

She tightened around his finger. He withdrew it and thrust again. She was so small, so taut. He needed to stretch her more so that when he pressed his length deep inside as little pain as possible came along with it. But she was wet and getting wetter by the minute. He removed his finger from her opening and she whimpered.

He then did something that made her eyes widen and her breath quicken. He traced her lips with the wet finger. "Lick your lips."

She looked at him, confused, scared, aroused.

"Lick your lips for me, baby."

She did as he requested and he felt his cock jump against his stomach as she did. She traced each coated lip once, then again, removing all the traces of herself from them.

"You like that?"

She nodded.

"Good," he replied, before letting his finger pass through her lips into her mouth. She didn't hesitate. She held his wrist so that he couldn't take it away. His gaze met hers and he felt himself grow harder.

"I want more." Her voice passed his ears and affected his cock. She licked down the side of his finger, back up and then down the opposite side. She smiled at him. He couldn't help but smile back.

"You want more?" he teased.

She nodded and confirmed, "I. Want. More."

Before he knew her intent, she rose to her knees and pushed him to his back. The blanket he had laid down was soft and warm against his back and she was soft and warm against his front. She lifted her face to his and sipped at his lips.

"I thought you wanted more?" He traced his hands along the line of her back, down her sides and rested on the smooth contours of her ass. He squeezed the round, firm globes and pulled her closer to him.

She braced her hands against his chest and ran them through the light swirls of hair. The movement of her fingers across his torso caused his muscles to contract. She glided her fingertips across his collarbone and let them drift to his flat, darkened nipples.

"I do. I want more of you." She lowered her mouth to his body and tasted him just as he had tasted her. She let her tongue flick against his nipple making it harden. Without pause she took it into her eager mouth. She moaned and the sound hit his insides. She gave his other nipple the same treatment as the first and then blazed a trail down his body and stopped at his navel.

He grabbed her shoulders and searched her eyes. "What are you doing?"

She smiled, flattened her tongue against his quivering lower belly and said, "You tasted me, now I want to taste you."

His head fell back against the blanket as his hands guided her lower and lower until she hovered above his straining cock. He opened his eyes and watched as she took it in her hand. It wasn't the first time she had touched him, but it was the first time she had touched him with her mouth. It wasn't the first time he had thought about the possibility.

She moved her hand from the base to the tip, causing a pearl of fluid to appear at the opening. The next thing he knew the tip of his cock was being treated to velvety strokes. One after the other. She licked the drop away and then licked her own lips. Her eyes caught his.

His hands moved to the side of her face and lowered her gaping mouth to his waiting flesh. He felt it throb in her mouth as she lightly sucked. She had no rhythm to her stoke and it drove him crazy. She would take as much as she could and then deny him the warmth of her mouth as she licked around the engorged head.

He fisted his hands in her hair and started to release them, scared that he may be hurting her. Her moan stopped his action. He tightened his hold and felt her take him into her throat. His hips bucked. He thrust shallowly into her mouth at first, and then *increased the depth as she increased the suction around him.*

Her hands were braced on his thighs, holding her body above his. Never breaking his rhythm, he thrust into her mouth. He took one of her hands and wrapped it around the base of his erection He then showed her how to pump. His hand covered hers and they both moved his flesh more into her wanting mouth.

"Harder." He moaned. Her eyes flew to his, questioning.

"Suck me harder."

She did as he requested. She sucked harder and took him deeper with each thrust. He felt his sac tighten and knew that at any second he would release himself into her mouth. He wanted to, but he didn't want to startle her by doing that. "Baby, you've got to stop." Her only reply was to moan. The vibration caused a jolt through his body. He tried to tear himself from her mouth but she wouldn't let him.

"Baby, if you don't stop I'm going to come in that pretty, little mouth of yours." He felt her smile against his dick. She wanted it. She wanted him to come. She wanted to make him come. Anything she wanted he gave her.

He let his head fall back to the blanket, his eyes drifted closed and he let her suck him off. Seconds later, he felt hot spurts of his orgasm fill her mouth. She took every drop.

Chase Kiel came awake with a groan and with his cock in his hand. His breath was ragged and heavy. Looking around his room, he found it draped in the pre-dawn shadows. His body was covered with a thin layer of sweat, his sheets had been pushed to his knees and his hand and stomach were covered with evidence of his release.

"Shit," he muttered. Kicking the covers further down his legs, he lifted himself from the rumpled sheets of the bed. He walked to his bathroom and flipped on the light. The intense glow caused him to squint. Making his way to the sink, he grabbed a towel that lay on the counter and turned on the faucet.

He washed away the traces of fulfillment from his hands and then rubbed the damp towel across his hard belly. He threw the used towel in the hamper, turned the light off and made his way back to bed.

It wasn't the first time he had woken up this way. It happened more times than he liked to admit to. It was Willa. Three years later, even by way of a foggy dream, she had the same effect on him—cock-hardening.

He passed by the mirror of his dresser and looked at himself. At twenty-eight, he looked tired. His hair was still the dark hue it had been years ago. Gray had yet to overcome the tresses. His body was still hard. He hadn't gone to flab around the middle like some of his classmates from high school. He attributed that to running the ranch. Seven days a week of riding fence lines, branding and vaccinating cattle and breaking the occasional stubborn colt kept him hard. Kept him as hard as Willa kept him at night.

He shook his head at his reflection and moved toward the inviting bed. Maybe an hour more of blissful sleep would pull her image from his mind. He doubted it, but it was worth a try.

He heard a door slam and he moved the curtain from the window to see who had caused the noise. There they were.

Nick and Hayden made their way across the yard, toward the porch of the house. One of the dogs that had taken up residence at the ranch greeted each with a nose to the groin. Hayden paused and petted the beast before taking the steps two at a time into the house.

Where in the hell have they been? They had both disappeared last night early in the evening. Nick he didn't worry about. Hayden he did. Hayden was so much like his brother Jason it was hard to tell what he might get himself into. Hayden always did better with Nick dogging his steps.

Wherever they had been they were no worse for wear. He heard them both climb the stairs and shut their bedroom doors. At least they made it up the stairs. There had been times in his youth, around Nick and Hayden's ages, when he, Brent and Jason had all slept on the porch, in the barn or in the truck because they couldn't make it any further.

Chase wondered at times how they had made it home. But those days were long gone. He'd stopped the hell raising he was used to when he met Willa. Hell, he stopped them the first time he saw her.

She'd spilled coffee on him. She'd burned his hand. She'd kissed it to make it better. He could still see her face when she'd realized what she had done. Her cheeks tinted the prettiest red color, her blue eyes twinkled as she laughed at herself and Chase Kiel had fallen in love.

At the time, she was seventeen to his twenty-two. He waited

for her. Waited until she was eighteen, waited until it was more respectable for them to see each other, waited until her aunt gave her consent to date him, waited for her to come to him. And she did. He spent three years courting her, wooing her, taking his time with her. He proposed, then she'd run—run faster than a scalded dog.

Three years, two months and one day later, Chase still didn't know why she'd run away. He had looked for her and every lead had ended with him coming up empty. He still thought of her, often. He still cared for her, too much, way too much. And he still loved her, against his better judgment. Loving her was the worst part of it all. How could a man hold on to someone who didn't want to be held? It was a question Chase Kiel would have given his bank account for, many times over, to find an answer to.

✶

"Will you snap out of it all ready?" Nick growled, trying to penetrate Hayden's hung-over mind.

"Man, I'm trying." He lifted a limb from the fence line and threw it on the ever-growing pile.

"What's with you anyway?" Nick heard him grumble something and stopped. Hayden walked to the back of the truck, grabbed one of the coolers of water they had brought with them and poured it over his head.

"I can't get her titties out of my head. Every time I close my eyes that's all I see." He wiped the hair hanging in his face away. "Man, if you could see the dreams I had." He shook his head as he whistled slowly.

"Stop it, dumbass." Nick brought the spout of the cooler to his mouth and took a healthy gulp. He hadn't drunk as many beers as Hayden had, but he still felt the effects of the night before. In every inch of his cock. If Willa wasn't enough to throw his hormones into a rage, Raven was. Hayden's dreams may have been erotic, but Nick was sure his own were illegal.

Nick put the palms of his hands to his eyes and pressed. Leather, lace, stiletto heels and welcoming mouths were all he saw. He growled again.

"You gotta quit that. You sound like that old bulldog we used to have. All he did was sit on his ass and growl, remember what happened to him?"

Nick did and glared at Hayden who was now smiling.

"Are we gonna have to neuter you too?" Hayden laughed at his brother. Nick ignored him and pulled the worn, leather work gloves back on. He clenched the wrist of one in his teeth and pulled. Leather. God, Nick thought. He was so screwed. He rubbed his face again and followed Hayden back to the fence row.

"When are we going back?" Hayden said with a grunt. Nick stopped and just stared at his brother.

"'Going back?' We're not going back." And they weren't. For Willa sake, or for theirs, Nick hadn't figured that part out yet.

"Why the hell not?" He dropped his end of the branch, making Nick drop his.

Nick swung around and glared at him. "Because I said so." He attempted to pick up the fallen branch and realized that it was too heavy for just one of them to carry. "You gonna help me or what?"

"Nope."

"Why the hell not?" He faced Hayden, hands on his hips, eyes squinted against the sun. Hayden only shrugged.

"Why can't we go back? She didn't say we couldn't. I think it made her feel good that we were there."

"If you think that you're dumber than I thought." He attempted to lift the limb by himself but then gave up with a frustrated sigh and kicked it instead.

"Am I?"

"Yeah. Dumb as a box of fucking rocks." Nick made his way back to the fence and grabbed a limb he could carry.

"What makes you say that?"

"If you think for one minute that she actually enjoyed seeing us, there is something severely wrong with you."

"I think she did. I think she liked seeing us. I know she liked seeing me. Now your ugly ass, maybe not so much." He was baiting him. Nick knew it but it still rubbed him wrong. He didn't want to be rubbed right now. He wanted to clear the fence row, get back to the house and close himself up in his room with nothing more than himself and his thoughts. Thoughts of leather, lace, stilettos and mouths.

"I think she put up with us to get us out of there. You saw

how she ran off that stage like someone was chasing her. You really want her to have to look out in the crowd again and see the two of us sitting there staring back at her?"

Hayden thought about Nick's question for a minute and then said, "Why don't you call her and ask?"

"How in the hell am I supposed to do that, shit for brains? I don't have her number. I gave her mine." He had done that for a reason, thinking that if it were her decision, she would call. Hopefully. Maybe.

"Well, when she calls ask her if we can come back." Hayden picked up his end of the fallen branch and waited for Nick to do the same. He did and, grunting under the weight of the branch, said, "She's not going to call."

"What makes you think that?"

"We haven't heard from her in years."

"So?" He grunted and Nick groaned as they tossed yet another branch away from the fence.

"So?"

"Yeah, so?"

Nick wiped his forehead with the back of his arm and stared at his brother who was worrying a rock with the toe of his boot. "She won't call." He was sure she wouldn't but there was a chance. "What makes you think she's going to call us?"

"Because she wants to know about Chase." Hayden's declaration stopped Nick in his tracks. He turned and gave his brother a look begging him to explain.

"All I'm saying is she wanted more than what she got last night from us."

"What did she get from us?"

"Not shit. That's why she'll call. And if she doesn't we can always call the club. You still have that brochure, right?" Hayden left the rock alone and went back to work.

Nick nodded. Hayden knew he still had it. Safe and sound in the glove box of his truck.

"After seeing her last night, I understand now why he had such a hard time getting over her. I mean can you image having that in your bed. I can and I like it." Hayden laughed to himself and tossed a few willowy branches over his head.

"Fucking or lack thereof was not the reason he had the time he did." Nick remembered. He remembered how Chase used to look at her. The way he'd patiently waited for her to turn eighteen. The way he'd paced around the house the night he proposed to her. He also remembered the nights after she left when Chase had come home drunk and cussing her. Not many men cussed a good fuck and nothing more.

"It had to be one of the reasons. You don't remember hearing them? I do. The walls weren't thick enough to keep out her screams and I was three doors down. Man, I worship him and envy Brent for having the bedroom next door."

"Shut up, stupid." Nick gave Hayden a playful shove and moved past him.

"I know you heard them. How could you not?" In a falsetto voice Hayden continued, "'More, more. Yes, yes, more'." He whistled and covered his heart with his hand. "A woman after my own heart." Nick laughed.

"How's that?"

"Any woman whose favorite words are 'more' and 'yes' is the kind I want in my bed. Of course, Chase wasn't any better. I swear to God I have never heard a guy scream like that. Scared me to death at first. I thought she was killing him, but what a way to go." With his last thought he collapsed to the ground.

Nick laughed at the picture he made. Laid out in the dirt, one hand over his heart, the other over his eyes chanting over and over, "yes" and "more" in that damn voice of his.

"Something funny?"

Nick turned quickly to find Chase sitting astride the large sorrel gelding he called Bandit. He heard Hayden scramble to his feet and then felt him standing beside him.

Chase had a smile on his tanned face but Nick figured it would disappear if he knew what they were both laughing about. No man wanted to hear how he screamed in bed, no matter how good it had felt at the time.

"Nothing," both of them replied at the same time. Nick saw Chase's eyes narrow and his mouth set in a thin line. Nick tried his best to explain the situation without betraying their real conversation. "You know this idiot—can't ever get him to act right."

Hayden giggled that damn nervous giggle of his. If anything, that would make Chase even more curious.

If he was curious, he never let it be known. He dismounted the horse, walked him so that he could relax in the shade and turned back to his brothers and the work they were doing.

"Looks good," Chase said, inspecting what part of the fence row was clear. "We had quite a wind storm last night. Of course, you two wouldn't know, would you?"

Nick swallowed, feeling a bit of guilt well up inside of him and Hayden kicked yet another rock that lay at his feet.

"Where did you two run off to?"

Hayden raked a hand through his hair and gave Nick a shove on the shoulder.

"Out," was all Nick could say. He heard Hayden groan and looked at him as if to ask, *you got a better answer?* Hayden gave a little shrug and went and petted Bandit on the neck. The horse, enjoying the attention, pushed his giant head closer to the moving hand.

"Out, huh?"

Nick just nodded. What could he say? *We went to a bar we heard about hoping to see some ass and titties and we did. They just happened to belong to the girl you wanted to marry. She looks great by the way. Hayden can't get her titties out of his head.* Yeah, that would go over well.

"Well it must have been a hell of a time. You didn't roll in until nearly four. I never thought I would see y'all out this morning. Damned sure wouldn't have seen me."

Hayden gave another nervous chuckle and Nick inwardly groaned. *Idiot,* he thought.

"Anyway," Chase said, moving away from the fence and toward where Nick stood. "How long you reckon you two will be out here?"

Nick looked at the fence and at the limbs that still lay across it. Then he took in the amount of fence that had been broken and was sagging and answered his brother, "A couple more hours at least. We need to get these fences back up so that Brent and Jason can move the herd into this pasture tomorrow morning."

Moving cattle was part of ranching. Every so often the herd had to be moved so that they didn't overgraze the land. Overgrazing caused too many problems and problems were something Chase didn't want on his ranch.

"Well, I've gotta meet someone in town in the next twenty minutes or so, and I don't want to be late. I need to borrow your truck. I'll be back before you two knotheads are even close to being finished."

Nick nodded again, walked to the bed of the truck and removed their coolers.

Chase passed him and asked, "Keys in it?"

"Yep." Nick replied as he placed the coolers beneath the large oak tree where Hayden was standing still petting the mammoth Chase called a horse.

"I'll see you two in a little bit." He pulled himself into the cab and slammed the door. He turned the ignition and leaned out of the window saying "By the way, family dinner tonight, so don't disappear. Mom wants us to be at her house at eight." Their mother, her new husband and his daughter lived thirty miles away from the Kiel ranch. "Do you two think you can stay out of trouble long enough for us to have a family dinner?"

The younger boys both nodded.

"Good." He drove slowly through the pasture before hitting the dirt path that led to the paved road. When he was out of sight and definitely out of ear-shot, Hayden asked, "How much do you reckon he heard?"

"I don't know. I'm pretty sure he got here around, 'More please, more'. Asshole." Nick said, shoving him again.

"You don't think he knew what we were talking about do you?"

Nick thought on it a minute, decided Chase couldn't have, and reassured his brother "No, if he had, you'd be a dead man right now and I would be digging your final resting place instead of replacing this fence."

Hayden nodded his head in agreement. Smiling again, he chased after Nick and in the same shrill falsetto voice repeated, "More, please, more."

"Stop it." Nick said, shoving Hayden away from him. Nick knew that Hayden gave it his best shot but he couldn't help himself.

The west pasture was filled with Hayden's voice shouting, "Give it to me, baby! Yes, yes, more, more."

It wasn't until much later that either one of them realized that Chase, the brochure from The Garden, complete with a vampy picture of Willa and Nick's cell phone were all in the same truck.

Chapter Five

The Garden opened its doors at ten p.m. sharp, never a moment before, never a moment after. Willa stood backstage behind the sheer curtains and watched as the tables started to fill. There were faces she recognized and faces she didn't, it was always the same.

"Looking for someone in particular?" Raven pushed the platinum locks of the wig Willa was sporting to the side and pressed their faces close together, allowing both of them a view of the growing crowd. Raven was still wearing her glasses, Willa noticed, so she could actually see the crowd instead of a blur.

"No."

"Liar." Raven laughed a rich, throaty laugh. She was right. Willa was looking for a familiar face in the crowd, a face she thought she would never hope to see again.

"Cheer up. It's still early they could show up yet. So did you grow a pair and call him like he wanted?" Raven patted her on the head like a child and then waltzed to the full length mirror set up for last minute adjustments.

"I did. But I didn't get an answer." Willa let the curtains fall back in place and made herself leave them alone. Walking to the mirror, Willa watched as Raven adjusted the straight, shoulder–length, black wig with the pink highlights. It suited her. Most things did. Raven could make gaudy look glamorous and slutty look sensual. Black was Raven's signature color, per Lady Sadora's request.

Lady Sadora, the owner of The Garden, made a lot of requests of her girls. It was her business. She was entitled. *Everything is an illusion.* Those were the words that Lady Sadora had spoken to Willa the day she'd gotten the job. *Your life ends at the door—your life ends and someone else's begins.*

It wasn't a bad way to look at things. Willa was left behind at the entrance and Willow took her place. Willa gazed into the mirror at the woman looking back at her. Thick platinum bangs covered the forehead she'd always thought was too big. A high ponytail let the fiery locks fall and swing down her bare back to her hips, which she'd always thought were too wide. Child-bearing hips her grandmother had called them. She smiled at the thought and then the smile faded and a slight frown crossed her face.

"Hey, what's with the sad eyes?" Raven turned from the mirror and stared at her.

"Nothing, just thinking." Smiling, Willa scooted her over and pretended to fix one of her long, false eyelashes.

"Just thinking, huh? Well we can't have that, can we?" Raven took Willa by the hand and led her through the throng of dancers that had assembled in the backstage area. It was almost introduction time. They passed a blushing bride, a geisha girl by way of Houston, one dirty cop—handcuffs and all—a very leggy Marilyn Monroe and others in different costumes, some barer than others.

Willa spoke to each of the girls as Raven pulled her along. Raven, dressed as the naughty school girl, which she probably had been once upon a time, climbed the stairs first with Willa not far behind her.

The introduction at The Garden was a big part of Lady Sadora's show. It was one of two ensemble performances at The Garden. Each and every dancer participated in the introduction and the conclusion. Willa started the show and Raven ended it.

Willa didn't mind opening the show, it got the nerves out of the way. What she hated was the short, almost nonexistent changing time. After each introduction piece, Lady Sadora would make her nightly welcome speech. It was theatrical, it was dramatic, it was ostentatious, it was everything Lady Sadora was. It was one of the things that made The Garden more than just a dance hall with dance-hall girls, as was Lady Sadora's vision.

Willa took her place close to the stage-left upper entrance and watched as Raven climbed one more set of stairs placing her in the center, Marilyn took stage right. When the music began each of the girls would enter in sync and on beat. Willa liked the introduction piece. It changed songs every so often, depending on what was popular and could make an impression. Recently, the Pussycat Dolls provided the music and vocals the girls danced to.

Raven thought the song was appropriate. She'd made the comment that they were just like the Pussycat Dolls, except with pasties. Willa tended to agree.

She adjusted the waist of her pink and white bottoms that hung low on her hips. Tonight she was playing nice next to Raven's naughty. She ran her hands to the corset that cinched her waist and displayed her breasts. The corset was tight, but it needed to be. The outfit was completed by white boots that ended just below the knee. Willa loved the fact that these boots had a stack heel instead of the stilettos she usually wore.

Raven caught her eye and then she flashed Willa the age-old Longhorn salute, pinky and index fingers in the air and tongue hanging out of her mouth. Willa laughed and sent the salute back.

She hoped for a good show. She hoped that everything went smoother than it had the night before and she hoped, hoped, hoped, hoped, that Lady Sadora was long-winded in her speech. And she hoped that there were no surprises waiting in the wings for her.

All of her thoughts ended as the curtains rose and the sound of a siren pierced the interior of the club. The siren was the signal for Willa to disappear and Willow to take her place. It was showtime.

Twenty minutes, a dozen Rockette kicks and endless swivels of the hips later, Willa came off stage a bit winded. She smiled as she passed the next dancer getting ready to take the stage and quickly made her way down the long hallway to her dressing room. She had a half hour before her next set. Those thirty minutes were just enough time to change outfits, replace the blonde wig with the black one and cool down just a bit. Even though The Garden was kept cool and refreshing, the lights that bombarded the stage were anything but.

She fanned her face with her hands and quickened her step. Sometimes she lingered backstage and spoke to a few of the girls, but not tonight. Tonight she needed the privacy of her and Raven's dressing room. But Raven wouldn't be there. Her first set started in a little under five minutes.

Reaching the door with the two pink stars that held her and Raven's names, she twisted the knob, stepped inside and stopped dead in her tracks.

"Nick?" Her hand flew to her chest and she realized it was heaving. There he stood, all six feet of him. Willa didn't know what inclined her to make the next move, but she didn't care. She ran to him and threw her arms around his neck.

When her body collided with his she felt a familiar warmth surround her. He was warm. He was male. He was Nick. She felt him tense underneath her hold and pulled her body from his and smiled into his deep brown eyes. But Nick wasn't smiling back.

"I got your message," was all he said.

"We both did."

*

Chase watched Willa's knees buckle and saw Nick slide an arm around her slender waist, helping her steady herself. Still holding onto Nick, she turned to face him. Chase watched as her caramel complexion paled a bit. He thought for a brief moment that she might faint, but the moment ended when she turned in Nick's arms and slugged him in the stomach.

She must have packed a punch. Nick sucked in a deep breath and bent at the waist a bit, releasing his hold on her. Chaos followed.

"You damn tattletale." She slapped at his shoulder which was a sight to behold since she stood nearly a foot shorter than Nick's tall frame. "I should have known better than to call you." Chase heard her say, or rather snarl, then she lit into Nick again. Nick just stood there and took it. Chase thought about saving his younger brother a time or two but decided against it. It served him right.

While Willa continued her assault on Nick, Chase took the time to look at her for the first time in years. She had changed. She was thinner in places, curvier in others, but she was still Willa.

Chase let his gaze rake over her tiny frame. White boots encased her legs. They made her look taller, but Chase knew that without them she would barely reach his chin. The pink and white striped bottoms of her outfit barely covered the well-curved ass she had. The corset she wore cinched her waist and made her breasts swell over the top. Her breasts. That was one of the major changes in her. He wondered for a second if she had had them done. The thought both intrigued and enraged him, almost as much as the sight of her on stage.

When Chase, Nick and Brent had entered the club he'd picked Willa out in a heartbeat. There was something about the way she strutted around the stage—confident, cocky and sexy. Too sexy. He was jealous. Jealous that every damn cowboy in that club was looking at what was supposed to be his and his alone. Jealous that she was showing it to them. Jealous that she'd never danced like that for him.

"Wait a damn minute." Willa's raised voice calmed and it pulled Chase from the wicked thoughts he was having about her ass.

"What the hell happened to your face?" Chase watched as she placed her small hands on the bruises that had started to form on Nick's eye and on his cheeks. In an instant, her anger at Nick had turned into concern for him and the rage was placed on someone else—him. "You hit him!"

"I didn't have to." Chase left the spot behind the door he had been occupying before and since she entered the dressing room. He closed the space between the two of them. He saw her breathing quicken and saw the pulse in her neck beat rapidly beneath the flesh he knew was soft there. He wanted to touch that spot with his lips. Wanted to trace it with his tongue and feel it jump under his teeth. Later, he thought.

"Who did then?" Her question stopped him in his tracks.

"Who did what, darlin'?"

"Who hit him? And I'm not your darlin'." She turned her back on him and went back to comforting Nick. The little bastard. She coddled him, just like always.

"It's nothing." Nick said, stopping her hand as it ran over the bruise at the top of his left cheekbone. He held her hand longer than Chase would have liked.

"Get your hands off of her," he growled. He didn't know where the thick jealousy or possessiveness was coming from. He shouldn't be either, but he was both.

Chase started to step closer to the pair when the door of the dressing room flew open and nearly collided with his face. Without looking up, the tall, black-clad figure made her way to one of the vanities, rambling ninety miles an hour as she went.

"Can you believe this?"

The three occupants of the dressing room watched as the image in black propped one long, booted leg on a chair and proceeded to remove the boot from her foot She was oblivious to the audience she had.

"I paid a fortune for these damn things and they run. Look at this!" She pointed to the long run in the silk stocking without lifting her head. "They run twenty minutes into a show. Just my luck."

Chase watched as she rolled the stocking down her thigh, her calf and then wadded in a ball and flung it in a waste basket close to her. From the corner of his eye, he saw Willa cover her eyes with a hand and saw Nick lick his lips and swallow. He had to hand it to the boy, he had taste.

"You don't have an extra pair do..." turning she finally saw that she had more company than she'd thought, "...you? Am I interrupting something?" Her voice was throaty and low, a bedroom voice, a good one at that. She didn't seem embarrassed by her state of dress or undress for that matter. She removed her foot from the chair and placed it behind the one that still was cloaked. She looked at Willa and asked, "Friends of yours?"

Chase saw a small grin touch her red lips and heard Willa mutter, "Hardly."

The lady in black chuckled. She took a seat in the chair and crossed her bare leg over the other.

"I remember you," she said as she pointed to Nick. She turned her back for just a second to rummage through the drawers. When she found what she was looking for, a package of new stockings, she turned her attention back to Nick.

"I remember you too."

Chase glanced at his brother and saw Nick was watching every move the beauty was making. She was putting on a show for Nick and Nick alone, whether she knew it or not. Willa, he noticed, moved away from Nick and was slowly making her way toward the vanity where the girl sat. She kept her distance from Chase as she edged closer.

By the time Willa reached her destination the leg was clad again in stocking and boot. She stood when Willa reached her side. Willa's friend crossed her arms over her chest, making her breasts swell more so than they had before. "Are you going to introduce me?" She still had that smirky grin on her face as she pointed in Chase's direction.

"I'd rather not," was Willa's reply.

Chase took the choice out of her hands. He crossed to them both and extended his hand.

"Chase Kiel." The girl looked at his hand, then to Willa, who rolled her eyes, and then shook his rough hand with her softer one.

"Chase Kiel?"

He nodded and she flashed him a full smile instead of a grin. "Raven."

"Ma'am." He tipped the brim of his Stetson as he said it.

"Is he the 'real deal' too?"

Chase was lost on her question but Willa wasn't.

"Oh, yeah. He's the 'real deal'." Willa supplied with a sneer in her voice.

"Nice."

Chase smiled at her remark. He saw Willa narrow her eyes and throw a glare his way. "Well," Raven said, pushing away from the vanity and strutting her way to the door, "I hate to leave good company, but I have a set to do and it appears as if you all have some things to sort out. Mr. Kiel..." she extended a lace-wrapped hand, "...it was a pleasure to meet you."

"You too." Chase grinned at her and then flashed Willa the same grin over the girl's head.

"And, Nick, come back anytime." She opened the dressing room door and started to leave the room, but Willa caught her arm before she could make it to the hall.

"What are you doing?" Chase heard her whisper in a hasty voice.

"What's it look like I'm doing? I'm getting the hell out of Dodge. Love ya, sugar, but you're on your own. Have fun." She blew a kiss in no general direction and closed the door behind her.

Once again, the three of them were alone. Chase hoped any minute that number would be reduced by one. Willa stood with her back to them both and Chase took the opportunity to motion his brother out with a nod of the head. Nick, ever perceptive, took the hint and made his way to the door and closer to Willa.

Chase watched his younger brother touch her lightly on the shoulder. She turned and peered up at him with questioning eyes. Nick looked back at him and once more Chase gave him the dismissing nod.

"I'll see you in a little while." He let his hand trace over her shoulder and down her arm. Chase's head knew that it was a brotherly, comforting gesture, but that didn't mean he liked it. That green-eyed monster was rearing its evil head.

Nick opened the door the vixen in black had closed and with a look of worry and concern did as his brother bid and left the dressing room. They were alone, at last.

It was several minutes before either one of them spoke. Chase watched her shoulders rise and fall with every breath but he couldn't see her face. He moved toward her. She heard him drawing near and she swung around to face him. Chase knew that look. She was pissed.

"What the hell are you doing here?" Her voice was calm with an undertone of rage thrown in for good measure. She brushed past him and took a seat at the vanity. She peered into the mirror and caught his eyes. "Are you going to answer my question or just stare at me?"

Chase took a minute. He liked looking at her, he always had. She never took her eyes off of him as he approached her chair. Placing his hands on the back of it he leaned in closer. Not only did she look good, she smelled good too—subtle and smooth.

"Are you surprised?" Quirking an eyebrow, he stared back into the blue depths that were trying their damndest to burn a hole through him.

"Shocked, I think, is a better word."

"Is it a good shock or a bad shock?" He was toying with her. He didn't know why. In the course of the last few minutes, he had gone from insanely jealous, to raging mad, to slightly intrigued. She intrigued him.

She turned in the chair, forcing him to take a step back, and glared at him. "Is there such a thing as a 'good' shock?"

Again he took his time in answering her. "What are you doing here, Willa?"

"I'm working. What does it look like I'm doing here, Chase?" His name came out in a slight hiss.

227

"I wouldn't call it working."

"What would you call it then?"

Chase leaned down, bringing his body and face closer to hers. He was only a breath away from her when he said, "You don't want to know what I would call it."

In a flash she jumped up from her chair, backed him against the wall and held him there while her finger jabbed into his chest.

"This. Is. Just. Like. You." To add emphasis, she poked his chest as each word passed her lips. "You think you can walk up in here and take that condescending tone with me?" She didn't give him a chance to answer. "I've got news for you, Mr. big-and-bad Chase Kiel—Mr. 'Real Deal' himself, you might have been able to rush me into things when I was younger, but a lot has changed since then. I'm not that same little, naïve girl I once was. And furthermore—"

He'd had enough.

Grabbing the hand that was bruising his chest, he braced her back to the wall and both of her hands at the side of her head. The action brought their bodies together and Chase could felt every soft curve her body had to offer.

"That's enough." His chest lifted with hers as she breathed in and out. "First of all, I never pushed you around. I would never push you around." His voice had harbored a bit of anger, but it was now back to its normal, low tone. The hands that held her wrists relaxed and stroked the skin under their hold— it was an automatic response to the silk that lay under his fingertips. Flinching at the touch, she looked at him with questioning eyes. Chase let out a ragged breath and sighed, "Dammit, Willa."

The words passed his lips, barely, before his mouth descended onto hers. He hadn't planned on kissing her. He had planned on talking to her, questioning her, getting answers from her, but all of those goals were pushed away when their lips met.

Slanting his mouth across hers, he planned to break the seal hers created. She struggled for a moment before Chase felt her relax against him. Then she opened her mouth. He took the invitation. Dipping his tongue inside, he tasted the sweetness she held. His tongue played a game of chase with hers for the barest moments before hers met every stroke he delivered.

God, he thought, she tasted good. Deeping his kiss and pushing his tongue further into her mouth unleashed emotions that had been pent up for years. Releasing her hands, he let his roam the length of her body. Her "costume" didn't offer much protection from his seeking fingers.

Chase received a small shock when she wrapped her arms around his neck and tugged at his hair. Her fingers played at his nape, sending shock waves of pleasure down his spine, up his thighs and through his groin. He felt his cock harden against her flat belly, heard her intake of breath, but never gave her the chance to deny or accept him.

Circling her waist, he lifted her until her back was pressed harder and higher against the wall and her legs were straddling his hips. "Wrap your legs around me." He broke the kiss for a second to make his request. She complied. He let a groan slip past his lips into hers as she tightened her legs gripping his body closer to hers.

He was lost. Memories flooded his mind—Willa underneath him, Willa on top of him, Willa with her lips sucking lightly, drawing his dick further into her hot, wet little mouth. The memories, combined with the feel of her and how her body coaxed and stirred his, caused his cock to strain and jump beneath her parted thighs. Chase realized he was not the only one affected.

She was wet. Hot and wet and growing even more so with every passing minute. She was also moving, rubbing her body across his, flexing her thighs, drawing him nearer to the heat that radiated from her pussy. His pussy. She pulled his hair, tugged at his shirt covering his shoulders and nipped at his lips with her teeth. He loved it.

Bracing his legs further apart, he held her to the wall without the aid of his hands. He needed his hands for more important pursuits. When they were free, he let the back of one rub against the barrier her underwear offered—it wasn't much of one. Teasingly, he explored the patch of material and felt his arousal grow, if it were possible, when he came in contact with the small bud of flesh beneath the silk.

With each pass of his hand she moaned and became more willing under his kiss. He could take her here. He knew he could. He wanted to. He wanted to rip those sexy, silky little panties from her body and thrust into her. Into her wet and hot core. He wanted to feel her muscles part and beckon him deeper. He wanted to feel her clench and come around his cock the way she had time and time before.

Chase was lost. Lost in the scent of her, the taste of her and the feel of her. He was losing his mind. Nothing made sense anymore—why she left, why she was here, why, instead of talking, they were going at each other the way they always did, or had. He was so lost he didn't hear their visitor arrive.

Chapter Six

The heat was gone. Willa felt his lips leave hers and she felt disappointment linger where their soft silkiness had been. Her mind was racing. *Why did he stop? Why did she kiss him back? Why did he kiss her in the first place? Why was she upset he stopped?*

Willa let her head fall and rest against his muscled shoulder. He smelled so good. He smelled warm and familiar and sexy—just like always. Pressing her face to his shirt, she inhaled the familiar aroma. It was the same scent that filled her dreams and her nightmares. Letting her eyes drift open, she quickly realized that he was not looking at her.

His head was turned and from what little of his face she could make out, she saw that he was not happy. Peeking around his massive frame, she saw why. They weren't alone—not by far.

The dressing room that had been a den of seduction and delight seconds before was turning into hell on earth faster than she would have liked. Willa pushed at Chase's shoulders, forcing him to release the grip he had on her hips. He let her go, but kept her sheltered from their company with his body. She poked at his ribs, willing him to move. He didn't. She poked at him again, this time harder.

He grabbed her hand, glared at her and growled, "Stop."

"Let me go." It was meant to be a whisper but it wasn't. Every person in the room heard her request. He stared at her for a minute and then did as she asked. Stepping to the side of him, she faced their company.

"Brent." Brent Kiel glanced at her but didn't speak or even acknowledge her existence. Of all the Kiel boys, Brent had always been the hardest to like. Brent was moody at times, withdrawn at others and a long way from friendly. He was a good brother, though. Willa knew that at a drop of a hat Brent would be at any of his brother's sides without asking for an explanation or expecting one. He was here now. That said it all.

"You about ready to go?" he asked his question over Willa's head. The fact that he ignored her presence irritated her more than the fact that he'd intruded to begin with.

"I was getting there."

"You were getting somewhere." The snide tone to his voice made Willa bite her tongue. A sound erupted from behind her and she turned to see the furious look on Chase's face. That was it. She knew that the Kiel boys brawled given the opportunity, the proof was written all over Nick's face, but she wasn't about to let the opportunity present itself. She sure wasn't about to let the two of them go at it and wreck her dressing room.

Walking on legs that could have been more stable, she moved from her spot in between them. The two didn't seem to notice her retreat, all the better. When she was a safe distance away, she said in the calmest and most authoritative voice she could muster, "I think you need to leave." She had directed the comment at both of them but Brent was the only one to reply.

"Gladly, as soon as I collect my wayward brother here." Brent propped a hip against the door he held open. "I told you this was a bad idea."

"Shut up, Brent."

"What did you think was going to come out of us showing up here? Did you actually think she was going to run into your arms and beg you to take her back? Is that what you wanted? Hasn't she caused you, us, enough grief as it is?" His words cut through Willa like a knife. Who the hell did he think he was?

"Grief?" Willa couldn't bite her tongue any longer. She charged him, actually charged him. He never retreated. "What the hell do you know about grief? I didn't ask you to come here. Did I? I didn't ask your two brothers, who are underage by the way, to show up in the middle of my set. The only grief I ever caused was to myself. Nobody else. Grief?" Willa's back was up and her courage was soaring. If it hadn't been, she would have never have done what she did next.

He watched as she drew closer, so close that he had no

choice but to look at her, to acknowledge she was there and that she existed. She saw his dark eyes slant and his jaw clench at her closeness. "You don't know a fucking thing about grief, you son of a bitch." Willa brought her hand back to slap the sullen look off his handsome face—the fact that it was a fine feature made the rage heighten even more.

Before her hand could connect, Chase grabbed it and turned her into his chest.

"That's enough."

She struggled underneath the arm that anchored her to him, to no avail.

"I said that's enough from the both of you."

"Me?" She was livid.

"Yeah, you. You can mangle him later. First, you and I have some things to discuss."

The hell they did. "The hell we do." Willa wiggled until she freed herself from him. "You need to leave. The both of you." She pointed first to Chase and then to Brent, who still stood looking bored and uninterested. *Bastard.*

"I'll leave when I get good and ready." Chase said. Once again, she stood between a rock and a hard place—between two Kiel boys.

"You'll leave now." Her voice betrayed her a bit as it wavered at the end. The control she had found was slipping. "Evidently you *two* have to discuss some things yourself and I have to get ready and go back to work."

"Like hell." Chase roared. He roared. She had heard him raise his voice before, but this was something totally different. This was filled with rage, determination and stubborn pride.

Willa cocked her head to the side and glared at him. She'd be damned before she let him boss her around.

"Like hell, nothing. You're leaving and you're leaving now." She angled herself toward her vanity, determined to rid herself of him and his irritating guard dog of a brother. Willa never made it.

Chase intercepted her and with surprising ease, flung her over his shoulder like a sack of feed.

"What?" She planted her hands on his back and pushed her body away from his. She kicked her legs and bucked her hips in her attempt to get free. She could see victory in sight and then she felt his hand connect with her backside. He spanked her. Not hard, but he spanked her like a child.

"Calm down." Again she felt his hand connect with her rear and hated the fact that he did it and hated the fact more that she kind of enjoyed it. She was losing her mind. "Now, I'm ready to go."

He made his remark to Brent, who grunted in reply. Chase carried her into the long hallway toward the back entrance to the club. She lifted her head and saw Brent following in that slow stride of his that drove her crazy.

"You can't do this!"

Chase never replied nor did his step falter. He heard her, she knew it. Just to make sure, Willa did the only thing she could, given her position at the moment—she bit him. Her teeth imbedded themselves in the hard flesh just above his belt. His intake of breath told her she now had his attention.

"Do that again and I'll turn you over my knee right here and right now." He smacked her ass again just for good measure. Willa felt her insides clench. She had never been into spankings but the connection of Chase's hand next to her barely covered flesh was causing conflicting thoughts to rage in her mind. This was nuts.

"This. Is. Kidnapping." She started to plant her teeth in him again but stopped when she heard the heavy metal door creak open and the brush of air hit her exposed skin. *Shit.* "Let me go."

"Not going to happen." His stride was steady across the gravel, even with her weight added to his frame, he never missed a step. Willa was thinking of ways to escape when she felt them both come to a sudden stop.

The next thing she knew, she was thrown into the passenger side of a truck. Righting herself and turning toward the driver's side door, she hoped to break free and run. That was out of the question. When she made her move to escape she collided with another hard body. Smiling sweetly and with a sour tone she said, "Jay."

Jason looked like he was trying his best to restrain the smile that lifted his lips. He tipped the brim of his Stetson in greeting and replied, "Willa."

"I should have known you would be driving this getaway vehicle."

He smiled broadly at her, flashing the set of straight white teeth he had always possessed. "Didn't know I was, but it appears I am."

Willa blew out a frustrated breath and felt Chase slide into the seat next to her. He slammed the door of the oversized pickup and ordered his brother, "Drive."

"You're crazy." She shoved his shoulders and wedged her body into his side and pushed with all her might. "Didn't you hear me? You can't just come into where I work and haul me off like this. It has a definition you know."

Her strength gave out under the strain of a body that would not budge. Looking frustrated, he ran a weary hand over his face. "I heard you the first time. Kidnapping?" She nodded her head in agreement. "Don't think of it that way, darlin'."

"I'm not your darling, you overgrown gorilla. If it's not kidnapping what would you call it?"

"Repossession."

His explanation confused her to the point she barely noticed they were leaving the parking lot and heading toward the highway; back toward Millbrook and back toward all the things she'd ran from before. "Repossession?"

He nodded.

"What the hell are you repossessing?"

"What's mine."

Chapter Seven

The two-hour drive to Millbrook, Texas, took an hour and twenty minutes, thanks to Jay's driving. He never did have the good sense God gave a goat. Willa thought the speed on the highway was bad, but it only got worse the closer they came to their destination.

A time or two she dug her fingernails into Chase's thigh. One of those times, she squeezed so hard, she thought she might have drawn blood. She saw Chase wince against the pain she caused. He took her hand and tucked it in between his. The size difference between her hand and the ones holding her's was amazing. Chase's hands were strong, hard and roughly arousing.

When the subtle strokes of his thumb across her open palm became too much to bear she pulled her hand away, or tried to. He wasn't letting go. The silence in the extended cab was tension filled.

Every once in a while she would hear a grunt from the backseat that held not only Brent and Nick but Hayden as well. She figured the grunting was due to one of the numerous bumps Jay refused to miss. The jarring was causing Hayden pain evidently. Willa had looked at him only once and noticed that his eye was also black and the fact that he was sporting a swollen nose that had tissue wadded up and shoved inside each nostril made her grin. It was more than likely broken.

The Kiel boys did like to brawl. Evidently Nick and Hayden had gone a round shortly before showing up at The Garden and ruining her entire night. The evidence was written all over their bruised, and Hayden's bloody, faces. He was in pain. Good, Willa thought with a smile. Why should she be the only one uncomfortable?

The uncomfortable feeling didn't diminish during the ride. It grew and grew. She recognized the terrain and knew without a doubt that any minute Jay would make a left turn onto the gravel road that led to the main house on the Kiel ranch.

Willa shut her eyes and willed herself not to think about it. Easier said than done. What would happen when they got there? Would they all pile into the house together for a powwow? She hoped not. She wondered if Chase would banish his brothers to one of the other cabins that sat on the property. Probably.

By doing that, he would ensure that he and Willa were alone. Being alone with Chase Kiel was the last thing she wanted, especially after crawling all over his body just a few hours before. It was a nice body though—too nice. She groaned. The noise broke the silence in the cab and caused every brother, except Brent, to look in her direction.

"Uncomfortable?" Jason asked.

"You have no idea." Willa let herself sink further into the seat and into its warmth, not that being warm was her problem. She was warm. She was hot and it was all his fault. She looked at the man who sat to her right and studied his profile. His eyes were focused forward but every so often he would cut them at her. "Could you scoot over just a bit?" she asked nicely.

"I don't see that happening." He squeezed the hand he held and smiled down at her. She hated him. Willa noticed that the truck turned, and praise the Lord, slowed down. Peering over the dash, she saw the house in the distance. It was breathtaking.

The Kiel ranch sat on thousands of acres of land. The driveway leading up to the main house was flanked by stone pillars with flagpoles placed in the middle. The flags flew every day, rain or shine, one American and one Texan. That hadn't changed over time.

The main house sat at the end of the drive and was majestic and quaint in the same breath. It was a simple farm house, a large one, but still a farm house. A porch filled with rocking chairs and tables, wrapped around all four sides and was accessible from every room on the main floor. The second floor held six bedrooms and four baths, enough to accommodate Chase, his parents and all of his siblings. Well, it had in Chase's childhood. Chase's father had built the house to please his wife. It stood strong and steadfast against the Texas backdrop, even though he did not. Bayer Kiel, the strong patriarchal figure Chase resembled so much, had fallen to a heart attack years before.

Willa couldn't remember exactly when, only that she had been young when she and her aunt had attended the funeral. At nineteen, Chase had taken the reins as head of the Kiel household and still held them today. It didn't surprise her. Chase had controlled every situation life ever threw his way, all except one. And now it looked like he was trying to right that wrong.

The truck came to a stop easily, surprisingly enough. Willa kept her eyes shut even though she heard all four doors open and felt the cab shift as its passengers exited the vehicle. All except one. She could feel him watching her—she didn't have to open her eyes to know.

"You plan on sitting here all night?" The rumble of his voice vibrated through her body.

"The idea has merit."

He laughed in reply. "Come on." He took her hand and tried to pull her from the cab, but she didn't budge. "I think you will be more comfortable inside."

Willa knew he was right but she couldn't force her body to move. Sighing, he put his hands on his hips and narrowed his dark eyes at her. Standing that way emphasized the size and even the shape of his cock under the worn denim of his jeans. Willa turned her head away from the package that made her mouth water and her inner muscles clench.

"You can either come out or I'm coming in. Which would you prefer, darlin'?"

Then he smiled. The smile made his tanned face look less hard and severe. His whiskey–hued orbs crinkled at the corners just a bit, but the lines didn't alter the perfection of his features. A girl had to admit, he wasn't hard on the eyes.

"Willa?"

"Huh?" Sounding like an idiot and feeling more like one, she was pulled from her thoughts and risked glancing in his direction.

"Out or in?" He propped an arm on the open doorframe and extended a hand. It was an invitation, *"'Come into my lair,' said the spider to the fly."* Willa shook the ridiculous thought from her head and scooted closer to the driver-side door. The way she figured it, she could have it open and make a run for it before he even got around the truck. Of course, he could probably leap the truck in a single bound. It wouldn't surprise her if he did just that.

"Willa," Chase warned, "don't even think about it."

Too late. Faster than she thought possible, Willa bounded from the door and took off into the night. Running as fast as her legs could carry her in her platform heels, half-naked, she eluded Chase and saw victory in sight. That victory was short-lived.

Glancing over her shoulder, she saw Chase launch himself toward her and then all she saw was the thick green grass that covered the Kiel front yard. He tackled her. Actually tackled her, in the front yard with all his brothers watching from whatever window they could find.

When he caught her, he rolled to protect the majority of her body from the force of the fall. She struggled against his hold for the briefest of minutes before he rolled again, placing her squarely beneath his body. He anchored her arms to the ground with his own and placed his thighs on top of hers, giving her no choice but to lie there—trapped underneath him. Willa thought for a moment that there were at least twenty other girls in Millbrook alone that would trade places with her in a heartbeat. She would willingly let them have it, well maybe.

"You about finished?" he asked, breathing a little deeply.

"Finished what?"

"Finished acting like the little fool you've turned into? Dammit, Willa! You could have been hurt running out there like that. Twisted your ankle, broken a bone, run through barbed wire. God, that was a stupid thing for you to do."

"Almost as stupid as you hauling me out of The Garden like a sack of potatoes?" While she was hissing at him, she also tried to uproot his body from hers. It wasn't happening.

"Now that's where you're wrong, darlin'. What I did at The Garden was necessary, not stupid."

"Necessary, my ass! And if you call me darlin' or 'Dammit, Willa' me one more time I'll..."

"You'll what, *darlin'?*" Drawing the last word out made her see red.

Niki Green

"I'll knock you over that big, fat, conceited head of yours. Now. Get. Off. Of. Me!" With each word she bucked her body beneath his.

"You really want me to get off?" Her movements stopped when she heard his tone—deep, sultry, alluring. "If memory serves, you used to like me on top, or on bottom, or even from behind." Whispering the last words in her ear made her shiver. "If I remember correctly you used to love me from behind."

"You've got a dirty mouth and an even dirtier mind, Chase Kiel." Half-heartedly she pushed his chest away from her own.

"You used to like my dirty mind and my dirty mouth."

"Did not!"

"Did too. As a matter of fact, you had a dirtier mouth and mind than I ever could hope to have. Not that I'm complaining. I did love it." His fingers were tracing circles over the skin of her wrists. The circles were making her head and her body spin.

"Stop."

He chuckled when the words passed her lips in a rasp.

"Now if you really want me to stop you're going to have to be more believable than that. I dream about you. I bet you didn't know that." Her eyes widened at his admission. "I dream about that mouth of yours licking me, sucking me. I also dream about that time in the front seat of my truck. Remember that?"

She did, but she wasn't about to admit it.

Admitting that she too still had dreams, vivid dreams, about being with him would not help her situation or the amount of moisture collecting in between her thighs. Opening her mouth to protest again, she found them covered with his.

The struggle went out of her completely. It didn't matter that they were in the middle of the front yard, it didn't matter that they had been apart, it didn't matter why she had left—it just didn't matter. All that mattered was that she was back in Chase's arms. Back where she belonged. Where she should have been all along.

Chapter Eight

He was dying. Dying to sink his cock as deep as it would go inside of her. Dying to feel those lips and that tongue wrapped around his cock just one more time. But he didn't want just one more time—he wanted a lifetime of it.

A lifetime of waking up beside her and slipping into her hot pussy. A lifetime of late-night blowjobs as they watched a movie or even a good old-fashioned roll in the hay. Hell, he had a barn and it was, at the present moment, full of hay. Soft, sweet-smelling hay that stuck to the skin and clung to the hair, if you did it right. Rolling in the hay was a hell of a lot better than rolling around in the damp grass of the front yard. She deserved better than that. They both did.

He pulled his lips away from hers, regretting the move as he did it. Those lush, wet, pink lips were heaven for sure, but he had other ideas.

"Don't stop." Uttering the words and trying her best to pull him back to his original position made Chase give a second thought to a better location. In the end, he stuck to his guns.

"I don't want to take you in the grass." Taking her hand and kissing the fingers lightly he explained his plan to her. "When I take you it will be in a nice, soft bed. Preferably the one with my name on it upstairs." He kissed her forehead and then rolled himself to his feet. When he stood she came with him. As he lifted her from the ground, he cradled her in his arms and began his journey toward the house and toward the threshold that called to him. He should have carried her across it years ago, but late was better than never in his book.

"What about your brothers?"

"If they have any sense at all they will hightail it out of

there before I reach the door."

"Chase, wait."

He stopped in his tracks.

"We need to talk about some things first. We can't just fall into bed like old times. That's what got us into this mess to begin with. We never talked about things." He kissed her lips, let his tongue trace them and took his time before saying, "We will talk."

"Before or after?"

"Before, during, after or all of the above. I don't care. The only thing I care about is getting you into that house and into my bed where you belong. Where you have always belonged."

Taking him by surprise, she wrapped her arms tightly around his neck and kissed him deeper than she'd ever kissed him before. He faltered for a moment, felt his knees go weak for a bit and then quickened his steps. The sooner he got to the house the better. If he waited any longer, he would have her naked and under him on the front porch swing. It wouldn't have been the first time, but this time was different. This time was important.

Chase reached the front door not remembering the steps he took to get there. One of his brothers, the one apparently raised in a barn, had left the door wide open. Chase wasn't going to complain though. Not having to put her down to turn the knob worked to his advantage. He wasn't about to give her the chance to run again.

Kicking the door shut behind him, he thought about taking the stairs two at a time and then thought against it. He didn't want her thinking he was in a rush, even though he was. The sooner he got her in the bedroom the better. The better for both of them. Just feeling her body pressed against his was making him crazy with need.

His door was the first one to the left on the landing. He crossed the threshold, closed the door with his booted foot and placed her gently on her feet just inside. The curtains had been pushed aside and the moonlight had an unobstructed path into the room. It was cast in shadows and dim light, creating a mood for seduction. Would he have to seduce her? He wanted to, but he figured they were way beyond seducing. They had already crossed the line way into want. The want for each other.

He rested his back against the door, took a few cleansing

breaths and allowed her to take in the room at her leisure. If she was looking for changes she wouldn't find many. The furniture was old and sturdy. Handed down from generation to generation. The rug that covered the butterscotch hardwood floors was new, new to her. The last time she had been in this room she had mentioned the need for one. And here it was.

The biggest change in the room was the bed. It was large and tempting. The bedspread was a deep chocolate color and his mother had placed tons of pillows, both caramel and cream, on top of it. Chase didn't know why he needed all of the pillows, but he had to admit the bed was inviting. He hoped Willa thought so. He had purchased it just for her.

"This is my bed," she said with wonder in her voice.

"Yeah." He smiled at her expression. She seemed confused and delighted all at the same time.

"Why did you...?"

Wrapping his arms around from behind and placing his hands on her waist, he whispered lovingly into her ear. "I remembered you said that you wanted it. You went on and on about it for months. So I bought it. It was supposed to be an engagement present, but we never got that far, did we?" She shook her head, bumping his chin as she did so.

"We messed everything up, didn't we?"

He barely heard what she said. "We didn't mess anything up. You're here now and I'm here with you. That's all that matters." Rubbing his lips against her neck, his cheek came into contact with the wig she still wore. Blonde was her color, but not this blonde, not this style. "Hey, can you do me a favor?"

"What?" She nodded first and asked second.

"Can we get rid of this?" Tugging one of the locks of the wig, he continued, "Although I think it's sexy as hell, I think the real thing is much sexier." Feeling her smile made him smile as well. Slowly and seductively, she raised her arms above her head and pulled pin after pin from beneath the platinum wig. After what seemed like forever, she pulled the wig away from her head by the bangs and flipped her head over, shaking out the mass of wheat-colored strands he knew she still had. The action caused the roundness of her behind to rub against his erection, bringing it back to life instantly.

Lifting her head and running a hand through the curtain

her hair created, she smiled at him once more, "Disappointed?"

"Never." Moving his hand through grain-colored hair, he massaged her scalp and let the silky texture caress his fingers. She pressed her head into his hand and moaned at his touch. "You keep making noises like that and we won't make it to the bed. I'll end up fucking you on the floor, and even though the rug looks soft enough, it could be hell on a man's knees."

"Or a woman's." Almost laughing, she spun away from him and placed herself in front of the open bedroom window. She made such a pretty picture—hand gently caressing the sheer curtains, head slightly inclined, body relaxed and at ease. "I love this place."

Her voice was full of memories. He heard it in her tone.

"I think I could sit at this window for the rest of my life and never get bored with the view."

"Do you really believe that?" He stepped behind her and they watched the clouds roll across the moon and place patterns onto the grass below. It was an amazing view, almost as amazing as the woman standing in front of him.

"Yes, nothing is ever the same here and yet it is." Giving a short grunt of laughter, she moved away from the window and perched on the side of the bed, not fully relaxing into the soft depths.

"If you liked the view so much why did you leave in the first place?"

"You know why I left."

"I don't. I never did and I never will unless you tell me." Moving forward, he came to rest on his knees in front of her. At this angle he could look straight into her eyes and she had to look into his. Trying to resist touching her was a wasted effort. His hand traced her delicate cheekbone, the gentle and stubborn line of her chin and the full, pouty plains of those lips he fantasized about so often.

When he touched her, her breath quickened and caught in her throat. He could see the pulse beneath her warm skin beat faster and faster. The simplest touch excited her—it always had. He wondered how many other men over the years had realized that it only took the lightest touch to turn her to putty in their hands.

"How many men have there been?"

She arched an eyebrow at his question.

"How many men have there been since me?" It was a simple question and one that was driving him crazy. Seeing all of those men at The Garden drool all over her hadn't helped matters. He just wanted to know it wouldn't change how he felt about her. He just wanted to know.

"Are you kidding me?" She pushed his hand away from her face as she asked her question.

"What?" He saw her nostrils flare, her eyes narrow and caught sight of her fist as it connected with his chin and knocked him to the floor. He felt sorry for Nick now—she did pack quite a punch. He lay back on the rug and stared up at her from the floor. Her hands were still fisted and the look in her eyes called for his blood.

"You are the most arrogant, conceited, egotistical, sorry...*humph!*" The wind whooshed from her lungs as her back connected with the floor.

Chapter Nine

He did it again. For the second time in one evening, Willa found herself trapped beneath Chase's body. Fighting tooth and nail to free herself from his hold was making her winded and more tired than she was already. Giving in was not an option. Beating at his chest and aiming for his crotch were her only defenses against the massive form on top of her.

"Would you calm down?" he said as he dodged a fist that was aimed at his perfect nose.

"Calm down? Calm down! Are you serious?" His defenses were down and she hit him again for good measure.

"What is your deal? I just asked a question." Wrestling her hands to her sides, he held them there until the fight went out of her.

"No, you just called me a whore!" She aimed her knee at his crotch and would have connected, but he was ready for her assault this time.

"Did not!"

"Did too! 'So, Willa, tell me, since we have been *broken* up, how many men have you fucked?'"

"I didn't say it like that. I was only asking because it was on my mind, that's all." He rolled away from her and sat up, placing his back against the frame of the bed and waiting for her to do the same. Willa was tired. She was tired of fighting, tired of arguing, tired of everything. She didn't move. She lay on the rug, which was very soft, and stared at the ceiling and tried to wrangle her breathing and her temper.

"Tell me something, Chase. Do you always ask every question that crosses your mind?" Titling her head the slightest bit gave her the ability to see his face from her position. Sitting with his knees drawn up, booted heels on the floor and one hand raking the hair on top of his head, he looked mouth-watering. Willa closed her eyes and tried to ignore the fluttering sensation in her heart and in her stomach.

"I've found that the only stupid question is the question that is never asked."

"Do you really want me to answer your question? What if you don't like what you hear?"

"Whatever the answer is, it won't matter. My feelings for you won't change. They haven't in the years you've been gone and they won't just because you might a have been with a few people while we were apart."

"What if it's more than a few? What if it's ten? Twenty? A hundred different men since you and I were together, huh? Could you handle that?" Studying his face, she found him studying her as well. He didn't look shocked, he didn't look horrified and he didn't look mad. He looked like he was deciding on the best way to answer.

"Were there a hundred men?"

She could lie to him. She could lie and say yes and pick a hundred names out of the air and fling them at his overinflated ego, but she didn't. In truth, there hadn't been anyone. Not a soul. Only him, always him.

"No. There weren't a hundred men." Finding the energy, she rolled from her back and onto her feet. Pacing the floor and rolling the tension from her shoulders helped ease her mind and the fury that boiled in her belly. "This is one of the reasons we broke up."

"What reason would that be?" He moved from the floor and took her place on the edge of the bed.

"We fight. We always fight. Always have, always will." That was the truth.

"Yeah, we used to fight, but we also made up. That is the part I remember, the making up. We were always really good at making up." Crossing to her, he pulled her into his arms. "Do you remember that? Making up?" His fingers lifted her chin so that once again she was staring him in the face.

"Yes. But that's not the point. A relationship cannot be based on the 'making up' part. What happens when the making up stops and the fighting keeps going?"

"That won't happen to us."

"It happened to my parents. Do you remember that?" When the words passed her lips, Willa wished she could take them back. She'd already made one trip down memory lane this evening and she wasn't ready for another. Especially a trip that passed by her absent parents.

"Is that why you left? Because of what went on between your mom and dad? Willa, I would never leave you."

"You can't say that. You can't say that and mean it. You don't know what could happen between us. Do you think my father ever thought, in the beginning, that he would up and leave my mother? Do you think that my mother ever thought about my father leaving? Leaving her, walking out on her and his kid." Tearing up at the thought, Willa swiped her hands over her eyes. Tears did no good. They didn't solve anything. They sure as hell didn't make things better or different.

"I would never leave you. I would never in a million years, no matter what, walk out on my wife or my children." At the first sight of her tears, Chase pulled her into his arms once more. She felt them supporting her body and his hands caressing her back. Even in her state his stroke could still make her shiver.

"It's not just that." She pushed away from him. "What if I'm just like her? What if I'm not strong enough to handle you leaving and I walk out on our kids? What happens to them then? Will your mother be left to raise them like my aunt raised me? Would Brent raise them? Jay? What would happen to them?"

Willa stopped herself from sobbing. The thought of leaving him killed her, but the thoughts of not being able to raise her children were worse. Men left. Willa's father did. Walked out without a word, leaving her mother young, broke and full of heartache. Willa decided long ago that leaving Chase, who was strong by all accounts, was better than leaving any children she might have.

It had broken her mother, left her a shell of a woman. That was when her mother's sister had stepped in and raised Willa. Her mother had grieved herself into an early grave. Willa wouldn't go through that. She wouldn't put any children of hers through that. She hurt the one she knew could survive—Chase.

"Just stop." He pulled her back to him, making her body collide and collapse into his. "Just stop. That won't happen.

You are not your mother and I am not your father. I will love you for the rest of my life and I would never even think about leaving any of my kids in the care of my brothers. Can you imagine? Jason would have nipples on beer bottles and I don't even want to think about Hayden getting a hold of them." He smiled through his speech—the gesture and the remark made her smile too. He was good at that. Making her smile. Almost as good as he was at making up.

"You do realize we are talking about kids who don't even exist?" She tried to laugh but the sound was muffled against his chest.

"They could. If you quit talking and let me get you into this bed."

"You were always good at that. Getting me into bed. I remember that."

"What else do you remember, huh?" He asked as he placed kisses along her chin and down the side of her neck. His tongue came to rest on her pumping pulse in her neck. He flicked and played along the point until her knees became weak and her pussy clenched inside her panties.

"Do you remember the first time I ate that sweet pussy of yours?"

She moaned at his words and nodded. She did remember the first time she'd felt his lips against her clit. He'd nibbled at the bundle of nerves and then sucked it into his mouth. She'd come instantly all over his mouth.

Embarrassment had followed the orgasm, but he'd given her little time to fully feel any of the humiliation. Seconds after her first orgasm, he'd brought another one down on her with his fingers. She could still feel the pressure they'd created inside of her small, tight passage. The memory was almost enough to make her come, standing there with only his lips and fingers on her neck.

"You tasted so good. So sweet. Sometimes I think I can still taste you. I want to taste you again. I want to lay you down, rip those panties away from that pussy, spread your legs and taste you. All of you. I want to lick and suck and devour every bit of you. Can I? Will you let me, Willa? I'll beg if I have to but I don't think I can stand here another minute without my tongue being inside of you. Will you let me, let me lick you, let me make you come?" he moaned the question into her slick mouth.

Willa answered his moan with one of her own and allowed him to move her to the bed. His mouth was fire on top of hers and she couldn't wait to feel that hot, wet tongue between her legs.

She kissed him again, the way he'd taught her—open mouth against open mouth, tongue against tongue. He groaned as her tongue made contact with his, the vibrations made her nipples ache and her clit throb.

She pressed her lower body closer to his, feeling the hard outline of his cock beneath the denim jeans. She whimpered. She kissed her way across his mouth and down the side of his neck. She saw his pulse beating beneath the flesh and couldn't stop herself from licking the throbbing spot and nipping it with her teeth.

She heard his sharp intake of breath, thought she'd hurt him and pulled back. He wouldn't let her. He pulled her down against his lap, bruising her with the force. She liked it. Grinding her hips slowly, she showed him how much she liked it.

"Are you wet for me?"

Blushing, she nodded her head.

"Let me feel." Leaning back on his lap gave him better access into the scrap of material she called underwear. He let his hands roam her body, rubbing her breasts, her arms and the top of her thighs. She tried to resist teasing him but couldn't. She hooked her thumbs in the sides of the panties and pulled just the slightest bit, lowering them on her hips, exposing just the barest bit of flesh beneath them. He watched every move. He licked his lips. He waited.

The pink fabric of her bikini panties was visible against her flesh. He sat up straighter on the bed. One hand grabbed her waist and he let the other slip between the material and her flesh. He touched her, caressed her and tempted her.

Even after all these years, he found no problem parting the lips of her pussy and thrusting a finger deep inside. Moaning, she moved to give him more access. He pressed his finger in and out of her body while his other hand instructed her how to move on him.

"Ride it for me, baby." He thrust the digit deeper, causing her to cry out. "Are you going to come for me? He groaned. "Are you?" Replacing one finger with two, he stretched her, making her small entrance burn with the assault. The blend of pleasure and pain made her crave more.

"I want you. I want you now."

Jerking his hands from her body, he moved them to the button of his pants. The task was done quickly. Buttons undone, zipper lowered, he removed his hard cock from his jeans.

Willa's eyes flared at the sight of it. It wasn't the first time she had seen it, touched it or sucked it—but it was the first time in quite a while. She'd forgotten how big it was.

Not only was it massive in length but also in thickness. She remembered now that she couldn't close her fingers around it. The thought made her wiggle to get closer to him and to that gorgeous cock her mouth wanted desperately. She watched as he stroked the flesh. Base to tip. His hand was tight, that was how he liked it. His movements became quicker and his grip became tighter.

"Willa?" his voice pleaded. "Willa, I can't take much more." His breathing hitched and he stilled his hands. Creamy drops of fluid appeared at the head and she ached to take it in her mouth. She licked her lips.

"Oh, no you don't." His hand grabbed hers and clamped it around his dick. "You can't use your mouth. I come every time you put your mouth on me." He did and she loved it. Here was this shy, timid girl who could make the man beneath her come minutes, even seconds, after sucking him into her throat.

"I want to be inside you. I want to feel you all wet, hot and slick around me. I want to come inside you—deep inside you. I want to make you come around my cock. Can I Willa? Can I fuck you?"

Before she could answer, his lips took hers. The kisses that had started out innocent and sweet were now carnal and destructive. Willa rubbed her body against his and stroked the heavy cock she held in her hand.

"Don't," she heard him say, but she couldn't stop. Tightening her grip, she pumped faster and faster. She could feel his pulse beating beneath her moving hand. He groaned a ragged curse. Willa felt his legs tighten beneath her and saw his head fall back. He was close, so close.

Moving quickly, she removed herself from his lap and knelt in front of him. With one hand still jerking him off, she moved her hair away from her face. Then she swallowed as much of his erection as she could. He tasted so warm and male. A salty, sweet mix flowed across her tongue and she tightened the hold she had on him with both her hand and her mouth. Taking him deeper than she had ever taken him, she let the head stroke the back of her throat.

His hands fisted in her hair and knowing he was close, she took the decision away from him. Chase's cock pressed to the back of her throat, her hand working rapidly up and down the length still exposed, Willa swallowed. The motion of her throat muscles contracting caused him to shudder and come. Hot waves of the salty, sweet mixture coated her tongue and glided easily down her throat.

His breathing was hard and shallow. His eyes were still closed and his member jumped as she let it ease its way from her mouth. She saw him smile and he pulled her close to him.

She'd satisfied him, or so she'd thought. Without missing a beat, Chase rolled Willa beneath him and captured her mouth. She couldn't get enough of him, and she remembered something else about Chase Kiel she had forgotten. He was nearly insatiable when it came to sex. He would match orgasm for orgasm, favor for favor and touch for touch.

Leaving her flat on her back, chest heaving, and pussy contracting and begging to be touched again he stood above her and gazed down at her. His jeans were still unbuckled and Willa could see that his hard cock was back to full form. The head peeked out at her from the opening in his jeans. Chase followed her gaze and stroked the member slowly and with purpose. He was ready again and she was ready for him.

With ease and practice she popped the buttons on the bustier without taking her eyes from his face. She saw his cock jump each time a button was released. It was the one time in their entire relationship Willa was in control. She took her time. Each button revealed just a hint of skin. When the buttons were completely undone all she had to do was part the sides and let the material fall away, exposing her breasts. They were bigger now—better she thought. What would he think? Would he think they were too big? They had grown in the years apart.

"Let me."

Willa still clutched the sides of the garment in her hands and watched as he moved her hands away and parted the material with his own. Sucking in his breath and moaning, Chase stared at her breasts longer than she would have liked. She started to grab the material and cover herself but he wouldn't let her.

"God, you're beautiful."

He lowered his body to meet hers. His torso rested between her parted thighs and he let his mouth connect with the nipple of her right breast. Her reaction was involuntary. Her back bowed off the bed, a groan erupted from her throat and her hands held him to her.

Lapping at one nipple then the other, at her request, he bathed them both before taking one plump peak between his lips and sucking greedily. The suction caused Willa's insides to clench and made her body writhe beneath his.

"You like that?" He asked, before taking the second nipple into his mouth and nipping it with his teeth.

"Yes!" She gasped. Her nails dug into his shoulders and she realized he still had the majority of his clothes on, which wasn't working. Levering herself into a sitting position, she broke the connection he had with her breasts.

"What?" he asked, confusion thick in his tone.

"I want you naked. And I want it now." Sliding her hands up his sides, she took the shirt with them. He aided her in the removal when the material reached his head. As Chase pulled the shirt from his head, Willa took the opportunity to return a bit of the favor. She flattened her tongue against one of the flat, brown male nipples that hid beneath the swirls of hair on his chest.

She heard his breathing change and felt his hands play with the lines of her back. He held her close as she worshipped his chest with her tongue. While she let her tongue play its tune against his flat stomach, she pushed his jeans down his hips with her hands.

"Willa?" Chase tilted her head back, stopping her actions.

"What?" Was he stopping her? No, they couldn't stop, they hadn't even started. "What?" she asked, haste and anxiety pushing her voice.

"You'll never get past my boots." He smiled at her and kissed her lips. He took a seat beside her on the edge of the bed and removed his boots, socks, jeans and boxers in almost one fluid motion. Willa started to do the same, but stopped when he grabbed the hand lowering the zipper of her boot. "Your boots stay on, but those panties have to go."

Willa let him push her back against the bed and watched as he raised her hips and slid the panties down her thighs and past the white boots that encased her legs. Throwing the wad of material over his shoulder, he spread her legs and placed his body between them.

"Now it's my turn."

Willa let her eyes close as his tongue made its first pass over the smooth flesh of her pussy. She wondered for a second if he liked the waxed flesh beneath his lips and decided he did. He did if his moaning was any indication.

She couldn't stop herself from watching him. Pushing her hands beneath her body, she relaxed as she watched Chase devour her clit. He was so good. He licked her, sucked her clit into his mouth and then licked it while it was there. Willa didn't think her pleasure could mount any more until he eased a finger into her pussy. Her breath caught in her throat and she began to move against his mouth and against his finger. She wanted more. The single digit felt thick inside of her body but she needed much, much more. She needed him. She needed his body on top of hers, his cock buried deep inside of her, and she needed it now.

"I need you." Her breath was choppy, making her words the same. He smiled against her pussy and kept licking at her clit as he added a second finger inside of her. He pumped them in and out, over and over again, making her frantic and wild.

"I need you inside of me."

"I am inside of you. See?" He pushed his fingers further into her pussy and her muscles clenched around them, not wanting them to retreat, but they did. "You're so tight, so soft, so wet."

"I want *you* inside me." His fingers thrust in and out of her body as she made her statement. She was getting close. She could feel it and she could hear the sucking, wet sounds her pussy was making against his seeking fingers. She loved the noises. Flesh against flesh.

"What part of me do you want inside of you? Fingers?" He pumped once more into her, making her cry out.

"No." She shook her head as she said the word, making her hair fly and go wild just as her body was.

"Tongue?" He removed his fingers from her body and replaced them with his probing tongue.

"No." Willa's head fell back against the mound of pillows on the bed. Why did a man need so many pillows? Who cared?

"What part do you want?" His tongue entered her body again, making her body arch against it.

"*You.* I want you." Pulling at his shoulders did no good. His body wouldn't budge from its resting place.

"Just tell me what you want and I'll give it to you. Just say the words and I'm yours."

He wanted the words. He always did. Chase was always very vocal in bed. The words seemed to turn him on as much as the actions. Truth be told, they did the same for Willa. In bed, actions spoke just as loudly as words.

"I want you. I want you to..."

"To what?" He slid his body along the length of hers until he was face-to-face, chest-to-chest, cock-to-pussy with her.

"I want you to—"

He silenced her with his mouth, then asked. "You want me to what?"

"I want you to fuck me." She grabbed his hair and pulled his face to hers, seizing his lips and winding her legs around his hips. Chase gave her what she wanted. In one fluid motion, he joined their bodies together. Willa saw bursts of light behind her eyelids when he filled her completely. It had been so long. Years since they'd been together. The years had changed a lot of things, but it didn't change how he felt inside of her. Right, he felt right. He belonged with her. She belonged with him. They belonged together. Willa smiled at the thought and flexed the muscles inside of her body, pulling Chase closer to her—mind, body and soul.

Chapter Ten

Chase was in Heaven. She was so tight. Even tighter than he remembered. He tried to control his movements. He was doing a pretty good job of it too until he felt her tighten around him. He was a goner.

Chase settled his mouth on top of hers, slid his tongue inside to meet hers and thrust and pumped his body into hers. He felt her rake her nails against the muscles of his back. He then felt those same nails sink into his ass and hold him close. She wanted more. She wanted faster, deeper and harder and so did he. Bracing his weight on his forearms, he looked down into her flushed expression. Her eyes were dreamy and at half-mast. Her breasts swayed and moved with each thrust he gave her and the lines her legs created around him made him harder than he was already.

"Look at me." He watched her eyes open and saw those beautiful blues travel the length of their bodies, finally coming to rest where they were joined. "Watch me fuck you." He withdrew his cock from her body and saw that her pussy had coated it in her thick juices. He watched her face as he withdrew and then plunged back inside. So tight.

"Do you like that?" he asked, placing a kiss on her parted lips.

"Yes." She kissed him back, letting her tongue duel with his and trace his lips.

"Do you want more?" He pumped in and out as they talked.

"Yes."

"Tell me. Tell me what you want, baby. Whatever you want I'll give it to you." Kissing her again, he waited for her to answer him.

"More, I want more."

"I can do that." He pumped faster. The action made his balls tighten and his dick ache for release, but he waited. Waited on her. He wanted to feel her come around his cock. Wanted to feel her sweet cream coat his body and hers.

"I want you to make me come." She grabbed his shoulders and gripped his body to hers. "Make me come, Chase. Make me come all over you." Then she started to move. Chase felt her grind her clit against his body, felt her pussy grip his dick and felt her nails bite into his back, holding him still as she rode him. Chase heard her panting begin and knew it wouldn't be long. He increased his speed and drove into her body time after time, kissing her lips, her cheeks, her nose, her neck, any part of her he could reach.

"Chase!" She gasped as she wrapped her arms around his neck.

"Yeah, baby? You about ready to come all over me?" He pounded harder into her as he asked.

"Yes, yes. More, please, more."

He gave her what she wanted. Thrusting his body as hard and as far as it would go into her, Chase felt her pussy twitch around him and then felt a flood of juice surround him. That was all it took. One more plunge sent him straight into release. He felt the hot spurts of his come fill her already dripping pussy. He loved feeling the mix of him and her coating each other's bodies.

"Chase?"

"Yeah, baby?" He pushed the few strands of hair away from her face and kissed her lush lips.

"I love you." Her eyes pooled with liquid as she spilled her heart into his hands, and then she said it again, "I love you."

"I love you too, Willa. I always have, always will." Hugging her body to his, he rolled them once, bringing her body to rest on top of his. "I never wanted you to leave."

"I don't want to leave. I want to stay here. Right here for the rest of my life. Can I?"

Chase pulled her to him and surrounded her small frame with his arms. Pulling her close, he slid them both beneath the covers and into the comfort the bed offered. He'd wanted for so long to lie next to her in this bed, their bed. It was better than he could have ever imagined.

"Willa, if you want to stay here, you know you can. I think you might find it hard to leave with me attached to you anyway. If I have any thing to say about it, I would keep you here forever. Hopefully wedded, bedded and bred as soon as possible."

She laughed at his statement and slapped his shoulders lightly and with a little bit of flirt attached to it. "Wedded, bedded and bred. Gee whiz, Mr. Kiel, you sure know how to make a girl feel good."

"I'll make you feel any way you want to feel as long as you're happy. When you stop being happy is when we need to sit down and talk. Talk. No more running off and letting things stay as they lie. You're right we need to talk more."

"I thought we talked enough." She said as she adjusted herself to a sitting position on top of him. Chase watched her take his cock in her hands and bring it back to life. God, she was good at that.

"Maybe we could talk a little more," he said between clenched teeth. "Or maybe not." She laughed at him, ran her tongue over the head of his dick. "Willa?"

"Yes?" Rising on her knees she placed the head of his cock against the entrance of her pussy and moved it back and forth repeatedly until it was wet with her.

"Please."

"Please, what?" Barely, she slid him into her body.

"Fuck me." Grabbing her hips, he impaled her body with his.

"You want me to ride you?" she asked as she moved slowly up and down.

"Yes." He lifted his hips and arched his back, bringing them closer together.

"You want me to make you come?" Lowering her chest to his, she let her nipples graze his and let her lips nip and tempt his.

"Yes." He fisted his hand in her hair and pulled her to him.

"What else do you want?" Her tongue traced the outlines of his lips and then dipped inside for a taste.

"I want you. I want you forever."

She stopped and looked deep into his eyes.

"Well, you've got me." She kissed him and smiled into his

mouth.

"Now," he said pushing her back into her seated position. "I believe you have a little riding to do." And she did. Up and down, she moved faster and faster. Harder and harder, grinding and rubbing her clit against him until her orgasms ran into one another. Chase lost count of how many times she came on top of him. All he recalled was screaming her name and his oath to love her for life as he spilled his come inside of her.

They fell asleep that way—her on top of him, their bodies connected. Chase fell asleep for the first time in a long time without any dreams of the woman who tormented him. Instead, that woman was resting peacefully with him. Where she belonged and where she would stay if Chase had anything to say about it.

Chapter Eleven

When Willa woke, she was startled for a minute but then she felt the warm arms embracing her and she relaxed. She was in bed. In bed with Chase.

Trying her best not to disturb her partner, she rolled away slowly and quietly. The clock on the bedside table read 4:03 a.m. Perfect, she thought. Knowing that her cell phone was resting safely in her purse back at The Garden, she reached for Chase's.

Flipping the phone open illuminated the room more than the moonlight already did. She dialed the number she knew by heart and listened as a song began to play in her ear. After the first verse and a chorus the call connected.

"Hello?" The low voice on the other end sounded sleepy and confused.

"Hey. It's me." Those were the only words Willa got out of her mouth before the caller on the other end started ranting and raving at her.

"Where the hell are you? Are you okay? I tried calling you and all I got was your damn voicemail. God, you scared me to death."

"I'm fine. Better than fine if you want to know the truth." Willa peeked at Chase's face to make sure he was still asleep. She couldn't stop her fingers from running down the middle of his chest and toying with the thin line of hair than ran beneath the sheet.

"Well, where are you? Do you need me to come and get you?"

"No, I'm in Millbrook."

"Millbrook?" There was a pause and then silence on the

other end and then, "Oh my God! You're with him aren't you? You are. Don't even answer that. So, what's going on? What's happening? Tell me everything."

Willa covered her mouth with her hand to stifle the giggle that was forcing its way up her throat. If the sound came out of her mouth she would wake Chase and even though the idea had merit, she really needed to finish this conversation.

"I don't have time to tell you everything. I just wanted to call and let you know that I'm fine."

"So...are there wedding bells in the future?"

Willa thought about the question for a minute. Were there? Maybe, but not anytime soon.

"I think I'm going to try and take things slower this time. Let us get to know each other again."

"Right. Lie to yourself, but don't lie to me. Just remember something."

"What's that?"

"I look great in black and I don't do ruffles. I do lace, delightfully well, though."

Willa couldn't stop the giggle this time. The sound made Chase move and he pulled her closer to his body. Willa felt his awakening erection caress the small of her back and thought it best to end the call and give all of her attention to it.

"I know. Listen, I will give you a call later. Do you have to work tomorrow?"

"Yeah, but I don't go in until late. You know that."

Willa did. But there would be no more late nights for her unless they involved Chase, her and a bed.

"I'll call you later. Sweet dreams."

"You too. You know you deserve them."

"So do you." Willa heard a snort on the other end and then heard. "Maybe, we'll see. Talk to you later."

"Yeah, later." Willa closed the phone and put it back where she had found it. Rolling once, she brought her body against his and rubbed slowly back and forth. Chase and his erection were wide awake and ready for her. Willa took what he gave her— body, heart and soul.

*

Niki Green

Underneath the Texas sky spotted with stars, Nick and Hayden Kiel sat in two of the rocking chairs on the front porch and waited for the muted sounds from the bedroom upstairs to cease. It had been ages since either one had spoken.

Brent had retired to the north cabin hours ago, mumbling something about Chase being a glutton for punishment. Jason had followed a few minutes later, after retrieving several beers from the refrigerator inside the main house.

This left Nick and Hayden alone, sitting on the front porch, waiting until it was safe to take to their beds. Even though the north cabin was furnished, it only had two beds and no couch, as of yet. Nick figured that would change shortly. Willa was back. And his brother was whole again.

"I told you so," Hayden muttered into the dark night.

Nick glanced his way and saw that Hayden's eyes were closed even though he wasn't asleep.

"Told me what?"

"I told you her favorite words were 'yes' and 'more'."

Nick watched the smile cross his brother's face and felt his own appear moments later. "So you did."

"Looks like we are going to have to find a new place to sleep here soon. I can't handle hearing that all night. Especially now that I know what she looks like half-naked. I'll turn into a walking hard-on."

"I thought you already were."

Smiling, Hayden nodded his head and replied, "Guess I am."

Minutes passed in silence and then Hayden broke the barrier again.

"You think it's safe to go in? I mean, surely they're finished by now." Nick considered making his way up the stairs to his room and thought against it. Chase and Willa needed their time alone.

"I think we best find alternate places to lay down for the night. It's a nice night. We could just sleep under the stars." It wouldn't be the first time they had. Some nights there was nothing better than sleeping beneath the stars and letting the morning light act as an alarm clock. They were cowboys after all. The real deal.

About the Author

To learn more about Niki Green, please visit http://nikigreen.wordpress.com/. Send an email to Niki Green at niki.green@hotmail.com.

LaVergne, TN USA
03 March 2010
174834LV00002B/98/P